The Fate of All Traitors

Rise of the Giants Series: Book 3

Theo Mann

The Invisible Publishing Company

Rise of the Giants Series

Contents

Chapter 1

H angman halted at the head of the valley and looked down at a bunch of shelters constructed to make a loose camp.

Steep, high cliffs thousands of feet high flanked the valley on both sides. The other two ends joined up with the mountain range that used to belong to Thunder's band.

Red and his men had led Hangman's party here when they fled the Renegade attack on the artillery battery. The Godless found this valley deserted and no trace of Thunder's band.

The party settled here four years ago. Hangman originally stayed to give the women a safe camp where they could give birth. One month turned into two. The band got comfortable here and never left.

The men of his band settled here, too. None of them wanted to leave, especially not the men with wives. They all just kept living here as if they had never lived anywhere else.

Hangman scanned the valley for any sign of danger, but he didn't see any. The men only had to defend this camp from two directions—the two farthest ends of the valley. Those were the only ways in.

The men patrolled the mountains every day and even ranged farther away for a week or more. They never saw any sign of the Renegade

Clan invading these mountains again—or any other people. The band was all alone here with the whole place to themselves.

Hangman didn't want to trust that. He and his men agreed privately that it was only a matter of time before someone came along to challenge their position in this territory.

The Renegades wouldn't give up that easily, but Hangman didn't need to think about that now. He set off down the long hill leading into the valley. The slope led to long stretches of jungle covering the valley floor.

The men had to travel through miles of dense country before they spotted the camp in the distance. A little boy saw the men coming, charged out to meet them, and collided with Hangman's knees.

"Father!" The boy turned up his face to grin at Hangman. Empty places dotted the boy's mouth where he had been losing teeth.

Hangman swung the boy up onto his shoulders. His son Zaedi laughed when Hangman grabbed hold of his ankles to hold him in place. "Don't fall off," Hangman told him. "Pretend you're riding one of the Ashtaws."

The boy shrieked with laughter, held onto fistfuls of Hangman's hair, and more children came running. They flooded into the group of men. The band had a lot of children now—a lot more children.

A little girl a year younger than Zaedi grabbed hold of Hangman's leg. "I want a ride, Father! Let me have a ride, too!"

"Sit down there." He pushed her down to sit on his foot. "Hold on tight. Don't let go or the Stalkion might step on you."

She burst out laughing, sat on top of his foot, and wrapped her arms and legs around his shin. He set off walking toward the camp with both children yelling and calling out.

The other men carried or swung their children around to play with them. They walked into camp in a loud procession. The women stopped what they were doing to smile at the parade.

Hangman smiled at Mora across the camp where she stood in front of their shelter. She held a tiny newborn baby boy in her arms wrapped up with a piece of hide knotted around her body.

She didn't come forward. She left Hangman to play with the older two children. "What did you bring me, Father?" his daughter Thena asked.

"I brought you.....a big sloppy wet kiss." He picked her up and gnawed at her neck making growling, grunting noises.

She shrieked and struggled. "NO!!" she screamed. "Get away!!"

He laughed, put her down, and she ran off back to her mother. Hangman put Zaedi down and the boy returned to playing with the other children. That left the men free to finally relax.

Hangman turned to go over to Mora, but he stopped when he saw another group of younger men gathered on the other side of the camp.

Kalo's boys had all grown up into tall, powerful, fearless warriors of the Godless Clan. They all wore their hair long now, dressed in hide loincloths, and fought as ferociously as any Godless men Hangman had ever seen.

They had all initiated over the last four years—all except for Kalo. He was still their leader, but as it turned out, he was the youngest of the bunch.

The Godless Clan had a rule that two boys couldn't initiate within three months of each other. Any particular family band wasn't likely to have more than two or three boys the same age, so they had to wait three months between initiations.

This never caused a problem before, but this band had so many boys the same age that it took a long time for all of them to initiate.

None of them minded waiting. Their initiations didn't change their status.

The other men accepted them, fought with them, hunted with them, shared information with them, and respected them as much as any men. The men had no reason to treat them as boys because they weren't.

Hangman turned aside and went over to them. "What did you find?"

"Nothing," Kalo replied. "The country is all clear to the east as far as the Far Cry mountain range. We didn't see any people of any Clan."

"How far north and south did you go?"

Kalo pointed to Pitch and Lucky, the twins who once had been Ethio and Hitro. "We sent two parties north and south as far as the cliffs to the north and the great Amber River to the south. If anyone is out there, they aren't on the eastern side."

Hangman frowned. "I didn't expect to find any Renegades there, but I did think another Clan or at least another Godless band might live over there. It doesn't seem possible that we're the only people in such a big territory."

"Maybe the population is getting smaller," Omen suggested. He was the twins' younger brother who used to be called Carro. "Maybe fewer people are inhabiting the country—because they all get killed by creatures. Maybe people will die out completely now because we're too few to defend ourselves."

Protests broke out among the group. Kalo's group—what everyone called "Kalo's band"—they all yelled and threw things at Omen to tell him that would never happen.

These men always went out together in a separate party from Hangman and the others. No one in the band treated this as unusual. Kalo's band had their own way of doing things.

Hangman remarked on it the least of everyone. Kalo and his men never gave Hangman anything to complain about. They never did since the first day he met them.

He left them to their own devices and returned to Mora. She kissed him once and sat down next to him to serve him some of the food she was cooking.

"How's the little Abnormit?" he asked.

She laughed and stroked her hand across her infant son's head. "He's a hungry monster just like his Abnormit relatives."

He grinned at her and stroked the baby's head, too. The little one didn't wake up. His name was Maeno and he still had a crumpled look like he was really displeased that he had to be born at all.

Hangman took the bowl out of Mora's hands and started eating. "We have to go back out for Kalo's initiation. We shouldn't be gone more than a few days."

"It's about time." Mora glanced across the camp. Alien returned to his own house to greet, hug, and kiss Cheina, cuddle up with their new young children, and then crossed the camp to talk to Kalo.

Kalo and Alien kept getting closer with every passing day. Kalo had grown almost as tall as Alien now. They talked and laughed as equals.

Alien beamed at Kalo with as much pride as if Alien had been gazing on his own son. They considered each other father and son as if they had never lived apart.

The other men of Kalo's band welcomed Alien as one of their own. He sat with them, ate with them, and talked with them in ways no other men in the band could.

Mora broke in on Hangman's thoughts. "When are you going to initiate Kuvik? Don't you think it's about time for him, too?"

Hangman glanced in the other direction. Kuvik had built a house for himself. He lived there alone and never made any overtures to any single women over the age of gathering about getting closer to them.

Kalo and his men would be approaching the age of gathering this year. They all stayed close to the girls they originally became fond of, but the boys who grew into men always stayed within the bounds of propriety and never took it any further.

Kuvik never did any of that. He never even looked at women or the older girls.

"I can't initiate him until he says he's ready," Hangman replied. "He always says it isn't time."

"You could convince him," she insisted. "He would listen to you."

"I don't think so. I've already mentioned it more than once. He doesn't feel he's earned the right to call himself Godless."

"If he hasn't, who has? He does more than anyone."

"We would have initiated him a long time ago if he only said he wanted to. He could fight a Gorlock. He could probably fight a Crusher. He's one of the most ruthless fighters I've ever seen. He would pass the initiation easily. He just doesn't want to."

"Doesn't he want to become Godless?" she asked.

"Oh, yes, he wants it more than anything. He says he would give anything to be Godless, but he doesn't want to bring shame on our Clan."

"Shame?! What shame?!"

"You don't have to tell me." Hangman put down his bowl. "Has anything been going on here while I've been gone?"

"That." She jutted her chin across the camp. "Not that you would be interested."

He followed her gaze and spotted Lonion, Cheina's younger son. He sat next to Vardetha, Choma's young daughter. Both of the young people were fourteen years old.

"Great," Hangman muttered. "I can see we'll have to initiate him next. He needs to get out of the camp."

"And that." She nodded in the other direction. Lonion's sister Aster stood against a tree near the edge of the jungle at a distance from the camp. One of the other young boys stood in front of her kissing her and grinding his body against her while he pawed at her sides.

Vuco had been only a child when his mother escaped from the Renegades with Hangman's band. Now he was nearing the age of initiation. Aster was a year younger.

"How do they grow up so fast?" Hangman remarked. "We were never that young."

Mora laughed and petted the baby's head again. "It's hard to believe this little grub will grow up to look like Kalo and his boys some-day—and then like Viking. I can't even picture Maeno getting that big even though I know he will."

Hangman leaned over and kissed her. "You look as beautiful now as when I first met you. I don't believe you will ever grow old or that your hair will turn grey. I believe you'll stay like this forever."

She blushed and laughed. "I sure wish you were right."

He got to his feet, left the camp, and strode up behind Vuco. The boy had his face so thoroughly plastered to Aster's that neither of them saw Hangman coming.

He grabbed the boy by the hair, yanked him off with a startled cry, and then grabbed Vuco by the arm and hauled him to a safe distance out of earshot from the camp.

Hangman gave him the same speech he gave Kalo and the boys about not crossing that line until he got to the age of gathering.

Hangman put the fear of God into Vuco by warning him that, if he did anything with a girl he wasn't married to, he could get thrown out of the band or barred from marrying anyone for the rest of his life.

Vuco got as apologetic and contrite as Kalo and the boys. Vuco swore up and down that he never did anything with Aster or any other girl and that he never would.

He gave Hangman his solemn word that he would toe the line always—like that meant anything to Hangman.

Then Hangman had to go track down Aster. She didn't make it easy. She hid from him at a distance from the camp so he already knew she was ashamed of what she did.

He gave her the same reprimand and warning—only harsher this time. He had to warn her about the consequences she could expect if she got pregnant from a man she wasn't legally married to.

It would be Hangman's decision how bad to make the punishment. He could throw her out of the band to wander the country alone if he thought the infraction deserved that.

Was this what being Kral was all about—policing these young people and making them tremble in their shoes in front of him? He couldn't remember Butcher or Shadow ever doing anything like this with any of the young people Hangman grew up with.

Butcher and Shadow didn't have to do it because everyone Hangman grew up with grew up Godless. They already knew the consequences of bad behavior.

Hangman couldn't even blame this on the young people's ignorance about the laws. They already knew they were doing wrong. They just lost control of themselves because they were young and wanted each other so badly.

Hangman had to go straighten out Lonion and Vardetha next. He reinforced to all four young people that, if they stuck to the rules and kept their noses clean, they could marry each other when they finally made it to the age of gathering.

They only had to wait four years. That used to seem like a long time when Hangman was younger. He used to think a year would last forever.

Now it seemed like just a few moments. He had a hard time believing that his band had been living in this valley for four years.

Chapter 2

Hangman returned to Mora's side and sat down with a heavy sigh. She laughed at him again. "What a monster you are," she teased.

"Never become Kral. That's all I'll say."

She blushed and stroked his forehead. "I'll try not to."

He lounged for the rest of the evening and pretended tomorrow would never come. He didn't want to be responsible—for anything—nor did he want to admit to himself that he was actually responsible for everything.

He fell asleep early. He fell asleep outside lying down next to one of the cooking fires. He didn't even go inside. He woke up alone in the early grey dawn. Mora wasn't around and neither were any of the children.

He peeked into his own shelter. Mora and the three children lay curled up asleep on the bed of hides. They all slept in a pile with little Maeno tucked against Mora's side with his mouth attached to her breast while he slept.

Zaedi and Thena slept on either side of her with their arms around their mother. Hangman stood in the doorway and stared in at them for a long time. He loved them more than anything. He loved them too much to disturb them.

He stayed away from the camp as much as he did because he loved them so much. He wanted nothing more than to protect them from anything that might be out there trying to harm them.

Maybe the power of his love even penetrated their sleep. Mora stirred while he stood there watching her. Her eyes floated open and she looked around before she bent over to check on the three children.

She spotted Hangman standing in the door, smiled at him, and sank back down into her place. She didn't move in any other way.

She lay there gazing up at him with all that pure understanding she always poured into him. She didn't have to say a word to understand exactly what she was thinking and feeling.

Coughing and crying broke out in the houses behind him. The noise startled Zaedi and Thena awake. Thena started crying and that woke up Maeno.

Mora struggled out of the pile to sit up and deal with all three children. Hangman left them there and retreated back to the fire.

More people came out of their houses. Alien ducked under his doorframe and shot Hangman a hard look across the camp. Today was a big day for Alien. It was Kalo's initiation day.

Zaedi burst out of the house a second later and came over to squat next to Hangman. "I want to initiate, Father," the boy announced.

Hangman couldn't help but laugh. "You will, my son—when you're old enough."

"I want to initiate now. I could fight a Gurlg chick."

"What man of the Godless Clan ever initiated by fighting a Gurlg chick? Wait until you grow some more. Then you can fight a Shriker like Wildling."

"I want to fight a Crusher like you did."

"You definitely need to grow some more for that. Do you think you could take a Crusher now? Please. Don't make me laugh."

Zaedi looked away. "You're right. Everyone would call me a coward if I fought a Gurlg chick."

Hangman rumpled the boy's long hair. It already hung past his shoulder blades. "I'm sure you'll make a great man of the Godless, but you can't initiate until you get to be fourteen years. You know that."

Zaedi frowned. "Why does it have to take so long?"

"I don't make the rules. I had to wait. We all did. Look at Kalo. He's been waiting four years too long already, but he doesn't mind because he knows he's a man."

"Let me come with you, Father. I want to watch."

"I'm sure Kalo would be highly insulted if he heard you say that. Initiations are for men, not little boys. Grow a little more. Then you can go to your own initiation. No one will be able to stop you after that."

They had to break off their conversation when the other men came out of their houses. They stood and slouched around waiting for nothing. Kalo's band showed up a few minutes later. They usually camped together out in the jungle, but Kalo didn't come with them.

The band gathered with the other men on the opposite side of the village. The women assembled together in one place apart from the men. The children kept running around everywhere. Most of them were too young even to understand what was happening.

Cheina finally came out of her house, cast one desperate glance around, raised both her hands, and let them slap down on her thighs. She opened and closed her mouth multiple times while she floundered in turmoil.

The other women surrounded her and she burst into tears when they drew her into their circle. Mora came out of the house with her children, took one look at the arrangement of everyone, and took all three children over there to join the women.

She had to stop and extend her hand to Zaedi. "You come, too, Zaedi," she told him. "You can't stay over here."

"I want to stay with Father," he told her.

"Go with your mother, my son," Hangman told him. "Your day will come—and when it does, I'll take you out to initiate you myself. I promise. Don't worry."

He took Mora's hand and went with her after that, but not without grumbling a lot. Hangman had to smile at the boy. He was only four years old and already planning his own initiation.

He planned to fight a Crusher. The boy had high ambitions. Hangman had to give him that.

Hangman stood up, but before he could move, Kalo came out of the jungle by himself. Cheina wailed even more loudly when he stopped there in sight of everyone.

Hangman strode over to Kalo and nodded to him. "Are you ready, brother?"

"I'm ready," Kalo murmured. "I'll be fighting a Blastidon."

Hangman nodded again to stop himself from cringing. Kalo couldn't have chosen a more formidable creature to fight. Then again, he was three and a half years older than most initiating boys. He had the size, weight, and experience to pull it off.

Hangman nodded over his shoulder. "Go say goodbye to your mother and let's go."

Hangman retreated and joined the men. Kalo went over to the women, hugged and kissed his mother, and then said his last farewells to his sister and all the other women.

Aster broke down crying when she hugged him. "I'll never see you again!"

"I love you," he murmured in her ear. "Take care of Mother for me."

Cheina wouldn't stop wailing. She grabbed his arm and tried to hold him back when he walked away. He had to use force to tear his hand out of her grip.

He didn't look back when he strode over to the men. They filed into the jungle before he got to them. He entered the middle of their group and all of them walked away in silence.

Cheina's wails and the other women's loud sobs followed the men into the trees. They kept going, crossed the mountain passes, left the valley, and entered more jungle before they camped for the night.

None of the men talked. Kalo's comrades stayed around him in a protective huddle, but no one could help him with this. He had to go through it alone.

The men camped on the ground, ate and slept little, and woke up early the next morning to start walking again. They climbed a high peak and surveyed the countryside. They stayed up there for four hours before they spotted a herd of Blastidons in the distance.

The band set off at a run to intercept them. The Blastidons entered a different patch of dense jungle. This place had no high rocks for the men to watch Kalo's initiation fight.

The party stopped a mile away from the herd. Alien turned to Kalo and squeezed both his shoulders. "We'll be watching everything. If anything happens, we'll get you out."

"Don't get me out, Alien." Kalo's voice trembled for the first time. "Let me die if I don't pass the test."

Alien compressed his lips and nodded. "I'm proud of you—more proud than I ever thought I could be. You're a man of the Godless Clan. Never forget that."

"You'll always take care of Mother and Aster, won't you?" Kalo choked. "Promise, Alien."

"I promise, my son." Alien sniffed, but he didn't let himself show any other sign of emotion. "I swear it. You never have to worry about your family—but that doesn't matter because you're going to win today. You'll go home a man and no one will ever call you Kalo again. I know it."

"Don't get me out," Kalo choked. "Let me die instead."

Alien nodded. "I understand. You won't leave here as anything but a man. I swear it."

Hangman took hold of Alien's arm. "Leave him be, brother. It's time."

Alien backed off. He and Kalo held eye contact for a long moment while Alien backstepped away.

The other men rocketed into the trees one after another. Hangman sprang up to follow them and then Alien came, too. They all left Kalo standing there alone on the ground.

Chapter 3

H angman perched in the high canopy where he could see the Blastidon herd. They were one of the creature species that only lived in the mountains. They didn't exist outside this country.

They were bigger than Stalkions and much more aggressive. The Blastidon got its name from a long trunk it could swing and crack like a whip to strike anything that attacked it.

The trunk ended in a ball of spikes that made it extra dangerous. The creature could also rear onto its hind legs and strike with its forelimbs. The front feet had sharp, flintlike hooves that could break a man's skull if the creature landed a direct hit.

Each front shin had another whip-like appendage with another ball of spikes the creature could crack at its enemy.

The Blastidon wasn't as thick-bodied and lumbering as a Stalkion. The creature had a long, narrow body and lean, muscular legs. The Blastidon could easily run down a man at his fastest speed.

A ridge of long hair hung from the back of the creature's neck. It would have given the creature a graceful, flowing look when it ran, but the Blastidons were too deadly for anyone to call them beautiful.

The men settled on the branches and everyone stopped moving. Hangman positioned himself close to Alien. The Kral was supposed to stay near the boy's father—mostly to stop the father from rushing in and saving the boy from his own initiation.

Hangman didn't worry about that happening here. Hangman entertained absolutely no doubt that Kalo would defeat whichever Blastidon he decided to fight. He wouldn't come out here unless he was ironclad certain of himself.

The men selected a spot in the canopy too high for the Blastidons to see anyone watching them. The Blastidons kept browsing in the leaves closer to the ground.

The females of the herd each stood taller than a man's head—taller than a Stalkion. Most of the females had juveniles at foot. Some of the juveniles were getting close to being fully grown.

One fully mature stallion stood guard over the herd. He growled and snapped at random insects that buzzed in his face. He even growled and snapped at the juveniles who came too close to him.

He kept shooting ferocious glances around at the surrounding jungle. His eyes flashed with menace and he pawed the ground for no reason.

The men sat in silence for several minutes before Kalo came striding out of the trees. He made no attempt at all to hide his approach.

In fact, he roared out in furious challenge even before he got near the herd. His enraged bellows echoed through the trees and startled all the Blastidons into looking up.

The stallion tossed his head and snarled low when Kalo broke through the undergrowth in full view of the herd.

The stallion spun around, tossed his head, and thrashed his trunk at the females and juveniles.

They all squealed, reared on their hind legs, and took off running into the jungle to get away from Kalo. That left him alone on the ground against the stallion almost twice his size.

Kalo didn't stop walking. He stormed through the jungle gripping his weapons in both hands. He still fought with the square blades the band stole from the Renegades all those years ago.

He started out by saying when he was younger that he wanted to fashion kukris like Hangman's, but in the end, Kalo got so accustomed to these metal weapons that he never used anything else. He gave up the idea of making his own.

He bared his teeth in pure blood hatred, braced himself for a showdown, and roared at the stallion. The stallion bellowed back, reared on his hind legs, thrashed his front hooves at Kalo, and then slammed down to paw the ground.

The stallion paced back and forth waiting for Kalo to get there. Hangman's chest tightened. He clenched his hands on the branch next to him. He would have to stop himself from going down there to help Kalo. Forget about Alien.

Kalo's men sat apart from everyone else. Hangman didn't dare to take his eyes off the combatants on the ground to make sure Kalo's men didn't intervene.

They wouldn't. They respected him too much. They had all been waiting a long time to call him their leader. They couldn't call him their Kral, but they treated him as one even though he was younger than all of them.

Kalo halted at the edge of the trees and faced down the stallion. The creature kept pacing back and forth and around in circles, rearing, and flailing its trunk and forelimb appendages at him.

He didn't step forward to enter the stallion's range. Neither of the adversaries moved closer to each other.

The seconds dragged by at an agonizing pace. Hangman couldn't take the strain. The tension going through the men around him spiked to the breaking point.

Kalo kept roaring at the same volume. His roars shattered the stallion's nerves. The creature bellowed and shrieked every time Kalo roared. The creature couldn't stand that noise.

That must have been Kalo's plan all along—to antagonize the stallion into attacking first. The creature reared one more time and charged.

The stallion scampered forward on its hind legs at the highest point of its rear. It got just a little closer to Kalo, swung its trunk to pulverize him, and then plunged down to strike him with its front hooves.

The stallion would have killed Kalo for certain if he hadn't expected the creature to do exactly that. Kalo darted out of the way just in time, took a flying leap upward, and twisted over to land on the creature's back.

Kalo straddled right behind the stallion's shoulder blades, dropped one of his blades to the ground, and used both hands to raise his other blade high over his head.

The stallion shrieked in a rage and tried to turn around to attack him, but the stallion only carried Kalo with him.

Kalo contracted all his muscles and drove his blade downward into the creature's body from directly above. The blade stabbed between the spine and the shoulder blades—right into the most vital part of the stallion's chest.

The creature screamed in a much different tone, but he didn't fall. He reared again and thrashed his forelimbs in the air so loudly that he threw Kalo off his back.

Kalo barely managed to pull his blood-soaked blade out of the creature's body before he tumbled off and crashed down on the ground.

He scrambled to his feet just in time for the stallion to wheel around and attack again. The stallion cracked his trunk at Kalo, but Kalo scooted away just in time.

He tucked, rolled, and grabbed his second blade before he raced out of range, but the stallion didn't want to accept that.

The creature dove for Kalo again and again. The stallion became more frantic and more deadly with every plunge as the creature felt itself starting to weaken.

Kalo reacted to each plunge by springing out of the way at the last possible second and coming to rest within inches of the stallion's sides.

Kalo executed the same maneuver each time. He dropped one blade on the ground and used both arms and all his weight and strength to drive the other blade as far as it would go into the creature's body.

The stallion held on a lot longer than Hangman ever would have predicted. Kalo wounded the creature countless times, but the stallion didn't seem to weaken at all.

Only his wild, bloodthirsty rage told the tale of how badly he was hurting. He spun faster, charged sooner, and cut his corners tighter.

Kalo weakened first. He staggered each time he had to jump anywhere. Sweat and blood coated him all over. He gasped for breath and he had to keep blinking the sweat out of his eyes.

On his last strike, he couldn't drive his blade more than a few inches into the creature's tough body. The blade fell out in Kalo's hand when he sprang away to save himself.

He took a position at a greater distance from the creature. Kalo panted hard. He moved slower and barely kept out of the creature's way.

Blood soaked the stallion's sides and ran down his legs, but that only seemed to make him more dangerous. Hangman's nerves threatened to snap.

Alien kept burying his face in his hands, groaning, and forcing himself to look up. Hangman didn't dare to look at anyone else.

Kalo and the stallion both came to a halt and glared at each other. Kalo's rasping breath echoed in the tense silence. All the men in the canopy heard him wheezing and straining for air.

The stallion actually seemed stronger and less winded right now. He hardly seemed aware of his own injuries.

The two adversaries eyed each other. Which of them would have the strength to finish the job one way or the other?

No one in the canopy moved to intervene. Hangman made up his mind then and there not to save Kalo's life if the stallion won. The stallion earned the right to kill this enemy. Hangman couldn't take that away from such a brave, noble, powerful creature.

Kalo seemed to come to the same decision at the same time. He let his arms go limp and lowered his blades in a sign of surrender.

The stallion bellowed one last time, reared, and scampered his hind legs to shuffle a little closer to Kalo before the stallion drove his hooves down to kill his enemy.

Kalo stood in perfect stillness—right up until the moment when he sprang sideways. Hangman couldn't tell in that moment if Kalo had been faking his fatigue all this time or if the stallion really did wear him down.

Kalo kept his blades down until the last possible second when the stallion came perilously close to cracking Kalo's skull in half. Kalo didn't raise his blades even then.

He dropped one blade as before, took another flying leap, and twisted over in midair again, but he didn't land on the creature's back.

He just lifted off the ground—just enough for the stallion to bring down all its weight on that one spot. The creature landed so hard that it embedded its sharp hooves in the soil where Kalo had just been standing.

The stallion's own momentum brought its head close to the ground—almost touching the ground. Kalo wheeled in midair and landed straddling the creature directly behind its skull.

The stallion's head sank so low to the ground that Kalo ended up standing on his own feet with his legs spread to leave room for the stallion's head between his knees.

Kalo didn't wait for the stallion to recover. Kalo raised his only weapon on high, gripped it by the hilt in both hands, and brought down the hard metal butt of the handle right on top of the stallion's skull.

The blow shattered the stallion's skull with a brutal crack that echoed all the way up through the canopy. The stallion collapsed onto his chest. His face hit the dirt, but Kalo didn't stop there.

He took one menacing step forward, raised his weapon again, and smashed it down just as hard on the same spot. Brain and ooze leaked out through the cracked skull. The stallion didn't rise.

Kalo delivered the same killing blow twice more before his arms gave out and the blade fell out of his hands. He staggered away and stood there wavering on the spot with his back to his fallen enemy.

The stallion didn't move. Its eyes glazed over and didn't close. The fight was over.

Kalo collapsed on his knees and his chin sank onto his chest. His back and shoulders heaved from the effort. He couldn't stand or raise his arms. Exhaustion weighed him down.

Alien whimpered under his breath, buried his face in his hands, and didn't look up again. Hangman gripped his shoulder and shook him. Kalo did it. He initiated. It was done.

His men recovered first. They swarmed out of the trees, soared through the canopy, dropped into the clearing, and surrounded him all talking and touching him at once. Hangman couldn't see him anymore.

Hangman, Viking, Alien, Kuvik, Red, and Red's men stayed where they were and let Kalo celebrate with his comrades. This one was all theirs. Cross went down there with them. He always traveled with Kalo's band nowadays.

Hangman and the others watched from a distance and didn't interrupt even to go congratulate Kalo. Hangman needed to come up with a name for him now.

Alien took his hands down and wiped tears off his face. He sniffed and ran his knuckles across his nose. His features contorted when he saw all the young men in the distance practically dancing around Kalo.

They pulled him to his feet, but he kept wavering. He smiled at them a lot, but he didn't jump around. He could barely move.

Hangman and the others stayed in the trees for hours. Kalo's men built a fire, butchered the Blastidon, and put the meat on the spit to cook. The sun went down and it got dark.

Their voices rang through the canopy a lot more loudly than they should have, but no one went down there to tell them to be quiet.

Hangman waited until nightfall. "We better go join them," he told the others. "Let's go."

He climbed down and waited for the others to do the same. They met up in a loose group and headed for the bonfire in the distance.

Dead silence fell over the group when Kalo's men saw Hangman coming. They stopped horsing around and straightened up to gather behind Hangman.

Hangman realized in that moment that this was no initiation. It never had been. None of these young men were boys anymore. He couldn't even consider them his subordinates anymore if they ever had been.

He halted in front of Kalo—the man who would never be known as Kalo before.

"You're a man of the Godless Clan," Hangman began. "But you've been a man for a long time—a man we're all proud to know and respect. Your name is Hammer—and let me be the first to call you Kral of your band here. We should agree to live together in harmony and share the same territory—you with your band and me with mine." Hangman held out his hands. "I offer my friendship and alliance for all our sakes. Join me and live side by side in the same territory."

Hammer compressed his lips to hold back emotion, shut his eyes, and then looked up fighting back tears. He clasped Hangman's hand. "I accept with honor—honor to call you brother and all these men brothers. We will share the territory and live together as one band with two Krals. Consider me and my men your friends and allies. We're stronger together."

The two men squeezed, let go, and everyone sat down together to enjoy a feast of the meat Hammer killed.

He and Hangman sat next to each other in honor of the occasion. Every passing moment sealed the deal. Hammer was as much Kral of his own band as Hangman was. Hangman would never be able to tell any of these young men what to do ever again. He didn't want to.

Hammer's men passed around the food and everyone shared it. They talked late into the night. Different men told stories about their initiations or battles they fought in the past.

Hammer's men told and retold the story of his fight against the Blastidon and all the tricks he pulled on the creature. Everyone admired the stallion and marveled at how close he came to defeating Hammer. All the men called the stallion a worthy foe who tested Hammer to his limit.

He stayed quiet through the evening. Hammer didn't engage him in conversation. A bunch of the men tried again to encourage Kuvik to initiate, but he refused for all the same reasons. No one could talk him out of it.

Chapter 4

H angman and his men woke up in the early dawn light. Hangman sat up and looked down at the remains of the fire. Some of Kalo's men stayed up to cure what was left of the Blastidon meat.

Now they slept on the other side of the fire from Hangman. Hammer rolled onto his back and stared up into the canopy. "We should take you home to your mother and sister," Hangman told him. "Do you feel strong enough to travel?"

"Of course." Hammer sat up and shot Hangman a grin. "That's the hardest part of the ordeal, isn't it—going home and having them cry all over me?"

Hangman laughed. "It is definitely the most dangerous part. Eat something before we leave."

Hangman and Hammer ate together while the rest of the men woke up. Hammer didn't act weak or tired. He just stayed much quieter than usual. He didn't even engage his comrades in conversations.

"You'll be near the age of gathering now," Hangman remarked. "You should consider getting married. Every Kral needs a wife."

Hammer didn't look up. "I still plan to marry Vina if you're still willing to let her go with me when the time comes."

Hangman's head whipped around. "I didn't know you still saw her."

Hammer nodded. "We keep it clean—always—but our feelings for each other never changed since we first met. We take walks and talk about our future. That's all we do." Hammer looked up for the first time. "Will you let me marry her—when we get old enough?"

Hangman could barely make himself heard. "Of course, brother. Be happy. I'm sure she'll give you a big, beautiful family."

Hammer looked away again. "I'm afraid that being Kral of my own band will mean I have to part from you."

"No!" Hangman breathed. "Not because of that. Circumstances might part us, but never that."

"Thank you," Hammer murmured. "You were always my Kral. I never wanted to replace you."

"You aren't replacing me. Either way, I can't think of a better man who would replace me. You're Kral of your own band. You have been for years. Just accept it. It's never easy for any man to become Kral. It's always easier to let someone else do it, but you're already a leader to these men. Just keep doing what you're already doing. They love you for it. They want you to."

Hammer nodded. "Thank you. I value your friendship."

"And I value yours. I never could have led this band for so long without your help. You must know that."

Their conversation came to an end as more men woke up. They all ate, drank, splashed water on their faces and necks in the streams, and divided up the leftover food for the journey back.

The men set off in another long, silent, single-file line. Hangman and Hammer mixed in the middle of the group. No one kept to any particular order even though everything had changed.

Hangman turned his head from side to side to scan the jungle. This jungle sounded different from the sounds he knew from Shadow's territory, but Hangman got used to the new pattern.

It told him just as much as before. All the men adapted, but Hammer's band adapted the quickest. They didn't have any history in Shadow's territory to contradict their experience.

Hangman felt closer to Hammer now. Making Hammer Kral of his own band erased a barrier between them. Hangman didn't realize the barrier even existed until now.

Initiating Hammer sooner wouldn't have been possible or even advisable. He initiated when he should have and he became the man he was always meant to be. He wasn't the same person as he was even yesterday. His initiation really did change him into a new man.

The party crossed the pass. The energy in the group charged with a thrill of excitement when the men saw home ahead. Hammer actually smiled at his men for the first time. Hangman could just imagine the celebration when they got back.

A few other men burst out in grins—until a weapon cracked in the nearby rocks. All the men spun around and drew their axes and blades when a party of Renegades swarmed out of the nearby cliffs.

They fell on the Godless way too close. Hangman sprang into the fight swinging both his kukris. So many men fought around him that he lost track of what they were doing.

He attacked any Renegade in sight. They used fewer firearms here. He didn't know why. They only fired from the rocks. They used regular weapons and fought hand to hand inside the pass.

The Renegades must not have planned to meet up with such a large body of Godless in one place. The two bands never traveled together the rest of the time. They only came together now because this was a special occasion.

The Renegades brought the number of men to overwhelm what they must have expected to be a much smaller party. The two sides locked together at a stalemate. Hangman attacked Renegades engaged with Red's men or any of Hammer's comrades.

Hangman slashed and whirled from one opponent to another. He spotted Cross backed against the rocks fighting three Renegades at once. The rocks saved him until three of Hammer's men charged over there to help him.

Hangman turned the other way just in time to see another four Renegades going after Viking and Alien. The two cousins got trapped right at the top of the pass. The downward slope fell away behind them toward the Godless camp.

Hangman leapt over there to help his cousins, but another three Renegades darted in front of him and drove him back. He fought them as hard as he could, but they overpowered him. Where were all these Renegades coming from? Did they bring in more men?

He glanced around and accidentally missed blocking one of their strokes. It slashed across his forearm and brought him back to his senses in a heartbeat.

He raised his weapons, but at that moment, Pitch and Lucky raced up behind the Renegades and stabbed two of them. The last remaining Renegade turned around to defend himself and Hangman stabbed him through the back of the head.

Hangman spun around looking for his next target. Pitch and Lucky did the same thing. The three men turned back to back, but the Godless men had cut down all the Renegades. No new enemies came out of the rocks to attack them.

"They ambushed us," Wildling murmured. "They were waiting for us—right at the crest of the pass—right where they knew we would come. How did they know?"

"They could have followed us another time," Butch pointed out. "They could have marked the spot, let us go through, and then laid the ambush."

"That's impossible," Hammer pointed out. "We've patrolled this country every day for miles around. We would have seen signs of Renegades before now. I agree with Wildling. They knew exactly where to come."

"How do you explain that?" Cross asked. "No one in our band would betray us. They're all loyal."

A broken murmur interrupted them. "Hangman.....over here....."

Hangman had to look around everywhere before he realized who called his name. Viking squatted on the ground right next to the pass.

Hangman went over to him and saw Alien lying on his back with a penetrating blade wound through the lowest part of his neck. Blood welled out of the cut and out of his mouth.

"No...." Hangman started to bend down, but Hammer collided with him, shoved Hangman out of the way, and fell on Alien. Hammer grabbed him by the shoulders and tried to pick him up.

"NO!!" Hammer roared. "NO....ALIEN—NO!!"

"My son...." Alien's eyes rolled back in their sockets. He choked on his own blood.

He tried to touch Hammer, but Alien couldn't focus well enough even to see where Hammer was.

Hammer seized his hand and placed it on the side of his own neck. "No, Alien!" Hammer whimpered. "You can't die! I need you!"

"....proud of you.....my son......" Alien coughed and spat blood all over the place. "......the best of men....."

"NO!!" Hammer wailed and burst into bitter tears.

Alien's eyes rolled back again. He started choking and he didn't stop—not until he burst into a fit of convulsions and then collapsed. He didn't move again.

Blood gushed from the wound and from his mouth. No one tried to stop it.

Hammer gulped down tears. He kept whining, touching Alien's face, and sobbing, "No! No!"

No one stepped in to comfort him. A thousand ideas collided in Hangman's head, but one thought boiled up higher than the others.

This was no accident. He would be inclined to believe that the Renegades followed the band here—except that no one in Hangman's band had seen any Renegades for four whole years.

The band crossed treacherous, rocky, barren country before they settled in this valley. That was years ago. The Renegades couldn't have followed the band's trail here—not after all that time—not with so little sign over such steep, rocky ground.

Hammer was right about one thing. Everyone in Hangman's band had stayed on high alert through four long years of patrols, scouting missions, and tracking parties to make absolutely certain no Renegades entered this country.

One of the Godless would have seen something—anything—any sign. No one knew this country better than the Godless. They searched tirelessly—every day—for years—and found nothing.

So how did the Renegades just drop out of the clear blue sky and wind up here—at exactly the right spot to ambush the band?

How did the Renegades know to attack today of all days—at this particular time? It couldn't be coincidence or accident. That wasn't possible.

Hangman stared down at Alien—and his adopted son sobbing over Alien's dead body. What a crushing blow for Hammer on the day of his greatest triumph.

Hangman couldn't even feel his own loss for the cousin he loved and worshiped as a brother and even something like a surrogate father.

Hangman shook himself back to his senses. "Pick him up. We have to take him home."

Some of Hammer's men took hold of his shoulders. He had been calming down for the last few minutes. He completely fell apart when Viking and Red's men picked up Alien and carried him down the slope toward the camp in the distance.

Hammer sobbed all the way down the hill. He let himself grieve, now when his men and comrades surrounded him.

He stopped when the party made it to the flat ground on the valley floor. He sniffed back his tears, rubbed his face, and his features closed up in a wall of solid granite.

He locked his mouth shut, narrowed his eyes, and gritted his teeth in smoldering fury. He showed no other side of grief at all as the party came out of the trees in full view of the camp.

Cheina screamed when the men walked into the camp carrying Alien's body. She screeched herself hoarse and didn't stop. The other women had to hold her back and restrain her.

She went into a hysterical fit of bellowing, thrashing, and even throwing kicks and punches at the women nearest her. She fought them, and when they wouldn't let her go, she turned on them screaming and raging her head off.

The men pretended not to hear her. They also ignored Aster and Lonion sobbing to one side. Aster kept screaming and tearing her hair until Vuco caught her and stopped her.

The men laid Alien's body on the ground in the middle of the camp. No one even acknowledged Hammer's return.

Hangman paced up and down next to his cousin's body. "Someone in this camp is a traitor!" he boomed. "Someone here sold us out to the Renegade Clan! They attacked us when we were coming through the pass. They killed Alien—which means whoever did this killed Alien! We'll find out who did it! Don't think you can get away with betraying us! You'll pay the ultimate price when we find out who you are! I hope you can sleep at night. You killed a good man who gave everything to protect you—and this is how you repay him!"

Hangman pointed down at the body, but he couldn't go on. His own despair threatened to break him in half. He returned to his own house. Mora stood outside it clutching all three of her children near her. Tears poured down her cheeks when she saw Alien dead.

Hangman couldn't look at any of them. He collapsed there on the ground, folded his arms, and covered his face with his hands. He couldn't break down—not now.

That was someone else's job. Cheina kept raging, screaming, and howling over there on the other side of the camp. Aster and Lonion both wept openly. Their friends tried to comfort them, but no one could comfort anyone from this.

Hammer squatted down next to Alien's body and glared at it in outright hatred. Hangman already knew what was going through the young man's mind.

Someone did this. No way could this be a random attack.

The Renegades had definitely not been wandering around in this country and just happened to locate the Godless band. That is exactly what didn't happen.

Hangman stared at the ground in front of him. He prepared to completely shut down all his brain functions when his son Zaedi broke away from Mora, walked over, and hugged Hangman around the neck.

Hangman's reserve cracked. He put his arms around his son, pulled the boy into his lap, and hugged him.

Hangman prayed to Almighty God that Zaedi never had to go through what Hammer went through today. Hangman prayed that he died somewhere far away from Zaedi—somewhere Zaedi didn't have to see it happen.

Was Shadow dead somewhere? Was Hangman one of the fatherless sons wandering aimlessly in the world with no older man to guide him?

Hangman couldn't think that. He had to keep believing that Shadow was still alive and that they would meet again someday. On the other hand, Hangman hoped he was hundreds of miles away when Shadow died. Hangman didn't want to be around for that.

Zaedi huddled into a ball in Hangman's lap and cowered in the shelter of Hangman's arms. Was Zaedi thinking the same thing?

Hangman would spend his life worrying about his children—especially his sons. Would Maeno be the one to go through that nightmare?

Mora sat down next to Hangman, rested her head on his shoulder, and cried. She did all the crying for both of them.

Maeno lay asleep in her arms with his mouth permanently attached to her breast. Did he ever take it off? He didn't really need to. He belonged there.

Thena sat down on Hangman's other side. She tried to hug him, but her little arms only went a third of the way around his torso. "Alien is dead, isn't he, Father?" she piped.

"Yes, my love," Hangman choked. "He died this morning. That's why Hammer is so sad."

"Who's Hammer?" Zaedi asked.

"Alien's oldest son. He initiated yesterday and changed his name to Hammer. Call him that from now on."

All eyes turned to Hammer. "He doesn't look sad," Thena pointed out. "He looks mad."

"He is," Hangman replied. "He's mad that someone killed Alien."

"Then why do you say he's sad?" Zaedi asked and shrank deeper into Hangman's arms when Hammer got to his feet.

"He's mad and sad at the same time." Hangman fell silent when Hammer shot one last death glare at Alien's body and barged over to Hangman's house.

He stopped there and glared down at Hangman holding his children. Mora didn't take her head off Hangman's shoulder.

"I'm going back out tomorrow," Hammer clipped. "I'm going to track them down and get some answers."

"Let us come with you," Hangman replied. "We're stronger together."

Hammer compressed his lips and finally nodded. "We should leave some of our men here to guard the camp—now that we know there are Renegades in this country."

"I agree. We'll leave six of Red's men and six of yours—the same number from each band."

Hammer nodded again and stormed off. He returned to his mother's house, ducked inside, and came out with a bundle wrapped in a hide and tied with string.

His mother didn't notice. She kept blasting off over there with five women surrounding her to make sure she didn't lose control and hurt herself or someone else.

They finally let her approach Alien's body. She collapsed on top of it wailing, screaming, and crying all over him.

Hammer walked out of the camp, entered the jungle, and disappeared without another word to anyone. His men followed him and left the camp partially empty.

Chapter 5

The men returned to the pass where the Renegades killed Alien. Silence fell over the group when they surveyed that horrible spot.

Hammer narrowed his eyes and glared at everything. He didn't soften. If anything, he became harder and more furious the longer this went on.

The men split up without a word. Hammer's band went off in one direction searching for any trace of the route the Renegades used to get up here.

Hangman Viking, Red, and his men went in a different direction searching for the same thing. These mountains only offered a certain number of viable pathways to those mountains.

The Godless traveled a lot faster than they did when they first entered these mountains. The men ran and scrambled over rocks and ledges, jumped down steep walls, and followed all the channels and byways they knew so well.

The Godless had that one advantage over the Renegades. The Godless knew this country better than the Renegades ever could.

That on its own made it so much more likely that someone from the Godless camp tipped off the Renegades and told them where to find the initiation party.

Hangman's group scaled the mountains almost all the way back to the battery. Hangman, Viking, Kuvik, and the others perched on a nearby peak and looked down into the deep canyons the Godless took so long to traverse getting into this country.

Hangman spotted Hammer and the others on another mountaintop a dozen miles away. The men could see the whole surrounding country from here.

Hammer's men spread out and scaled different hilltops at different vantage points. Red and his men did the same thing. Everyone kept an eye out for any sign of movement.

Hangman's sharp eyes darted everywhere. The Renegades had to be here somewhere. They wouldn't carry out a surprise attack like that if they didn't plan to follow it up.

They wouldn't travel all this way and take four whole years to penetrate this country—not without some credible intelligence to let them know the Godless were here.

He didn't see anything. None of the other men signaled that they saw anything.

Hangman started to turn away when he spotted a Shriker wheeling in the air. He had noticed the creature earlier. It circled in its usual hunting patterns high above the canyons.

The creature dropped a thousand feet for no reason, stalled, and dropped again. Hangman stood up to get a better look.

"Do you see something?" Red asked.

Hangman spun around and flagged Wildling on one of the other peaks. Wildling was looking away in the opposite direction.

Hangman pointed to the Shriker. Wildling squinted into the distance just as the Shriker stalled, lifted off, circled, and stalled again over exactly the same spot. The creature must have been eyeing something on the ground.

Wildling waved down some of his comrades, pointed at the Shriker, and spun his arm in the air above his head. Butch, Carnage, and Jolt took off running one way. Wildling sprang down from the peak and sprinted into a different canyon.

The whole party raced back down the byways to get back to that one spot. Hangman kept catching glimpses of the Shriker. It didn't attack, but it didn't leave, either. Something was down there.

The Shriker would have attacked if whatever was down there had been its normal prey. The Shriker might get that interest and not attack if it saw people exposed on the valley floor.

Hangman raced behind his friends. None of them slowed at all. Wildling and the others led the pack on a dead course for that spot, but they didn't run all the way there.

They scattered into the hills again, scaled cliffs, and took elevated positions where they could observe the ground from a safe distance.

The band clambered through the rocks as easily as they once traveled through the jungle treetops. The Godless adapted their methods to the terrain.

They drew up on a series of high points and looked down at a group of twenty Renegades. They had set up a semi-permanent camp in a closed box canyon where they probably hoped the Godless would never see them.

Hangman's people had searched this area recently. The Renegades must have entered these mountains less than two weeks ago.

This canyon was nowhere near the route the Godless used to enter the mountains. The Renegades couldn't have wound up here by following the Godless.

Hangman could only think of one explanation. Someone who knew these mountains must have told the Renegades to camp here thinking they would be safe from Godless scouting parties.

Hangman didn't like to suspect anyone from Red's party. They had been Godless long before they ever met up with Hangman's band.

Red and his men traveled to the ammunition store to defeat the Renegades. Red and his men gave up their homes and families for the chance to protect their loved ones from further attack. The men probably thought they were sacrificing their very futures to go on that mission.

Hangman bet that the traitor would be one of the former Renegade captives—someone who joined his band when he rescued Mora—someone who might have acted like a former captive but who actually liked the Renegades more than they let on.

He didn't like to suspect them, either, especially not any of the men's wives, but he had to consider all the possibilities. He couldn't rule anyone out until he knew for sure.

He did rule out Viking and Cross—and Mora. They were the only ones he really trusted. None of them would have done anything to put Alien in danger—or anyone else in the camp.

Hangman found it impossible to believe that any of the men would tip off the Renegades. None of the men had acted squirrely after Hammer's initiation.

All the men acted as surprised as Hangman himself when the Renegades attacked. That supported the idea that the traitor was one of the freed captives—but it didn't prove anything.

The Shriker kept bombing out of the sky, screeching at the Renegades, and then pulling back when the men on the ground raised their weapons to defend themselves.

One of the men aimed a firearm at the creature, but his comrades stopped him from shooting. The sound would have brought the Godless running if nothing else did.

The Shriker gave the Renegades away. The creature swooped in wipe circles to gain altitude, came to a standstill, and hovered there to eye the Renegades. They saw the danger and stood ready to defend themselves if the Shriker attacked. It didn't, but it kept threatening.

The Renegades held a hasty conversation while they held the creature off. Hangman couldn't hear them from this distance. They backed against the cliffs and then decided to retreat into one of the side channels where the walls would give them more protection.

The Shriker followed them, but it couldn't dive or threaten them once they got inside the channel. The creature circled higher and took up a holding pattern high above the party where it could watch their movements.

The Shriker also spotted Hangman's men. They offered much easier targets, now that it saw them standing on the exposed rock.

The Shriker moved off to focus on the Godless instead. The Renegades took advantage of that by running for it to get away from the creature.

Hangman signaled his friends. They all dropped into side canyons and fissures for protection, too, but they didn't retreat. The Godless used the labyrinth of cliffs to work their way around in front of the Renegades.

The mysterious traitor didn't tell the Renegades everything about these mountains. The Renegades didn't know where they were going. The Godless ambushed them easily.

Hammer's men and Red's men split up again. Hangman and Viking stayed with Red's party. Cross stayed with Hammer's band. The two groups converged where all the cracks and fissures opened into a wider, sandy canyon buried deep in the mountains.

The Renegades never realized the danger they were in until they blundered out into the open ground. The Godless emerged from their own channels at the same time and flanked the Renegades from two sides.

The Shriker knew the mountains much better than the Renegades did, too. The Shriker must have been watching the Renegades run straight into the creature's trap.

The Shriker dove the instant the Renegades came out of the channel. The creature plummeted at incredible speed, slammed its giant talons down on five men in the back of the group, and closed its claws around them to pick up three of them.

The men screamed in terror as the creature lifted off carrying them with it. The men thrashed around and tried to strike at the creature's talons, but the Shriker's tough scaly legs protected it.

The rest of the Renegades spun backward to defend themselves against the Shriker. The Godless attacked from behind.

Hangman struck out with his kukris, sank his blade into his first victim's shoulder, and then chopped his other weapon into the man's thigh.

The Renegade collapsed in front of him and Hangman lunged for the guy. Hangman seized the injured man by the hair and dragged him kicking and screaming toward the fissure the Godless used to get here.

The other Godless did the same thing. They attacked to injure and capture as many Renegades as possible.

The Shriker flapped its huge wings, rose as high as the nearby mountain peaks, and let his victims fall screaming to their deaths. They splattered on the rocks and the Shriker left them there to come back for more.

The Shriker circled at altitude while Hammer, Burn, and Prodigy also dragged their injured prisoners into the canyons. They barely made it before the Shriker plummeted again.

It aimed for the thickest cluster of men this time and would have grabbed Viking and Lucky along with the Renegades. Hangman dove for them just in time and tackled Viking out of the way. The Shriker grabbed Lucky and started to carry him away along with four Renegades.

Hangman raced back, grabbed Lucky by the ankle, and pulled so hard that the Shriker's claws loosened just a little bit. Lucky tumbled out and landed on top of Hangman on the ground amongst all the remaining Renegades.

The Shriker screeched in a rage and turned back, but the creature couldn't attack the men without loosening its talons the rest of the way. It lifted off and let those men drop from altitude, too.

Hangman and Lucky charged for the cliffs. The Renegades tried to give chase, but the other Godless came out and drove them back while Hangman and the others escaped into the canyons.

They dragged their four injured prisoners with them. Some of the prisoners put up more of a fight than others.

The Godless drove the injured men away at blade point. One of the Renegades collapsed. Viking picked the guy up and carried him for miles until the party retreated to the safety of a high cave on a cliffside far away.

Chapter 6

Hangman stood off to one side and waved at Hammer. "Go on. Question them. Get the answers you want. Don't spare their feelings."

Hammer clamped his lips shut. "I don't trust myself to do it slowly enough. You should do it."

Hangman had to smile at the young man. "You earned this. Do it as quickly or as slowly as you want to. Make them feel what you feel inside. I'm sure you can do that."

Hammer hesitated again, but he finally went over to the four injured men. The one Hangman injured was by far the healthiest of the bunch.

Hammer measured the others. Pitch had stabbed one of them through the ribs. The guy panted and sweated while he clutched his side. His skin turned ashen and his eyes darted around in wild panic. He wouldn't last much longer.

Cross had cut another across the back of the thighs so the guy couldn't walk. He was the one Viking had to carry. Blood poured down his legs. He wouldn't last much longer, either.

"Which one of you wants to tell me how you found us?" Hammer murmured in a deadly undertone.

"Die, Godless scum!" Hangman's victim bellowed. "You'll all die and the Renegade Clan will rule this territory!"

"You'll die first, my friend." Hammer strode over to the man with the stab wound in his chest. "We're going to find out one way or the other. If you tell me what I want to know right now, I won't torture you. I'll kill you quickly. You don't have to die screaming in pain and begging for your mothers."

"You foul vermin will never defeat the Renegade Clan!" the first man thundered. "We'll never tell you anything!"

Hammer strode back over to him, squatted in front of the guy, clamped his hand around the man's shoulder wound, and squeezed.

Hangman had to look away and shut his eyes when the guy screamed out. Hangman retreated to the outer cave open, but nothing could block that sound out of his head. He gulped down the urge to puke.

Hangman didn't give himself the option to go over there and stop Hammer from doing what he had to do. These Renegades threatened the Godless band. They threatened Mora and the children.

The guy kept screaming until Hammer let go. Then the injured man collapsed sobbing on the ground.

Hammer paced back and forth in front of all four prisoners. "Which one of you wants to be next? I can keep going like this all day. Some of you will probably live a long time."

He stopped in front of the same man with the stab wound. Hangman expected Hammer to try to reason with the guy and tell him again that he was going to die anyway.

The guy didn't give Hammer a chance to reason with him. "The signs...." the guy panted. "We followed....the signs....."

"What signs?" Hammer demanded. "Do you mean you tracked us—over bare stone after four years of hard weather? I don't think so."

"The signs....on the rocks....signs....left for us.....to follow.....to the pass.....and messages....arrows.....symbols....."

Hammer squatted down and got right in the guy's face. "Who left the signs for you to follow? Who led you to us?"

The guy shut his eyes, shook his head, and gulped. "I don't know...... someone..... met with Agrenon...."

"Who's that?" Carnage asked.

"One of our....one of our leaders.....met with our contact......"

"So you never met the contact? You never saw the person?"

The guy shook his head fast. "Agrenon......camps....to the south. He doesn't come into the mountains."

"How is that possible?" Wildling asked. "How could one of ours travel all that way south to meet with one of yours?"

"I don't know.....don't know.....anything about it......He wants you.....only you.....your band....no other......" The man's eyes glazed and rolled back into their sockets before he dragged his vision back into focus. "The signs...we follow the signs.....that's all I know."

Hammer stood up and shot a death glare at the other three Renegades. The man with the slash across the back of his legs cast a terrified glance over his shoulder at Hammer and looked away.

"Do any of you know anything about this contact?" Hammer asked. All three shook their heads.

"We all follow the signs.....all of us.....in that party....."

Hammer went back over to the man with the shoulder injury. "What about you? Do you know something you aren't telling me?"

Hammer started to extend his hand toward the guy's neck. The guy screamed before Hammer even touched him. "No! No! I don't know anything! I only know to follow the signs. The contact has a series of marks they use to tell us where to go, where to wait, and where to camp."

Hammer stood up, looked up and down the group, and then pulled his blade and slashed it across the man's neck. Hammer went down the line and cut all their throats one after the other. He left their bodies there bleeding.

All the Godless turned their backs on the bodies. Hangman left the cave mouth and rejoined his comrades. It was over now, but he still felt cold sweat running down the back of his neck.

"Someone is leaving signs all over these mountains for the Renegades to follow," Prodigy remarked.

"It must be someone who leaves the camp often and is gone for long periods," Hammer pointed out. "None of us could have done it. We're always together."

"Anyone could be leaving the camp undetected," Jolt added. "Everyone is too busy to pay attention to what everyone else is doing."

"Not anyone could be leaving the camp undetected," Cross interjected. "You can't tell me mothers like Mora who have three little children to tend would leave the camp for hours or days at a time. Are you telling me she takes her children with her—and baby Maeno wrapped around her chest—and goes trekking across the country to leave signs on rocks for the Renegades to ambush us? Excuse me, but that is just not happening."

"That rules out half the women in camp," Wildling reasoned. "Who else is there?"

"All the young people," Hammer replied. "They have plenty of free time. They leave the camp all the time and no one notices. The women and whichever men stay behind think the young people leave together, but no one really knows what they do."

"There are also the older women—Hicia and the others," Viking added. "They don't have children."

"We can't go back to the camp and start interrogating these women," Red decided. "For one thing, we would leave the country unguarded if we kept a constant watch on our own women."

"We might not have to interrogate them," Hangman suggested. "We could tell the few we trust to keep an eye open for anyone who stays away from the camp for a long time or anyone acting suspiciously."

"We all trust our own women," Prodigy pointed out. "We couldn't tell them all. That would tip off the traitor."

"We would be able to keep an eye out ourselves if we went back," Legacy suggested. "The traitor wouldn't be able to go off without one of us seeing."

Hammer glanced over at Hangman. "What do you think?"

"I say we track down what's left of this party and finish them off," Hangman replied. "I say we destroy any Renegade we find in this country. This Agrenon will never find out what happened to his men. They'll disappear into the mountains and never return."

That settled it. The men picked up the dead Renegades and took turns carrying them over the mountaintops.

The Godless returned to the place where the Shriker attacked the Renegades. From there, the Godless tracked the Renegades back the way they came.

They returned along the same route they took to get here. They went back to the box canyon, but they didn't camp in the open this time. The remaining Renegades huddled in the canyon where they would be safe from creatures—airborne creatures, at least.

Hangman, Hammer, and most of the party descended to the ground. They split their party into two. Hammer took his men into the box canyon.

Hangman climbed down into the fissure, but he did it far enough away to stop the Renegades from finding out he was there. Then he snuck as close as he dared until he could hear their conversation.

They were talking about taking precautions against the strange creatures in this country. The Renegades knew nothing about them. The Renegades didn't have a group of locals to explain everything to them and how to defend themselves against these creatures.

Hangman counted down the seconds. He didn't see anything at first until, without warning, Viking, Carnage, Red, and Butch tossed the dead Renegades down from the cliffs.

The bodies thumped onto the canyon floor within inches of their startled comrades. All the Renegades jumped up, seized their weapons, and spun around to stare at their slaughtered friends.

Hangman and his men attacked from there side at that moment. Hammer's band attacked from the box canyon side and the two parties met in the middle. They overwhelmed the Renegades and cut them all down in a few seconds.

Chapter 7

Mora adjusted Maeno's position in his wrap. He almost never left it. He liked it in there. He nursed constantly and slept the rest of the time.

Mora learned a long time ago not to take a baby out of the wrap as long as they were comfortable and happy in there. She went through a torturous ordeal when Zaedi was small before she learned this lesson.

She eventually resigned herself to leaving him in there until he learned to walk if necessary. He didn't. He grew and spent more and more time outside the wrap. He sat up, crawled, and eventually walked.

Mora knew better by the time she went through the same process with Thena. Morea didn't try to take Thena out of the wrap.

Life was so much easier, now that she knew how to do all of this. She supported Maeno with her left arm while she used her right hand to do her work.

She hardly noticed Zaedi and Thena playing around the camp with the other children. The women worked together where they could all keep track of each other's children.

Cheina sat off to one side and glared into space. She didn't talk or smile at anyone, not even her own children. Choma held Cheina's baby daughter Raria.

That baby would never know her father. Alien died before Raria even learned to walk. Mora didn't see Aster or Lonion much around the camp anymore, either. They both kept to themselves since Alien's death.

Mora had to stop herself from thinking about Alien. She got too sad and heartbroken if she thought about him too much.

He lived almost his entire life alone. Then he found a wife and adopted her children. Alien found the greatest happiness he could imagine—and then he died before he could even enjoy it.

He lived just long enough to see Hammer initiate as a man of the Godless Clan. That must have been Alien's proudest moment—and his last. What a tragedy.

She shook that thought out of her head, but not fast enough. Zaedi came up to her just then and squinted up at her. "You're sad again, Mother," he announced.

She did her best to smile at him. "I was just thinking about Alien, my son. I'm all right. Make sure you stay inside the camp. Children are a favorite treat of creatures out there. The Boultars might come for you."

"I would fight them." He picked up a stick, swiped it back and forth like a blade, and made slashing sounds with his mouth.

She laughed at him. "Tell your father to teach you how to use that thing before you poke someone's eyes out."

Choma stood up just then and looked around. "Someone take this little treasure for a while. I need to go get water."

No one spoke up. Cheina didn't turn around. "I'll take her," Mora offered and held out her right arm.

Choma transferred Raria into Mora's arm. Maeno opened his eyes when he felt the pressure of another body against his in a way he wasn't used to.

Mora put Raria into the wrap with him. "Get used to it, my son," she told him. "Get used to sacrificing a little discomfort for the sake of the band."

Zaedi wandered a little farther away still parrying and stabbing with his stick. Mora would definitely have to tell Hangman to give the boy some lessons.

Maeno settled down with his new wrap companion. He didn't care about the cramped conditions as long as he stayed attached to Mora's breast at all times. Nothing was more important to him than food.

Mora went on with her work, and in a little while, a bunch of other women went down to the nearby river to get water, too. Mora went with them and took her children with her.

Choma went with them, too, even though she had already fetched water. She took Raria back and carried her in another wrap.

Zaedi, Thena, and the others played on the bank. The women filled their water skins. They couldn't use gourds because this country didn't grow gourds. The women made water bags out of stitched hides.

The women sat on the bank and talked for a while about what to do about Cheina. "She doesn't eat," Aliva remarked. "She'll die soon if she doesn't snap out of it."

"What are we supposed to do?" Choma asked. "We can't force her to eat."

"I say we just leave her alone," Hicia suggested. "She'll come out of it eventually—or she won't. It's up to her. It's cowardly to give up on life because you lost your husband."

"How can you say that?! Aliva gasped. "None of us would want to go through what she's going through."

"The Renegade Clan slaughtered my husband right in front of me—and my father, my brothers, and four of my cousins," Hicia went on. "I didn't give up on life. I kept taking care of my children. Someone had to and I was the only one left to do it. Cheina is a coward for letting another woman raise her daughter in her place—and now her older children are old enough to initiate and get married and she won't pay any attention to that, either. She should die if she wants it so badly."

No one answered. Mora couldn't exactly argue with that. She didn't have any experience of losing her husband like that—thank God.

Hicia went through the same tragedy herself—and much worse. She could talk about it much better than Mora could.

Mora wouldn't let her children go without if Hangman died. She would never let another woman raise Maeno just because Hangman wasn't around anymore. That was just foolish. What was the point of being a mother if she didn't care for her children when they needed her most?

Now Raria, Aster, and Lonion were losing their mother along with Alien.

Lonion would initiate soon. Then he would go out with the men and Hammer would take his younger brother under his wing, but what about Aster?

The group fell into a thoughtful silence. No one wanted to talk anymore, so the women gathered their water skins and headed back to the camp.

Mora got Zaedi and Thena to carry one skin each. That lightened her load a little bit, but not much.

She let her thoughts wander, but all the women jolted to high alert when they heard a long, high-pitched scream coming from the sky directly above them.

Mora didn't even have to look up to see what it was. She dropped all her water skins and grabbed for her blades.

She almost dropped Maeno, but she managed to drop her blades instead, unhooked the wrap from her shoulder, and lowered him to the ground before she snatched her blades again.

She straddled the baby. He immediately started crying the way he always did when he lost body contact with his mother.

She cast one glance around. "Zaedi! Thena!"

She didn't have to say a word. The children knew that sound too well. It was their greatest fear.

They dropped their skins and raced back to her, skidded in the gravel, and huddled next to her legs and underneath them. The children crowded close with Maeno directly between them.

All the women around her did the same thing, dropped their skins, grabbed their weapons, and stood their ground to defend their children as a dozen juvenile Shrikers plummeted out of the sky.

The juveniles weren't as dangerous as the adults, but the juveniles came in force. They liked hunting this way and they always went after unprotected children.

The young Shrikers used a different strategy than the adults. The adults dropped from much higher and used their weight to flatten their prey before lifting off with it.

The juveniles didn't have the weight to pull that off, so they made fast, swooping passes trying to snatch their prey on the wing.

Mora saw the Shrikers coming. She had fought them before and developed her own strategy to combat them.

She measured the distance, let go of one of her blades so it hung from its wrist strap, and extended her hand to her daughter Thena.

Thena grabbed one of the water skins, used the carrying rope to pull it toward her, and pulled the top off so the water gurgled out onto the gravel.

Thena drained the bag just as the first Shrikers descended on the exposed women. Mora snatched the bag from Thena's hands and flipped it backward to hold it by the sack.

The Shrikers spread out—one attacker to each woman. The young Shrikers were still big enough to easily carry off an adult human.

They just had to get their talons around a person's body. One of their claws could impale a child through the torso and it would be all over.

Mora left her second blade dangling and held her breath for the coming attack. One Shrikers swooped at her and tried to snatch her. The creature couldn't get to the children as long as she stood her ground.

She counterattacked at the last second, tossed the rope of her water skin around the creature's neck as it soared past her, and flexed her knees to twist and yank down with all her might.

The creature plowed headfirst into the gravel. She leapt out of position, landed near it, and chopped her blade across its neck to kill it.

She untangled her rope and sprang back into position just as another Shriker streaked in to grab her children. She didn't have time to hook that one with her rope.

The creature stalled just long enough to swing its talons forward to grab Zaedi. Mora struck without mercy, hacked into the back of the creature's head, and the Shriker fell dead right on top of the children.

They both screamed. Maeno bellowed his head off, but the Shriker's body actually did more to protect the children than Mora could.

They couldn't push the Shriker off. "Stay under the wings!" she hollered. "Stay under the Shriker's wings! It will protect you!"

Zaedi understood her first and stopped his sister from trying to push the creature off. Another Shriker raced in to attack Mora. She didn't care as long as they didn't go after her children.

She didn't have time to pick up another water bag and drain it, so she used the same strategy in a different way. She waited until the creature dove for her, timed her movements, swung her arm to knock the creature's beak aside, and chopped at its neck.

She looked around everywhere in search of the next Shriker to come in for the attack. Her blood ran cold when she saw a party of Renegades coming down the nearest hills on a dead run for the Godless camp.

Mora snatched up her second blade and pivoted closer to her children. "What's happening, Mother?!" Thena whimpered. "I'm scared!"

"Stay under the Shriker!" Mora roared. "Don't you come out for anything!"

Sobbing sounds came from under the creature's body. Maeno's enraged howls echoed across the riverbank. That would definitely give away the children's hiding place, but Mora couldn't do anything about that now. She needed both hands to defend the children.

The other women scrambled to get ready for the attack. Thirty Renegades poured down the hill. They would overrun the camp, kill all the boys and the few men standing guard, and then carry off the women and girls.

Mora swallowed hard and prepared to go down fighting. She couldn't make up her mind if she should let herself get captured again. She didn't want to die if she could still help Thena or any other young girls in case the Renegades captured them.

She wouldn't get a chance to decide. The Renegades came in force, too. They would be the ones who decided what happened to her—and everyone else.

She couldn't just stand here and watch Zaedi and Maeno die. The Renegades didn't care if they killed a newborn baby as long as he was a boy.

She raised her blades to strike fast and hard. She would just have to do her best and prepare for the worst. She probably wouldn't be able to stop what was about to happen.

The Renegades saw the women on the riverbank and split into two flanks. Most of them headed for the camp. The rest came toward the river to capture the women.

Mora stood guard over her children until the Renegades got there. She bent her knees to take a deeper stance and raised her blades to destroy as many attackers as she could.

Five Renegades rushed her and widened their formation to circle her. They raised their blades, too. They fought with metal blades the same as hers. At least they didn't bring firearms this time.

One huge guy brought down his blade with a ringing smash against hers. The force of his stroke knocked her arm down. She couldn't defend herself against even one of these men, let alone all of them.

She raised her other blade, but at that moment, another beefy Renegade charged her from behind and grabbed her around the waist. He lifted her feet off the ground and started walking away with her toward the river.

She kicked and screamed, and when that didn't work, she spun her blade around and tried to stab him under her own arms.

The men in front of her leapt forward and grabbed her blades out of her hands. She couldn't stop them from taking her. The nightmare was happening all over again—except that now she was leaving three children behind.

Her children screamed out for her, but she couldn't get to them. She couldn't do anything but flail her arms and legs around in helpless desperation.

She saw the Renegades taking her farther and farther away from her children. The huge guy who initially engaged her and knocked her blade down turned to the dead Shriker. He lifted one of the wings and looked under it to see the children hiding there.

Mora went ballistic. She flew into hysterical rage trying in every possible way to return to her children, but she couldn't move. The man holding her clamped both his muscular arms around her and restrained her easily.

She couldn't look. She turned her head aside so she wouldn't see her sons put to the sword and her three-year-old daughter carried off into captivity.

At that moment, a fully grown Shriker plunged out of nowhere and landed on the man about to capture Mora's children.

The Shriker attacked hard and fast, squashed the man flat right on top of the children, and the adult Shriker flexed its talons to lift off its prey.

The man screamed and tried to roll over to fight the creature, but he couldn't get hold of his weapons from this position.

The creature's talons closed and picked him up along with the dead juvenile underneath him. Mora feared the worst, but Zaedi wriggled out from under the dead Shriker and protected Thena and Maeno from getting caught.

The adult Shriker lifted off and left the three children lying there totally exposed and unprotected. Mora became aware of more creatures all over the camp. The man holding her let go and she fell hard on the gravel.

Another young Shriker attacked him. She twisted over and scrambled away just as a fresh group of juveniles soared in all over the camp. The Renegades had to stop what they were doing to fight the creatures instead.

Mora staggered to her feet, rushed back to her children, and scooped up her blades the Renegades had dropped on the ground. She stumbled into position straddling her children again, but no Shrikers and no Renegades came near her.

She panted for air—and then stared even harder as the Godless men rushed into the camp. They attacked Shrikers and Renegades in fury, wiped out the Renegades, and drove the Shrikers off.

Chapter 8

Hangman charged over to Mora and grabbed her by the shoulders. "Are you okay?!" he yelled in her face. "Are the children okay?!"

She nodded fast, but she couldn't speak. Her whole face trembled with agitation. She kept trying and failing to move her lips.

He patted her down, but she didn't seem injured. The children huddled on the ground at her feet. They didn't come to him when he approached them.

He held out his arms. "Come, my son. It's over now. Come on. Help me take Mother to the camp."

Zaedi recovered first, got to his feet, and let Hangman put his arms around the little boy. Thena huddled on the ground and burst into loud, hysterical sobs. Maeno lay on the gravel staring up at the sky in confusion.

Thena's cries brought Mora out of her shock. She spun around, gathered the girl in her arms, and covered her in kisses. "It's all right, my love," Mora husked. "You made it! We made it! You were so brave! You helped me so much. I love you!"

She scooped up Maeno, looped the hide wrap over her shoulder, and he latched onto her breast as though he never had been anywhere else.

She kept trembling all over. She had a hard time standing up once she got her arms around her children. She kept petting them, kissing them, and gasping and whimpering in terror. She looked around everywhere at dead Renegades and dead Shrikers.

Hangman found himself doing the same thing. He couldn't stop touching all four of them just to satisfy himself that they were actually okay.

"What happened?" he finally asked.

Mora waved behind her. She couldn't answer for a second while she struggled to form words. "The Shrikers.....they came in first......then the Renegades....."

Thena started crying again. She crushed her arms around Mora's neck way too tight.

"They tried to take Mother," Zaedi half-whispered.

"You were all so brave." Mora blinked back tears. "I'm proud of all of you."

"Mother!" Thena shrieked. "Mother!"

"I'm here, my love." Mora kissed the side of the girl's neck. "I'm here and I'm okay. We all made it."

"The Shrikers came back while the Renegades were here," Zaedi went on.

Hangman looked at him. "How did you get away from them?"

Zaedi waved behind him, too, but he didn't seem to be able to come up with the words to explain exactly what happened.

"Never mind." Hangman got to his feet. "Let's go back to the camp. We need to check on everyone."

He took hold of the boy's hand. Mora stood up, but her knees kept wobbling. Thena wouldn't let go of her mother's neck.

The girl's body kept bumping into Maeno. Hangman tried to take Thena away, but she only cried louder and held on tighter.

Mora caught Hangman's eye and shifted Thena to her other hip where the girl wouldn't crush the baby. Mora carried both of them back to the camp.

More women and families assembled from all over. Hangman took a quick head count. He didn't see anyone missing.

Hangman, Mora, and their children had to pass through the camp to get to their own house. All the other men held onto their wives and children. The incident shook the Godless. No one talked about anything else.

Mora stopped in her tracks halfway across the camp and her eyes fell out of their sockets when she saw Cheina sitting in her usual spot. She hadn't moved from that spot since Alien's death.

Hangman looked back and forth between Mora and Cheina before he realized why Cheina shocked Mora so much. Cheina must have been sitting there through the whole Renegade attack. She would have let them carry her off without any resistance.

Hangman had to get Mora moving to cross the rest of the way to their house, but they didn't enter it. The whole family sat down there in front of the walls to rest and catch their breath.

No one went near Cheina, not even Choma who still carried baby Raria as usual. Hammer finally went over to his mother, squatted in front of her, and got right in her face where she couldn't ignore him.

He talked to her, stroked her cheeks and hair, and didn't leave her alone until she started crying. Her sobs escalated to wails and then to howls. This was the first time she let it out since the night of Alien's death.

Hammer put his arm around her shoulder, pulled her to her feet, and marched her back to her own house. Everyone heard her crying through the walls.

Hangman left Mora and the children sitting where they were, went over to the cooking fire, and added a bunch of wood to it to build it up. He stacked it into a bonfire. All the other men pulled their families over to the fire and they gathered around.

No one said anything for a long time until Hammer came out of his mother's house. He went over to Choma. "She wants her baby back."

"Of course!" Choma handed the baby over. "I'm glad your mother is coming back to herself."

"Thank you for taking care of my sister. I'm forever in your debt."

He took the baby back to his mother's house. Cheina's crying didn't stop, but the tone changed. Hammer came back out and squatted on that side of the fire with the rest of his men.

That was Hangman's cue. He got up and raised his voice so everyone could hear him. "We're going to leave this valley."

Protests erupted all over the circle. "Why do we have to leave?!" Aliva demanded. "We're safe here."

"We *were* safe here," Red corrected. "We aren't anymore."

"Today proved that," Viking added. "The Renegades attacked the camp itself. They'll do it again."

"We have a traitor among us," Hangman went on. "Someone sitting here right now is going out into the canyons and leaving signs on the rocks for the Renegades to follow. That's how they found us. Someone here is selling us out. This traitor is responsible for Alien's death. The traitor could have been responsible for all our deaths—and for all you women and girls to get taken back as captives. I'm charging each of you to keep an eye on each other to find out who this person is."

"How *can* we find out who it is?" Hicia asked. "None of us has time to watch everyone else's movements."

"All our lives depend on exposing this traitor. Whoever it is leaves the camp alone and stays out for a long time. They have time to trek all over the country leaving signs for the Renegades to follow. I'm sure you can all imagine who in this camp has time to do that."

Hangman didn't have to look around him to see who had time to do that. Most of the women were far too busy raising multiple children. They never had time to eat or sleep, much less wash their hair or even to gather water for their children.

Others were too heavily pregnant to walk more than a few steps. Hangman really didn't want to leave here to go traveling across the country with them again.

His only consolation was that they would give birth on the journey. They would travel more quickly after that, but giving birth didn't reduce the danger.

All these children would offer an irresistible temptation to every creature for hundreds of miles around. The creatures would be far more dangerous than the Renegade Clan.

"I say we head south," Hangman went on. "We don't know how far we'll have to travel, but we can meet up with another Godless band there. If worse comes to the worst, we can head east and rejoin my father's band. Then my family will take us in."

"You would do that, Hangman?" Lonion murmured. "You would give up being Kral to go under another band?"

"I would do much more to get all of you to safety. I don't know if we'll ever find safety, but maybe we can make it far enough south that the Renegades can't follow us. I don't know if that's possible, but I have to try."

"But we'll take the traitor with us," Aliva pointed out. "The person will lead the Renegades to us even there."

"Not if we find out who the person is," Hammer growled under his breath. "We'll find out who it is and feed them to the ants. Then we can travel more safely."

His word cast another chill over the group. Silence answered him.

"All of you relax with your families tonight," Hangman decided. "We'll take tonight to butcher these Shrikers, smoke the meat, and try to get some sleep. We'll pack up and leave in the morning."

No one moved for a second. Everyone sat there stunned and staring, either at each other or into the fire. The men didn't try to make this any easier for their wives.

Hammer's band broke away from the fires one man at a time. The young single men went out into the gravel beds, butchered the Shrikers, and brought the meat back to the fire to cook.

The cooked meat made the rounds and everyone ate in subdued silence. The men occasionally murmured to each other to give each other instructions or ask each other for help with something.

Their voices brought everyone else back from the brink. More men stood up to help and then the women started moving.

Mora sat next to Hangman eating and sharing her food with him and the children. She answered them in an undertone when one of them asked her anything.

Maeno fell asleep in a little while and she laid her hand on Hangman's arm. "I better take these little ones inside to bed. Are you staying up for a while?"

"Not long," he told her. "I'll be there soon."

He pulled her in to kiss her before he let her go, but sitting out here alone only made him want to go inside. This might be the last night he got to spend in something like peace and quiet with his family.

Plenty of men butcher and smoke the meat. They would all stay up late tonight. They might even stay up all night to get the job done in time for the band to leave tomorrow.

He didn't need to stay. No one would care if he went in. No one even noticed that he was here. He stayed a little longer and watched the men at their work, but after a while, he went inside and stretched out in the bed of hides with Mora and the children.

They fussed a lot. She spent another hour tending to each of them before they finally fell asleep.

He couldn't get close to her with all of them jammed around her on both sides, but he didn't need to get close to her. Just lying in the same bed under the same roof with the four of them—it was the greatest blessing of his life.

He never would have wanted to spend his life alone if it meant he couldn't feel this. He didn't know it back then when he married her. He didn't find out until after it happened. He didn't think at the time that it would mean this much.

He grew up watching parents and children living together. He lived with his brothers and his parents. He didn't think it meant anything. Everyone did it. It was just what everyone did. Now he found out that it meant everything. Nothing else meant a thing.

Or it would be more accurate to say that everything else subordinated itself to this. This was the most important thing. Everything else served this, supported it, and made it possible.

Finding this out—actually getting married, having his own children—and now seeing all of them in danger he couldn't protect them from—this made all his efforts worthwhile.

His struggles, his battles, his losses—it all came down to this moment—this moment when he looked across the bed and saw Mora's eyes drifting closed—this moment where he could look down and see the angelic light glowing in his sleeping children's faces.

He would do a thousand times more if he could only feel this—just for one night. He might lose all four of them tomorrow.

Losing them would destroy him now. He wasn't alive before they came here to be with him. He wouldn't be a man without them. He would be some hollow shell of nothing—a shell waiting for life to fill it up.

He would work harder, fight harder, risk more, and face more danger for them—just for the chance that he might feel this again some other night—just one more night.

Every day's battle won him one more night. Every day's struggle earned him one more night of seeing his children grow up. His wife's and children's survival hung on every battle. He had to win. Losing wasn't an option anymore.

Chapter 9

M ora struggled over rocks, ledges, and sharp corners. Traveling south through hundreds of miles of canyons while she was pregnant would have been a lot harder than this.

Traveling with a baby and two little children turned out to be plenty hard enough. She had to hold onto Zaedi and Thena by their hands—which meant she couldn't use her hands to hold onto the rocks to pull herself up.

She also had to hold onto Maeno in his hide wrap. She had to keep letting go of the children so she could support him or herself depending on where she happened to be climbing that minute.

The rest of the band had the same problem. All the families here had little children. They didn't understand how to travel. Most were too young to take care of themselves or to climb very well.

Zaedi did better than Thena, but not by much. They tripped a lot or didn't understand how to climb over the rocks. All the children slowed the band down.

The men surrounded the party and kept their weapons drawn the entire time. The men climbed into the rocks on either side and kept constant watch.

The men spent the first half a day watching for Renegade Clan pursuers coming after the Godless. After that, the men kept watch for creatures coming after the children.

Every creature in this world hunted humans, but every creature favored children. The women kept watch for creatures, too, but the women mostly had their hands full just trying to keep the party moving at all instead of coming to a standstill every few minutes.

The women had to keep stopping to pull their children under the shelter of rocks from Shrikers, Boultars, and other creatures coming out of the mountains to hunt the children.

Things got so much worse when the party traveled through valleys growing thick with jungle. The band entered the jungle every time they had to travel through a valley. The band could travel faster down there, but more creatures came out to hunt the children.

Then the band had to climb up treacherous passes again to cross more mountains before the group descended into more valleys choked with jungle.

Hangman didn't stay near Mora and the children on the march. He constantly circled the band and usually split off to climb into the rocks or travel through the surrounding mountains to search the area.

Mora didn't look for him very much. She had to concentrate on the children, but he always circled back around eventually before he left again.

The party entered another patch of jungle. The sun was starting to go down. Only some of the children were old enough to camp in the trees, so the adults had to carry the younger ones to safety. Spending the night on the ground would be too dangerous.

The men usually came back at sundown to help with this process. Hangman dropped out of the branches and landed near Mora.

She caught his eye. "Is everything okay out there?"

His sharp eyes shot to the rest of the band. "We aren't seeing any Renegades, but we know they're there. The traitor will keep leaving signs." He lowered his voice. "Keep an eye on the other women. See if any of them breaks away to leave any marks."

"I haven't seen anything yet, but I'll try to watch. Everyone has to stay with the group while we walk."

"I mean when we stop." He clenched his jaws and shot another flinty glance at the surrounding families. "Like now."

He covered up his comments by picking up Zaedi. Hangman slung the boy onto his back. Zaedi held on by wrapping his arms around Hangman's neck from behind.

The boy wrapped his legs around Hangman's waist. Hangman picked up Thena and she strapped herself around his torso from the front.

"Are you both ready to go?" he asked.

"Ready," Zaedi replied.

"Ready," Thena added.

"You both need to learn to climb as soon as you can," Hangman told them. "You should be doing this yourselves to save Mother the extra work."

"Mother isn't doing it," Zaedi pointed out. "You are."

"That's my point." Hangman nodded to Mora. "After you."

She tightened Maeno's wrap, but she still had to support him. Climbing with one hand took longer. She had to be careful that she didn't slip on the branches or drop the baby.

Hangman climbed slowly to stay near her. They and the rest of the families scaled to the high canopy.

Hammer's band didn't come with them. They went hunting as usual. Lonion, Vuco, and two other boys nearing the age of initiation went with Hammer's band. The younger boys spent a lot of time with Hammer's band now.

This band fell into the same pattern of following different rules from the Godless of Shadow's band. Shadow's band didn't allow uninitiated boys to go out with the men. The boys had to hunt and fight on their own until they earned their places as men in the Clan.

This band did things differently. Mora couldn't explain this away by saying the band didn't have enough men because it did.

Hammer and his men grew up fighting alongside the men. None of those boys had a choice about fighting and hunting with the men.

Hammer had every reason in the world to let the boys go with him. He and his men understood better than anyone how to train up boys to become good hunters, good fighters, and good protectors of their female relatives.

Mora found herself some solid branches where four limbs twisted together to make a wider base of support. She sat down and Hangman lowered Thena into Mora's arms. Then he put Zaedi down and they all settled into the branches for the night.

Mora and Hangman both took food out of their bags to share with the children, but he kept casting sidelong glances at the people around him. All the other families climbed up and settled into the branches, too.

Cheina moved around normally now. She carried Raria in a wrap around her chest and shared food with Aster in the usual way. Hammer must have finally talked some sense into his mother about taking care of her family.

Kuvik and Viking settled on branches near Hangman and Mora. Both men searched the band for any sign of suspicious behavior, but they didn't see anything. Everyone here behaved normally. No one could leave without everyone in the band seeing.

"Did you scout farther south like I asked you to?" Hangman asked after a while.

Kuvik nodded. "The mountains get smaller and turn into hills, but it will still be the same country for a while before we get into the solid jungle."

"And you're looking out for other bands?" Hangman asked. "We have to alert them that we're passing through."

"There is no one in this country except us and the Renegades," Viking told him. "We don't have to alert anyone."

Hangman frowned. "It's strange. There should be someone here."

"It makes me wonder what happened to Thunder's band," Kuvik added. "Did he leave the area—or did the Renegades penetrate this far and destroy his band?"

"The Renegades only found us by the traitor leaving signs," Viking pointed out. "That valley would have been the first place they looked."

Kuvik shrugged. "I suppose."

Hammer returned just then. He returned alone and didn't bring his men and boys with him. He traveled fast through the canopy, balanced and swung from branches, and dropped lightly onto the limbs near Mora's family before he approached the rest of the way.

His weight bounced the branch under Mora before he squatted down next to Hangman. "How is it?" Hammer asked.

"It's fine. How are your new boys working out?" Hangman asked.

Hammer nodded. "They're good boys. They try hard and they have good skills. Growing up with this band helped them a lot. They don't need extra training the way we did."

Hangman looked up at him. "Can I help you with something?"

Hammer raised his head and the two men locked eyes. "I'm the age of gathering now. I want to marry Vina. You said we could when we got old enough. The others are all over the age of gathering now, too.

We want to take wives, but the girls are all in your band. We need your permission."

"I did say that and you are all over the age of gathering," Hangman replied. "My objection isn't your ages—not anymore. My objection is the girls' ages. Vina is a year younger than you are. She isn't the age of gathering yet. You need to wait another year—and the girls your men want to marry are all younger, too. I can't let you marry them—not yet."

Hammer looked away. "I forgot about that."

Hangman rested his hand on his shoulder. "You've all waited this long. Another year is nothing compared to a lifetime you'll spend with your wives. Just wait a little longer."

"Don't say anything about matching the girls to boys their own age," Hammer growled. "They wouldn't go with us if they went to the gathering."

"I wasn't going to say that," Hangman murmured. "We don't have a gathering here and we won't find one. There are no girls your age and the boys their age are all interested in girls already. The girls who will be your wives won't match with anyone. You don't have to worry about it."

Hammer only nodded, but he wouldn't make eye contact again.

Mora didn't know if they had ever had this conversation before, but it must have been hard for Hammer and the others to wait. They had known these girls all their lives.

Hammer and Vina developed their romance years ago. They spent all that time waiting. Now they found out they had to wait another year for Vina to come of age.

Hammer accepted Hangman's ruling in silence. Hammer didn't really have a choice about that. Hangman was Vina's Kral. He could have outright refused to let Hammer marry her at all.

Hangman wouldn't refuse, but he would have no choice but to stop the marriage if Hammer and Vina did anything too soon. That would be outright illegal.

Mora found herself glancing around the band with the same sharp eye. Someone here was a traitor. Someone here left signs and clues for the Renegade Clan to catch up with the Godless, follow them, and attack them.

This band was bound to get a whole lot bigger as soon as Hammer and his men married and started having children of their own.

That would make an even bigger target for the Renegades to attack. It would make even more children for all the jungle creatures to come out and hunt.

The band had to hurry up and get south—somewhere safer and better protected than this. Traveling through the wilderness with these children was dangerous enough. Traveling with that many would be disastrous.

Chapter 10

Mora sat up on her branch and straightened Maeno inside her wrap. Hangman had woven smaller branches between the tree limbs to make a bed for Zaedi and Thena to lie on.

Hangman wasn't here. He must have gone out patrolling again. The two children didn't wake up. That gave Mora a few precious seconds to just sit here in the silence and think.

The rest of the band settled in the canopy nearby. Most were still asleep or just beginning to stir. Viking stretched out of the notch where he'd fallen asleep. He yawned loudly and then coughed.

A few people moved around on the ground far below the band's camping place. Aster and another teenage girl named Yoa walked together across the ground. They carried dozens of water skins belonging to a bunch of different families.

The band had developed a routine of sending everyone in pairs to gather water or to do whatever other chores anyone needed to do away from the rest of the band.

This way, no one could split off and go out alone to leave signs for the Renegades. The rule seemed to be working. The Renegades didn't follow the band.

Kuvik came back just then. He must have been out scouting with Hangman, but Kuvik came back alone.

Yoa broke away from Aster and crossed the jungle floor to intercept him. Aster kept going and disappeared into the trees.

Yoa walked up to Kuvik and started talking to him. Mora couldn't see Yoa's facial expression from here or hear what she was saying.

Mora did see Kuvik's expression. He looked down at the ground and away from Yoa. He squirmed and shuffled his feet like her attention made him uncomfortable.

Mora had seen this before Yoa took a special interest in Kuvik, but he always pushed her away. She even complained to the other girls that he said she should find herself a real Godless man.

Their conversation only lasted a few minutes this time. He shook his head and kept walking before he swung up into the branches to rejoin the band. She stormed off in the other direction to catch up with Aster. Aster wouldn't go for water alone after all.

Mora turned back to her children. Zaidi woke up and then Thena did the same thing. They both fussed and complained a lot.

"I don't want dried meat!" Thena moaned. "When will we get some fresh meat?"

"I'll eat it myself if you don't want it." Mora stuck the food into her mouth. "You won't catch me saying no to food. I don't care if it's dry or fresh."

Thena sulked. Mora didn't offer the girl any food after that. Thena would start complaining about being hungry soon enough. Then Mora would offer the girl more dry meat. Thena would learn sooner rather than later that dry food was better than no food at all.

Zaedi learned that lesson quicker, but he had an extra year to learn it. He ate what Mora gave him and never said a word about what he wanted instead.

The men came back and helped carry the young children down to the ground. Traveling through the treetops wasn't an option with all these babies and young children in the group.

The party set off heading south as usual. The men kept separating into patrols, forming different positions around the travelers, and adjusting their configurations according to changes in the terrain.

The party left the jungle and started climbing toward another steep, rocky pass. Mora held Zaedi and Thena by the hand as long as they traveled over level or slightly sloping terrain.

The party had to travel single file when they came to the narrow cliff defiles. The path twisted and turned every few feet. The path switched back again and again working its way up the cliffs.

Mora steered her children in front of her so they wouldn't fall behind. All the women took extra pains to keep their children near them at all times.

Some of the women who had their hands free drew their weapons just in case. It wouldn't be the first time some creature attacked from the air when the band could least defend itself.

The men climbed into the rocks to stand guard. The men had to continually swarm up the mountain to find better vantage points and search the surroundings.

Rocky passes had become the men's least favorite place to get caught unawares. The men sent some of their number ahead to check the pass and make sure the band wouldn't encounter anything unexpected there.

The party struggled to the top of the pass and paused there to look down. A bunch of Hammer's men raced down the other side and fanned out to search the country ahead.

Mora stopped to catch her breath. The wind blew stronger here and cooled the sweat on her face and body. Jungle covered more of the country south of the pass. The mountains fell away from here and didn't rise again.

Sighs and gasps of relief went through the group when everyone saw the downhill slope and the flat landscape in front of them. The band wouldn't have to climb any more mountains after this—not as soon as they climbed down this one.

Hangman said, "Let's go," and started down the hill. Mora took hold of the children's hands. Hopefully she wouldn't have to use her hands to climb anymore—or not much more.

A loud screech brought everyone to a halt as another Shriker plummeted out of the sky to land on top of the party.

Mora instantly dove for the nearest rocks—and just in time. The Shriker came after her and her children. The creature would have snatched them, but its grasping talons hit the rock instead.

She crouched underneath it while the bird flapped and scratched at the rock trying to grab her or one of the children. Zaedi and Thena screamed their heads off and cowered between her and the rock behind them.

She couldn't get out and the bird didn't go away. It kept pumping its giant wings with deep, thumping strokes. None of the men could get near the creature.

Mora reacted automatically, ripped her hands out of her children's grasp, and drew her blades. She couldn't even see the Shriker well enough to decide where to hit the thing.

She stabbed upward in no particular direction above her head. She thought she might be able to stab the creature in the foot to win herself a few more inches of space so the creature wouldn't be able to get a hold of her.

She missed the talon completely and wound up stabbing the Shriker in the body. Her blade went straight through the creature's feathers.

She didn't see or feel how deeply she stabbed the creature, but it exploded away from her in seconds. The bird lifted off with a few more powerful wing beats and launched away from the rock.

The Shriker didn't take off into the sky. It hovered ten feet above the ground and widened its claws to make another dive for its target.

Lightning quick, before anyone even realized he was there, Wildling sprang out of the rocks and threw a length of rope around the creature's foot.

Wildling always carried rope no matter what. It had become his trademark—a personal idiosyncrasy left over from his initiation.

The Shriker didn't even notice when he cinched the noose tight around the bird's ankle. The Shriker dove sideways to avoid the rock this time. Mora turned around to fight the bird off a second time, but Wildling acted faster.

He yanked the rope hard and jerked the bird out of position. Mora was too focused on the Shriker to see until it was all too late.

Wildling threw one length of the rope behind his back and flung himself over on his back. The force of his weight against the rope ripped the bird sideways. It lost control of its wings and landed flat on the ground in a heap.

Butch sprang off the rocks just as fast and hacked his axe down on the creature's neck to kill it. The Shriker burst into a fit of twitching and thrashing. Butch had to dive out of the way so it didn't knock him over.

"That was amazing!" Zaedi breathed. "I want to fight a Shriker for my initiation."

"You won't be initiating anytime soon, my son." Mora stood up and faced the men in front of her. "Thank you so much. You saved us."

Wildling got to his feet and started winding up his rope. "We'll take care of this. You should all get down to the valley floor. We'll catch up with you."

Hangman only nodded and got the women and children moving again. Mora took hold of her children and led them to the pass.

Zaedi hung back and looked over his shoulder. Wildling, Butch, Legacy, and Prodigy started cutting up the Shriker and tearing off its feathers. The band always needed a lot of food. The meat wouldn't go to waste.

Chapter 11

Hangman crouched in the branches and peered out over a flat grassland stretching to another wall of jungle on the other side. He and his band had been traveling through this country for a month and still hadn't seen any people.

Keeping constant watch on everyone around the clock wasn't possible anymore—not for the men. They had too much ground to cover in their scouting patrols.

The women didn't see enough suspicious behavior in anyone to report someone who might have been the hidden traitor.

Hangman made a conscious effort not to let himself start thinking that their vigilance might have stopped the Renegade Clan from following the Godless. He would be stupid to trick himself into believing that.

Kuvik squatted down next to Hangman and looked through the foliage at the flat country beyond. "How far do you think it is to the jungle over there?" Kuvik asked.

Hangman shrugged. "A couple of hours maybe—at the most."

Kuvik glanced left and right. "At least we'll be able to see creatures coming—if they come."

"They're bound to. We'll be out in the open with a bunch of little children."

"That's the only jungle around. Going west or east will only leave us exposed for longer. We have to go straight across and get under the trees as quickly as possible."

"I know," Hangman replied. "I guess I just want to delay the inevitable as long as possible."

"There's a herd of Crammers over there," Kuvik pointed out. "We should hunt some of them for food. We can camp over here under the trees and then get across as quickly as possible."

Hangman found himself smiling at the man in front of him. "All right. You convinced me."

The two men retreated and met up with their comrades in a different part of the canopy. "How does it look?" Red asked.

"Very exposed," Hangman replied. "Very, very exposed. Kuvik spotted a herd of Crammers to the east. We're going to hunt some of them, process them for food while the jungle still gives us some cover, and then cross to the other side. Then we won't have to stop on the way or in between."

"Good idea," Cross exclaimed.

"Hammer, you take your men through the jungle to the east and come at the herd from that side," Hangman ordered. "Red, you and your men follow, but don't get in front of the herd. You'll attack from the tree line. The rest of us will approach the herd from this direction. We'll drive them toward you. Red and his men will attack from the side and Hammer's band will cut off the Crammers from escaping eastward."

Everyone nodded and split up. Viking, Kuvik, Cross, Lonion, Vuco, and two other younger boys stayed behind. The boys' names were Ziti and Thuron.

Hangman and his group returned to the same place where Kuvik first spotted the Crammers. The herd grazed in the open fields. The creatures didn't notice anyone sneaking up on them.

"How do we do this?" Lonion asked.

"We do it head on," Hangman replied. "We walk out there in plain view, let them see us coming, and the Crammers will threaten us. Some will attack. Others will try to fall back and they'll run into Red and the others. Hammer's band will distract the creatures and then we'll all attack."

Lonion took a fresh grip on the Renegade blade he always used. Most of the freed captives still used the same weapons they took from the Renegade camp years ago.

"You boys will do fine," Hangman told them. "We'll have enough men to wound the creatures, at least. Then we can bring them down."

"Just leave the young ones," Cross added. "Let them escape. Go for the adults instead."

Hangman said, "Let's go," and the party jumped down to the ground.

The boys fell in line as soon as the men stepped out of the trees. Everyone drew their weapons. Viking took his enormous axe off his back.

The group strode across the planes and got the Crammers' attention right away. The males stopped butting their heads at each other and turned around to face the Godless instead.

The boys tensed for the fight. Hangman had seen them all fight before. He didn't doubt their abilities or their courage.

Hammer was right about these boys. They were growing up Godless and learning from the best about what that actually meant.

The Crammers snorted, roared, and pawed the ground. They lowered their heads and tossed their horns at the approaching men. Hangman clenched his fists around his kukris, but at that moment, he heard a distant rumble coming from the south—or more like the southeast.

He didn't see anything at first. The Crammers heard the noise, too. They stopped snorting at Hangman's men and the creatures turned to look in that direction.

The noise didn't stop. It got louder—and before anyone could move, a massive herd of Blastidons thundered out of the jungle to the south—the jungle where Hangman had just been planning to take the band to safety.

He didn't think Blastidons lived this far south. Red's men thought creatures like Crammers, Blastidons, and Shrikers only lived in the mountains.

They must have lived here in even greater numbers. None of the Godless had seen a herd this big. What looked like hundreds of Blastidons charged out of the trees and stampeded onto the planes. The Crammers broke and ran for it.

They ran straight into the jungle where Red and his men hid and waited for Hangman to open the confrontation. Did Red and Hammer see the Blastidons?

Hangman couldn't see Red, Hammer, or any of their men. Hangman didn't have time to warn any of them. He hesitated for a second. The Blastidons kept on coming. They were running too fast and in too great numbers to stop.

"Run!" he yelled and all the men and boys spun away toward the trees.

He judged that his group probably made it level with where Red's party should have been hiding. Red and the others would see Hangman's party coming. He only hoped they saw the Blastidons coming, too.

Hangman stuck his kukris into his waistband on the run and launched himself into the trees. The men and boys swarmed up after him and the Blastidons pounded down the planes and exploded into the jungle.

They streaked between the trees by the hundreds. Hangman could see the open grassland from here. The herd kept coming out of the opposite patch of jungle. The Blastidons covered the fields in a million pounding hooves.

He glanced east and west. Red's men squatted in the branches a few dozen yards away from Hangman's position. None of Red's men descended from the trees to go after the Crammers. Hangman only hoped Hammer's band was all right.

The stampede went on for a long time—a lot longer than Hangman expected. He, Cross, Viking, Kuvik, and the boys stayed where they were.

They probably could have joined up with Red's party, but no one moved until the last Blastidons galloped out of the opposite jungle. They streaked down the grasslands, plunged into the jungle underneath the men, and the Blastidons raced away.

Silence returned except for the usual sounds of creatures and insects buzzing and scratching under the trees. Hangman didn't move for a second.

"The Crammers are gone," Kuvik pointed out. "I suppose we have no reason not to cross the fields now."

"You're right." Hangman got up. "Let's go get the women and children moving. The sun will be going down soon. We won't get a better chance than now."

Chapter 12

Hammer jumped down from the branches and approached the tree line to look out across the grasslands. "The Crammers are gone. Hangman will take the women and children across the fields now. We should go back and help protect them."

Omen called down from the high branches above where Hammer had just been sitting. "I don't see him or Red's party."

"They may already be heading back." Hammer waved to the rest of his men. "Let's go."

They stayed in the branches. They could move faster that way without putting themselves in danger by coming down to the ground.

He turned his back on the grasslands. He could have climbed up there and traveled through the branches, too. He didn't understand why he stayed down here on the ground.

He kept casting backward glances toward the open fields behind him. Taking women and children out into such exposed terrain would be dangerous—even more dangerous than taking them through the mountains.

Hammer would make the same call if he was in charge of this band. Hangman made a point of telling Hammer at his initiation that he was Kral of his own band, but that only applied to these men with him right now.

Hammer wasn't Kral over women, children, and families. All those people still came under Hangman's protection and followed his orders.

Hangman treated Hammer as an equal, but they both knew they weren't. Hammer still followed all of Hangman's suggestions as if they were orders.

No one questioned this. None of Hammer's men ever implied that he should contradict whatever Hangman wanted to do.

Hangman was Kral. Everyone knew it. He was Kral to Hammer and his men as much as anyone else. No one understood this better than Hammer.

He didn't want to be his own Kral. He never wanted to live under any Kral other than Hangman, but Hammer still found himself questioning if he would make the same decision in Hangman's place.

Would Hammer take women, children, and babies out into those fields if Hammer had been Kral over this band? The sun was going down. Now would be the best time if there even was a best time.

He turned back. His men raced far ahead of him, but he didn't hurry to catch up with them. He wanted to spend some time alone to think.

He had been all set to marry Vina, now that he finally initiated. He was a man now.

Then Hangman knocked him down by pointing out that she wasn't of age yet. Hammer kicked himself for forgetting that and getting his hopes up. Now he had to wait another year.

Hangman was right. A year was nothing. He and Vina loved each other as much now as they did when they were young. That wouldn't change.

He sure wished he could take her home. He ached for her, but he never showed it on the outside. He never said a word about it to anyone other than Hangman.

Hammer only hoped Hangman didn't notice how disappointed Hammer was by the decision. Hangman couldn't possibly have let Hammer marry an underage girl. That would have been outrageous.

Hangman was too upright to let something like that happen under his watch. He wouldn't have been the Kral Hammer admired so much if Hangman let Hammer get away with that.

It still stung, though. This was the first time Hammer got a chance to be alone and really feel the crushing blow of that decision. It drained the life out of him.

He turned aside to go get a drink from the stream. He didn't need to hurry.

Hangman and the others would bring the women and children through this part of the jungle to get to the grasslands. Hammer would meet up with them then.

He made a mental note to check on his mother and baby sister. He had been so busy with all these patrols, scouting parties, and helping train up the younger boys.

He had to balance all of that. His men still kept their habit of staying apart from the band. Hammer had his own obligation to spend time with his mother. She needed him more now after she lost Alien.

Hammer was the man in her life now. She needed someone to talk to and express her feelings to. She needed someone to talk about all her turmoil and how difficult it was to raise Raria knowing the little girl would never know her father.

Hammer would have to step into that role and be the older brother Raria needed him to be. Alien would want that.

Hammer's own words came back to him from his initiation. He made Alien promise to take care of Cheina and Aster if anything happened to Hammer.

Now Hammer was the one fulfilling that promise to Alien. Hammer didn't make that promise to Alien, but the promise wound up applying to both of them the same way.

He squatted down next to the stream, cupped both his hands, and lifted the water to his lips.

That was the moment when he heard scratching and scraping sounds behind a stand of rocks nearby. The scratching didn't sound like any creature he knew.

Red and his men had spent the last four years educating everyone in the band on the habits, sounds, and behavior of every species in the mountains.

The band passed out of the mountains and entered the jungle, but the creatures here represented a strange mix of both habitats.

Hammer listened with the water still cupped in his hands. The scratching kept going. It didn't stop.

He stood up, pulled both his blades, stepped across the stream, and eased around the rock to see what was making that sound. He had to find out if this was some creature he didn't even know existed until now.

He stopped and stared in horrified disbelief when he saw a young girl standing in front of him. She had her back to him while she used a rock to scratch long lines in the rock in front of her.

She raised her arms, drove her stone into the rock face high above her head, and scored downward to the left to the height of her hip.

Then she did the same thing scratching a line straight down toward the ground and a third line to the right. The three lines met at the top to form an arrow.

Hammer's stomach clenched in knots. He didn't need to see the girl from the front to recognize who she was. It was his sister Aster.

He gulped when he realized the truth. She was out here alone leaving a sign on this rock. She was drawing an arrow on the north-facing side of the rock. The arrow pointed south—the direction the Godless would travel to cross the grasslands.

Hammer's first instinct was to turn away, bury himself in the jungle, and do something to block this knowledge out of his mind. His own sister was the traitor. She had been leaving signs for the Renegades to follow the Godless band.

She finished scratching the arrow, threw her stone aside, brushed off her hands, and stood back to survey her work.

Then she turned off to return to the band—and saw Hammer standing there. She stared at him with a million different emotions racing across her features—and then her eyes dipped to the blades in his hands. He was still armed.

She recovered from her surprise first, compressed her lips, and threw back her head in defiance. "Well?" she snapped. "Go on. Feed me to the ants. That's what you want, isn't it?"

He took a step forward, but he couldn't stop looking back and forth between her and the arrow behind her. "You....you're the one. You're the one leading the Renegades to us...."

"So what if I am?" She spun away, but she didn't leave. "What are you going to do about it?"

He took another step. She no longer stood between him and the arrow. He stared up at it struggling to straighten out his own thoughts. "You....you're the one....."

"You can stop saying that," she snapped over her shoulder. "Just do what you're going to do and leave me alone."

"You.....you led the Renegades to attack the camp.....All those boys could have gotten killed. All the women and girls and even babies could have gotten carried off. *You* could have gotten carried off."

"You don't know what you're talking about!" She whipped around to confront him. "We are Renegade Clan! When are you going to wake up and realize that? We aren't even Godless!"

"You......" He blinked at her as the last stone in the wall crumbled away to powder. "You killed Alien."

"He killed Darso!" she snapped. "Did you forget that? Darso was our father—not Alien! Alien and the Godless killed him! We would be with him now if not for these Godless animals!"

"Darso!" Hammer gasped. "You think Darso was our father?! Are you insane?!"

"He was!"

"He captured Mother from her family band in the Followers Clan!" Hammer heard his voice rising. He was not having this conversation with his own sister—but he was. "He stole her from her people, carried her off to Renegade country, and took her by force! Don't you realize that?! Do you not realize that you, Lonion, and I were all conceived that way?! Darso was not our father! Mother only had one husband and that was Alien! He was the only man she ever truly married!"

Aster whirled away in the other direction. "I don't have to listen to this!"

Hammer shocked himself by springing for her. He would have attacked her, but he kept his head enough not to.

He jumped in front of her instead. "You aren't going anywhere! You better listen to it. What do you think will happen to you if the Renegades catch up with us? They'll kill all the men and boys—including Vuco! Is that what you want? Vuco will be dead and the Renegades will drag you off to their territory and hand you off to whichever of them wants you. He'll have his way with you, beat you, whip you, break your bones, assault your daughters—anything he wants. That's what you're doing to all of us. You're bringing that fate on all of us—and you don't even care!"

She tossed her head at him. "You don't know anything about it! They promised me they wouldn't. They said I would be spared."

Now he was the one who snorted. He couldn't even bring himself to answer her. She was completely deranged. She wasn't thinking clearly about any of this, but that didn't excuse her behavior.

He seized her arm, turned her the other way, and marched her around the rock heading back toward the stream.

She struggled, but he only tightened his grip. "Leave me alone!" she shrieked. "Just get it over with and feed me to the ants! Let go of me, Hammer!"

He realized in that one moment that she called him by his real name. She didn't call him by his boyhood name—the name he got in the Renegade Clan.

She really was Godless. She grew up Godless in Hangman's band the same way Hammer did. She followed Godless customs by dropping the name when Hammer initiated.

She said she was Renegade Clan, but her actions told a different story. Her mind must have snapped somewhere along the way.

"Hangman is your Kral," he muttered. "He'll be the one to decide what to do with you."

She yanked her arm harder, but he crushed his fist onto her and didn't let her go. No way would he let her get away with this.

"You only care about Hangman!" she spat. "You serve him as your Kral—like his loyal little pet!"

"That's right," Hammer snarled. "Some of us still hold loyal to our Clans and bands. That's something you'll never understand."

Chapter 13

H angman glanced around him to make sure the women and children stayed together. Red and his men flanked the band on the west side. Kuvik, Viking, Cross, and the younger uninitiated boys brought up the rear to make sure no one fell behind.

Hammer's band took the east side. The whole party traveled slowly enough to keep everyone collected into one group. No one straggled or lagged.

Hangman went in front and led everyone to the edge of the trees north of the grasslands. The open fields spread out in front of him. The whole place breathed with danger and menace.

He couldn't see any creatures out there. He didn't need to. Every creature would be able to see these women and children as soon as they stepped out of the trees.

He looked over his shoulder one last time to make sure everyone was in position. That was the moment when he saw Hammer and Aster coming out of the undergrowth to the east.

Hangman didn't notice them missing until now. He had gotten used to Hammer and his men going off in different directions on their own business. They didn't tell him or explain themselves to him ahead of time.

He didn't understand what Hammer and Aster might have been doing over there, but Hangman trusted Hammer to handle whatever it was. He would manage his sister better than Hangman could.

Hammer pushed his sister into the group of women. Hangman had his own concerns right now. He cast one glance into the group to make sure Cheina was okay. She had come back to herself, now that Hammer was taking care of her in Alien's place.

Hangman faced front, stepped out onto the open grass, and glanced up, around, and behind him for any sign of any creature. He didn't see anything, so he kept going and waved to those behind him. "Let's go! Let's move!"

The women and children followed him. He cringed when Mora, Zaedi, and Thena passed Hangman on their way into the open.

He kept his kukris drawn in front of the group. He pressed forward alone, but the other men would jump in to back him up if anything came from that direction.

The party streamed out onto the grasslands and started to cross. The jungle looked a long way away from here. Hangman picked up his pace and had to slow himself down to keep pace with everyone else.

The children hurried as fast as they could. Everyone hurried. No one wanted to stay out here any longer than they absolutely had to.

The band walked for an hour. Hangman looked behind him to check on everyone. They all stayed in the same positions. The men kept turning right, left, and backward to survey the fields in all directions. The lull couldn't last.

Viking pointed eastward. Another herd of Crammers stood over there five miles from the band. The Crammers didn't put the Godless in danger and Hangman didn't dare to stop to hunt the Crammers now. It was too late. He'd already played his hand.

The group kept going, but at that moment, Cross and the uninitiated boys leapt around backward and raised their weapons. Lonion shouted something and everyone else turned to see a mob of Demonex loping out of the jungle behind the band.

Half the men rushed over there to help defend the party's rear. "Keep moving!" Hangman roared. "Don't stop! Get to the jungle!"

Everyone picked up speed. Some of the children tried to run, but their mothers stopped them and forced the children to stay inside the group. The men had to leave Viking, Kuvik, Cross, and the boys to face the Demonex alone.

The remaining men surrounded the women and children to keep defending them. Hangman would have liked to stay with Cross and the others, but he had to keep leading the band.

Seven Demonex paced back and forth behind the party. The Demonex took a few threatening steps forward, but they couldn't get near the band with the men standing guard. Lucky and Omen dropped back to support them.

The men and boys backed up as well as they could to protect the party from behind. The group loosened its formation, but it held—for now.

Hangman measured the distance to the jungle ahead. It looked a lot farther away from here. The band wouldn't make it there before nightfall. The Godless would travel through the darkness. That was the best way to stop any creatures from seeing everyone walking unprotected in the open.

A yell made him look behind him. The Demonex sprang for the men and boys back there—and at that moment, at the worst possible time, a flock of Boultars dropped out of the sky and attacked the party, too.

These creatures couldn't have planned their assault to catch the Godless more unprepared. The men and boys fought tooth and nail against the Demonex. Hangman and his men couldn't even break off to go support them.

Boultars plummeted on top of the group and tried to snatch any children not standing close enough to their mothers.

All the mothers planned for this, came armed, and kept their children near them. The women reacted quicker than anyone. Some of the Boultars hit the mothers instead.

Aliva and Hicia got into hand-to-hand battles against Boultars trying to attack the women and get away from them at the same time.

Those scuffles gave the other women enough time to arm themselves before the men moved in. Hangman hacked a Boultar that attacked Cheina. He fought his way to Mora who already straddled Zaedi and Thena crouching between her legs.

A giant Boultar kept swooping in and trying to either peck or grab her with its claws. She slashed the creature, but it kept darting out of the way in time to save itself. It didn't see Hangman coming until he chopped his kukri into its neck and brought it to the ground.

"Keep moving!" he bellowed. "Get to the jungle! Go now!"

He had to turn around fast to face another four Boultars coming out of the sky. Mora seized her children and ran for it.

All the families got separated into a long, straggling, stretched out line running for the distant trees. Hangman took down another Boultar and came face to face with a giant male rushing straight for Hangman's face.

He dodged in time to save himself from getting impaled by the creature's beak. Then the Boultar collided with him, knocked him flat on the ground, and kept on rushing over his head to pass him and go after the fleeing women and children instead.

He reacted on pure adrenaline, dropped his kukris, flipped onto his back, and grabbed the Boultar by the feet just as they brushed the top of his face. He held on with all his might, took a page out of Wildling's book, and brought the creature crashing down on the ground.

Hangman didn't waste time picking up his weapons. He scrambled on top of the creature, pinned one of its wings to stop it from launching, and punched the creature across the side of the face.

The Boultar's skull turned out to be a lot harder than he thought. He hurt his hand, but he stunned the creature long enough to climb on top of it, straddle its body, and snap its neck to kill it.

The two battles escalated by the second. All the Godless took off running across the fields to the distant jungle. How many of those people would actually make it?

Cross, Kuvik, and the boys kept battling the Demonex behind the party. Hangman's shattered brain registered just how well Lonion, Vuco, and the others were fighting. They didn't back down one inch. Hangman couldn't ask for better fighters than this.

He had to turn his back on them and race to catch up with the others. He was the last man here not fighting the Demonex.

He picked up his kukris and took off running for the trees. They vanished into the darkness long before he got near them.

Chapter 14

The Godless band huddled in the undergrowth and waited for night to come on the second day. They made it this far in pairs and family clusters. It took a long time for everyone to rejoin, but at least the band didn't lose anyone.

The party camped on the ground this time. No one could muster the energy to climb into the canopy.

Hammer sat off to one side and observed his sister Aster talking to their mother. Cheina and Aster shared food and handed baby Raria back and forth between them whenever one of the women needed to do something.

Hammer didn't see Aster behaving any differently than usual. She didn't look in his direction to see if he was watching her. He still hadn't told Hangman about her. Maybe she thought he wouldn't. Maybe she thought he would go soft on her and spare her.

He didn't understand his feelings toward her. He had been moving away from her and the rest of his family ever since they joined the Godless. He and his band of boys separated themselves and went with the men. He even separated himself from Lonion.

Now Lonion would become a man of the Godless. Hammer couldn't ask for a fiercer, more dedicated fighter.

Lonion gave his all to defend the band against those Demonex. He and the other boys took their share of injuries. Viking, Cross, and Kuvik couldn't say enough about the boys' conduct.

Hammer would always protect his mother and Raria. He saw himself stepping into Alien's role in everything except for the part about him being Cheina's husband.

Hammer didn't know where he stood with Aster. He still saw her as a little girl he had to protect and take care of. He got himself punished and hurt countless times when he tried to protect her from Renegades before the captives joined Hangman's band.

Now Hammer barely saw her as his sister at all. He felt absolutely nothing for her.

Alien's death and all of Cheina's despair that came from it—it was all Aster's fault. The attack in the valley—the crushing ordeal of leaving and traveling again once the men realized the Renegades were coming for them—that was all Aster's fault, too.

She did all of this. How long had she been leading the Renegades here? Did she lead them through the gulley to find the artillery battery in the mountains? Was she responsible for the band having to leave the battery, too?

He was still sitting there thinking things over when Vina came over and sat down next to him. He really should spend more time with her, but more and more of his time got taken up with tending his mother.

Vina rested her hand on his arm. "You're troubled," she murmured. "Tell me what's bothering you."

He looked across the camp at his mother and sister. Vina wouldn't know the real reason why. "I'm just worried about the band—and what's going to happen to all of us. The Renegades are still following us. They'll follow the traitor's signs and find us again."

"Cheina seems much better," Vina remarked. "She needs you now. Don't think I don't see what you're doing."

Hammer winced and looked away. Of course Vina understood, "I'm sorry I haven't been around for you as much as I should have."

"Of course I know," she murmured. "Don't worry about me. I'll always be here."

He couldn't look at her. He really wished he could bury his head in her lap and shut his eyes—just once. "I asked Hangman to let me marry you." His voice broke. "I forgot that you have another year before you come of age."

"I'll still be here then." She slipped her hand into his and squeezed. "That won't change between us."

He lowered his voice so only she could hear him. "You have no idea how much I need you."

"You already have me. You have me in every way that counts. You might not have my body until then, but you have the rest of me now. Never doubt that."

"How could I doubt it when you tell me all the time?"

She rested her head on his shoulder. They both looked out at the band. "You would think we would have spotted the traitor by now," she remarked. "It doesn't seem possible that any of these people could betray us. I don't want to believe that about any of our people."

He answered by kissing the top of her head. He didn't need to tell her the real truth. "I have to go," he murmured. "I love you. We'll be together very soon."

He kissed her hair one more time, got to his feet, and stalked into the party of women and children sitting around resting.

He strode over to where his mother and sister sat, took hold of Aster's arm, and dragged her to her feet.

She started protesting and struggling again. "Hey! Hammer—let me go! Leave me alone!"

"I don't think so." He shook her and yanked her into the middle of the camp.

"What are you doing?!" his mother cried.

He raised his voice so everyone could hear him. "Aster is the traitor! Aster is the one leaving signs for the Renegades to follow us! I found her scratching an arrow into the rocks on the other side of the grasslands. She is the one who keeps showing them where we are and how to follow us."

Gasps and cries ran through the group. A bunch of people jumped to their feet until the whole band surrounded Hammer and Aster in the middle.

Hangman stood up and the other men gathered around. "Are you sure about this?" Hangman asked. "There's no mistake?"

"She admitted to me that she considers herself Renegade Clan. She's doing this in revenge for all of you killing the man who captured Cheina—the man Aster considers her father. The Renegades promised her safety and protection in exchange for her help. You can send your men back across the fields and I'll show you the rock where she scratched the arrow. That will prove it."

"I don't think we need to do that." Hangman turned to Aster. "Did you do this, Aster? Are you the one who led the Renegades to us?"

"You're animals!" Aster spat. "You're vermin—all of you!"

"You....you killed Alien...." Cheina's voice rose to a broken scream. She aimed an accusing finger at her daughter. "You killed Alien! You were the one who did it! You killed him!"

She broke down crying and screaming the way she did when the men first brought Alien's body into camp. The other women surrounded her and started to pull her away.

Aster yanked her arm against Hammer's grip, but she only wound up hurting herself when he held her tighter.

"Did you leave signs for the Renegades?" Hangman insisted. "Tell the truth."

"Yes!" she roared. "I saw the battle before we left Ceon! Alien was the one who killed Darso! I saw him with my own eyes!"

"You killed him!" Cheina shrieked. "You killed Alien!"

"He deserved it!" Aster bellowed back. "You all deserve it! You'll all die and I'll go back to Renegade country where I belong!"

"Your baby sister will go back to Renegade country, too," Hangman told her. "She'll become a slave to some man who mistreats her—and so will you and your mother. Is that what you want?"

"You're scum—all you Godless!" She bared her teeth at everyone. Hammer didn't recognize her like this. She actually looked like an animal herself.

Hangman nodded to Vuco and the other boys. They took off running through the trees and vanished. Lonion stayed behind. He stood in one place staring at his sister in blank horror. Hammer didn't blame him.

Hammer wouldn't have been able to pass judgment on Aster. Hammer didn't know if he would have the guts to pass that sentence on any living person—not even his worst enemy.

Hangman turned to Red's men and murmured, "Take her."

"NO!!" Cheina shrieked. "NO!! YOU CAN'T!!"

Everyone ignored her except the women restraining her. She kept fighting to break their hold and run forward. Hammer didn't know what she would do if she got near Aster. He didn't want to find out.

Red, Wildling, Prodigy, Butch, Burn, and Carnage surrounded Hammer and Aster. The men pulled her out of Hammer's grip and immediately moved her away from him so he couldn't intervene. He didn't plan to, but he backed off anyway.

He retreated and took his place standing next to his brother. Aster burst into a fit of screaming, kicking, and struggling while the men hauled her to the center of the camp.

The band had camped in the first small clearing they found. It was barely big enough to hold all these people.

Everyone backed off. People started climbing into the trees and carrying their children high enough off the ground. The remaining men went to help their wives carry the children to a safe distance.

Red and the others fought Aster down onto the ground, tied ropes around her wrists and ankles, and staked her out where the Godless had just been sitting.

Hammer didn't hear a single child crying in the canopy above him. They better learn the fate of all traitors.

Cheina kept thrashing and shrieking the whole time. Her cries got a hundred times worse when she saw the boys coming back.

They walked backward sprinkling pollen on the ground to lead the ants into the clearing. Hammer tugged his brother's arm and the two climbed into the branches. They stayed low where they would be able to see everything.

Aster screeched her head off. She kept spitting curses, threats, and insults when she saw the ants coming through the trees.

The women climbed into the branches and tried to drag Cheina up there with them. She fought them every step of the way and kept breaking their grip and trying to run back to Aster.

Hammer gave it up, jumped down, and went over there to restrain her himself. She was already far enough out of the ants' path. They wouldn't put her in danger.

He didn't take her into the branches nor did he use his body to block her from seeing what happened to Aster. He wanted his mother to see. He wanted to give her the satisfaction of seeing the band get justice for Alien.

The boys backed up as far as Aster, tossed a few handfuls of pollen over her, and then bolted into the trees before the ants got there.

Aster shook the pollen out of her face, but she couldn't free herself. She screamed louder as the ants started to crawl up her legs and bit into her flesh.

Her voice changed and they smothered her face chewing her down to the bone. It was all over.

He stood with his arms around his mother through it all. She howled with loud, broken sobs until Aster fell silent. Her body imploded as the ants devoured every part of her.

Cheina collapsed and twisted like she wanted to turn around in his arms. He adjusted his grip to hold her and comfort her. At that moment, she tore out of his embrace, charged away too fast for him to catch her, and threw herself into the mountain of ants.

Hammer lunged for her, but she got away from him and vanished under a thousand biting mandibles. He realized a second too late that she took Raria with her and they both crumbled under the ants' mouths, too.

Hammer stood there stunned and staring into the pile. He didn't see this coming—but he should have. He should have taken more care to stop Cheina from doing this.

He should have seen her trying to get to Aster—probably to save her. Cheina had been falling apart ever since Alien's death. This was her last act of hopeless despair.

He couldn't look up into the trees at Lonion sitting there. Lonion saw all of this, too. He saw Hammer's failure.

Hammer barely noticed when the boys came down from the trees and sprinkled more pollen on the ground to lead the ants away. The ants trooped out of the clearing and left nothing behind. They devoured bone, ropes, stakes, Aster's clothes—everything.

Hammer couldn't stop staring at the spot. He wouldn't have to take care of his mother or Aster or Raria now.

Lonion would become a man. The two of them would vanish into the world of men. They would hardly be a part of this band anymore.

That would never happen because Hammer would marry Vina in one year. She and their children would keep Hammer connected to this world of family and feelings. He wouldn't be able to lose himself in hunting, fighting, and tracking his enemies.

Someone moved in front of Hammer's eyes. He had to struggle to recognize Hangman standing there. "Come up to the canopy," Hangman murmured. "You and Lonion come eat with me and Mora tonight. We'll be your family now."

Hammer had a hard time focusing his vision or his attention on anything. He knew beforehand that Hangman would feed Aster to the ants. Hammer never imagined it would end like this.

He should have. He should have seen this coming. He should have worried about his mother doing something like this. She didn't want to face the world without Alien. She didn't want to raise Raria without a father.

Hangman laid his hand on Hammer's elbow and steered him back to the trees. Hammer climbed up in a daze. Lonion went with them, but Hammer couldn't even bring himself to check how Lonion reacted to this situation.

Did Lonion blame Hammer for Cheina's death? Hammer blamed himself—and yet he already expected it. She didn't want to live—so why should she?

He squatted on the branch across from Mora and her children. Lonion squatted next to Hammer. Hangman, Kuvik, Cross, and Viking joined them and they all passed their food around to share it.

The two children did the same thing. They showed no sign of distress that someone they knew just went down to the ants. This was all normal and right according to Clan law.

Chapter 15

H angman raised his head and immediately stiffened when he saw Hammer and Lonion sitting on a branch at a distance from Hangman's family.

The two brothers stayed here and went to sleep at the same time as everyone else. Kuvik, Cross, and Viking also stayed and slept near Hangman's family.

Now Hammer and Lonion sat over there whispering with their heads together. Hangman didn't even have to ask what they were talking about.

Hammer was too smart not to sense someone watching him. He glanced over his shoulder and saw Hangman sitting there with his eyes open. Hammer shut his mouth and Lonion didn't ask any questions, either. The brothers got up and turned around.

Hangman pushed himself to his feet, tiptoed along the branch so he didn't wake anyone up, and went over to the two brothers.

"We want to lay a trap for the Renegade Clan," Hammer whispered without any introduction.

Hangman raised his eyebrows. "We? You....and this boy..... want to lay a trap for the Renegade Clan?"

"All of us!" Hammer whispered. "The Renegades are still in the area following Aster's signs. We need to eliminate the Renegades before they try to ambush us again."

"We should veer east," Lonion interjected. "Aster's signs pointed south. The Renegades don't know she's gone. They'll keep going south. We can go east and head back south somewhere they won't be looking for us."

"Did you both just come up with that plan right now?" Hangman asked.

"Yes, of course," Hammer replied. "I only found out about Aster the day before yesterday—before we crossed the grasslands. I didn't say anything because I didn't want to interfere with the band getting across."

"I'm not asking about that," Hangman interjected. "Did you see Aster leave any other signs?"

"No, that was the last one." Hammer pointed toward the north. "The arrow on the rocks was the last one she left. I kept my eye on her the whole time after that."

"I mean before. Did you see her leave any others before that?"

"No, only that one."

Hangman studied the man in front of him. Hammer didn't react to his sister's execution. He went into a numb trance last night after his mother's death.

Now he got that hard, murderous glare on his face—the same one he got after Alien's death. Hammer wanted revenge.

Lonion also went into a numb trance last night. Now he looked as placid and steady as he did before. His mother's and sisters' deaths didn't seem to touch him at all.

Hangman really needed to initiate this young man. Lonion and the other boys acquitted themselves beyond Hangman's wildest dreams against those Demonex.

Hangmen didn't hesitate for an instant to put the boys in the most dangerous positions to guard the band on its travels. He trusted these boys as much as any of the men.

He found himself thinking of the boys in the same category as Hammer's band when they were uninitiated boys. They never had been boys. They had been men from the outset.

They initiated themselves. What happened after that was just the formality to mark a process that happened long ago. Now the same thing was happening to Lonion, Vuco, and the others. Hangman couldn't treat them as boys. They became men even before they initiated.

He waved Hammer and Lonion forward. "Come over here and sit down. We'll discuss this when the other men wake up."

"Just tell me if you think it's a stupid idea," Hammer blurted out. "Don't patronize me."

"I wasn't trying to patronize you," Hangman replied. "I'm saying we should tell the other men so we can discuss how to lay this ambush of yours. I think we should lay some more of Aster's signs. The Renegades will follow the signs straight into your trap."

Hammer stared at him. "You're actually going to do it?!"

"Why wouldn't I? You're Kral of your band. I told you that. You can make these decisions as well as I can. Now come sit down. We won't be laying any ambush on an empty stomach."

The three of them returned to the circle just as Kuvik, Viking, and Cross woke up. They sat together and ate until the rest of the men gathered to discuss what to do that day.

Hangman didn't open the discussion. He nodded at Hammer to indicate that Hammer should explain his idea.

"So our plan is to make some more of Aster's marks in the surrounding jungle on this side of the grasslands," Hammer began. "The Renegades think we're heading south, so the women, children, and one party of men will cut eastward before turning back south once you get to a safe distance."

"Who will go with the women and children?" Omen asked.

"Red's men can do that," Hammer replied. "We'll post watchmen here in the canopy to keep an eye on the grasslands. The watchmen will raise the alarm when the Renegades cross the fields to catch up with us. The rest of us will divide up, scout the area to the east, and come up with a suitable place where we can trap the Renegades and stage an ambush. Once we pick out the location, we'll come back here, leave the signs, and direct them where we want them to go."

"Did you come up with all of that just now?" Vuco asked.

"Just a little while ago," Hammer replied. "Any other questions?"

"Whose idea is this—yours or Hangman's?" Omen asked.

"It's everyone's idea," Hammer replied. "But that doesn't matter because that's what we're doing."

"So who's going where?" Pitch asked. "Who's standing watch and who's going scouting?"

"Lonion, Vuco, Ziti, and Thuron can stand watch. I'll take my men east to scout the location. The rest of you can stay here and get the band moving. Then Red and his men will escort the families eastward and we'll divert you once we know the location for the ambush."

The party broke up. Hangman got busy helping Mora prepare the children and carry them to the ground. Cross went with Hammer's band. Viking and Kuvik worked through the band helping anyone who needed it.

The party assembled on the ground. Hangman checked that the uninitiated boys were all in position and keeping watch on the grasslands. Then he, Kuvik, and Viking joined Red's men in surrounding the women and children and moving out toward the east.

Traveling in any direction other than southward felt strange. An air of tension hung over the band this morning—an air more tense than the one that usually dogged the party everywhere they went.

Everyone in this band lived under the constant threat of Renegade attack. Last night's execution and Cheina's death put everyone on high alert. Traveling in the wrong direction only made the tension worse.

Hangman's nerves threatened to snap as the day wore on. He was just started to fear the worst when Lucky came hurtling out of the treetops to tell Hangman that Hammer's band had found the location for the ambush.

"He says to tell you we'll handle it on our own," Lucky told Hangman. "The location is in a gorge southeast of here. He says you and the other men can stay with the band and continue leading them due east. You won't run into the gorge or the ambush. Hammer is laying out the marks now. The Renegades will enter the gorge and we'll strike."

Hangman stopped himself from overreacting. Hammer and his band had been becoming increasingly independent as they aged.

Hangman wanted them to be independent. He wanted Hammer to make his own decisions and carry them out, but Hangman wasn't prepared to just sit back and hand over the reins entirely.

"Go back and tell him I'm coming," he told Lucky. "Tell him not to do anything until we get there."

Lucky left. Hangman told Red what was going on. Then Hangman, Kuvik, and Viking broke away and headed back to the west where they came from.

"He's getting mighty big for his breeches," Viking muttered under his breath. "He's got some nerve ordering you around and telling you to stay out of a battle that was your idea in the first place."

"Not exactly," Hangman replied. "We're equals. He can't order me to do anything."

Viking snorted. "You aren't equals—not at all. You're the only one who thinks that. Not even Hammer thinks it."

Hangman didn't answer that because he already knew it was true. He, Kuvik, and Viking returned to the same place where the band camped last night.

They found Hammer using a rock to scratch shapes into a wall of rock. The uninitiated boys showed up a minute later.

"The Renegades just left the jungle and walked out onto the grasslands," Vuco reported.

"Good." Hammer scratched some more lines onto the rock. "This should send them to the right place."

He had scratched three large long lines joined at one end. They formed an arrow pointing southeast. Then he scratched the outline of a steep gorge with some distinctive rocks on either side.

He threw the rock away, dusted off his hands, and turned to face Hangman. "What do you think?"

Hangman nodded. "I think it looks good. Let's go."

The men took off running through the jungle and vaulted into the canopy to cover the distance more quickly. They came up on the gorge a little while later. It looked exactly like the drawing Hammer scratched in the rocks.

Outcroppings and rock formations hung over the gorge entrance to form a channel. Only one or two men could enter at a time.

Hammer pointed up at the cliffs. "My men are over there. You three should stay down here. We'll pull the same maneuver on the

Renegades that we pulled on the Crammers. We'll attack from the rocks. Then you three cut them off from behind so they can't get out of the gorge."

Hangman didn't argue, not even when he saw Hammer maneuvering himself into taking charge of this ambush exactly the way he originally planned.

Hangman made no objection. Hammer and his men left and took the uninitiated boys with them. Cross must be up on the cliffs, too. He would take part in the ambush, but Hangman wouldn't.

He sighed and led Kuvik and Viking to a hidden place in the nearby rocks. "This is stupid," Viking muttered under his breath. "So we just sit here while they get all the glory?"

Hangman had to laugh. "There is no glory in death, brother. Besides, we'll fight them plenty of Hammer's band overpowers the Renegades and they try to flee. Then it will all come down to us."

Chapter 16

Hammer returned to the caves where he left his men. Cross came with them as usual. Hammer had always treated Cross as one of his own men. Hammer never thought anything about Cross coming with them when they went out hunting or scouting.

It seemed to make sense because Cross was the same age as all the men in this party. Now Hammer found himself wincing that Cross was here. Cross should have been down at the gorge entrance with Hangman.

Hammer caught some of his other men casting sidelong glances at Cross, too. Did Cross sense something wrong that Hammer wanted to carry out this ambush by himself—apart from Hangman? Would Cross view that as betrayal of their Kral?

Cross didn't seem to notice any problem, but the others did. "Is he down there?" Lucky asked.

"Yes, he's here," Hammer replied. "He, Kuvik, and Viking are guarding the gorge entrance. They'll move in as soon as we engage the Renegades. Then Hangman and the others will stop the Renegades from escaping the way they came in."

"We should have fortified this place better," Pitch suggested.

"We didn't have time," Hammer replied. "Anyway, they're down there so we don't have to worry about the enemy getting out through the gorge entrance. Now let's check this side and make sure we have everything in order."

He approached the cliff edge. It fell away to a pinprick on the ground far below. A tiny path led from the gorge entrance through the hills along the valley floor. Sheer cliffs flanked the path on all sides. The Renegades would come that way.

Another path led back and forth down countless winding turns from this cave to the canyon bottom. The Godless planned to take that path to attack the Renegades. The cliffs and rocks would hide the Godless until they could spring their trap.

Cross came up to Hammer and stood next to him looking down. Cross didn't mention anything about Hangman being here or not being here.

The men prepared their weapons and waited around until Omen came springing down the cliffs from higher up. He leapt into the cave all out of breath. "They're coming!" he panted. "The Renegades are just entering the gorge now!"

"Let's go!" Hammer started down the cliff path. All his men followed him with the uninitiated boys in the very back.

Hammer raced down the path as fast as he dared without making any unnecessary noise. He darted around rocks, sprang over ledges, and drew his weapons before he crept into position behind a steep vertical pillar.

His men gathered around him all bristling with weapons. No one breathed. They all heard footsteps coming closer.

The setup led the Renegades deeper into the gorge than Hammer planned. He thought he would be able to attack them right there at the entrance, but it didn't work out that way.

Would Hangman and his men follow the Renegades in here? Would Hangman really hold back, wait at the entrance, and leave Hammer's band to do all the fighting?

Hammer didn't believe that for a second—so how far behind the Renegades would Hangman follow them?

Hammer counted down the seconds. He heard the Renegades long before he saw them. They didn't understand the need to be quiet. They must have thought they were miles behind the Godless.

The gorge bottom followed the undulating banks of a river course. It tumbled over rocks, log jams, and small waterfalls.

The surrounding banks and paths rose and fell in gentle curves. The rocky cliffs blocked in the banks on both sides. The outcroppings and pinnacles didn't come all the way down to the water's edge.

Ten Renegades strolled along the banks at their leisure. That was all they sent—ten men. This must be just a scouting party to tail the Godless and see where they went. Then a larger war party would come in and attack later.

None of the Renegades even held a weapon. They didn't suspect a thing.

The path dropped into a hollow and turned a few more corners before it climbed in front of Hammer's hiding place. He tensed to spring—and the whole band attacked at once.

They fell on the unsuspecting Renegades and cut down four of them before the others had a chance to defend themselves. Two of the remaining six fell in the first couple of minutes.

The last four broke and ran for it back the way they came—and ran straight into Hangman, Kuvik, and Viking coming in from behind.

The three men must have been following right on the Renegades' heels. The three Godless burst out of nowhere. Viking hacked one of the Renegades to the ground with one punishing sweep of his massive axe.

Hangman and Kuvik engaged the others three against two. Hangman and Kuvik held the last three Renegades there until Hammer's band could move in and finish the job.

The men stood over their fallen enemies and wiped the blood off their weapons. "We better get back and catch up with the others," Hangman decided. "I don't want to leave Red short-handed."

Hammer nodded. "Let's go."

The party retraced the Renegade's steps out of the gorge and back toward the south. The men picked up the trail of all the women and children.

Hammer and his men ran scouting forays into the trees to cover the surrounding terrain and make sure no more Renegades came along to follow the band.

Aster wouldn't leave any more signs to direct them. The band could slip away undetected in the Godless territory farther east.

The band would still have to keep watch for the Renegade war party that planned to follow these scouts. The Renegade threat would always loom over the band.

Hangman, Kuvik, and Viking picked up their pace when they realized they were getting close to rejoining the band. Cross and the uninitiated boys went with them.

Hammer set off to catch up with them, but one of his men caught his arm and held him back. "Wait a minute, Hammer."

Hammer turned around to look up at the guy. His name was Stray. He had been one of the boys that escaped from Ceon with Hammer and the others.

"What's the matter?" Hammer asked. "You heard Hangman. We have to catch up with the women and children. Red and his men won't be able to defend the band on their own."

"Don't you ever think about doing something other than what Hangman tells you to do?" Omen asked.

Hammer's jaw dropped. "What is your problem with Hangman all of a sudden?"

Another man named Ant spoke up from the back of the group. "We don't need to stay with him. We can form our own band."

"By ourselves?!" Hammer fired back. "Are you insane? Our girls are all in his band. We can't leave without them and none of them are the age of gathering yet. Besides, we couldn't betray Hangman."

"Leaving to form our own band isn't betraying him," a man named Earthquake pointed out. "He was the one who said you were Kral of our band. You can come and go whenever you want."

Hammer turned away. "I won't go anywhere without Vina and I can't get her until she comes of age—so that's the end of the discussion."

Stray caught his arm to hold him back. "We could take our girls and go. No one would be able to stop us."

"We would be marrying underage girls and that would be a blatant violation of Godless Clan law—and all law," Hammer fired back. "Our children wouldn't be able to go to the gatherings. We would be outlawed by every Clan. We couldn't do that. I won't do it—and I won't betray Hangman. He's our Kral. He's my Kral. You can all betray him and become outlaws if you want to. Go on. Go choose yourself another Kral. It won't be me."

"He's a stranger," Ant pointed out. "We aren't even the same people as him and his family band. We should make our own band."

"We aren't our own band!" Hammer fired back. "When are you going to realize that? He's far more qualified to be Kral than I am. He has much more experience—and he's smarter!"

"He isn't that much older than we are," Earthquake pointed out. "He was our age when we joined his band. His own cousins voted him Kral...."

"And that doesn't tell you something?" Hammer countered. "Viking and Alien were both almost ten years older than Hangman when they voted him Kral over themselves. Wake up, all of you. Red and his men made Hangman Kral, too. None of them would ever support us if we challenged him."

"We wouldn't have to challenge him," another man named Bugs interjected. "We're free men of the Godless Clan. We can leave whenever we want. We have no reason to follow his orders."

"He plans to take us to his father's band in the south," a man named Scarecrow reminded them. "If we go with him, we'll go under a completely different Kral—a stranger. Hangman will become his father's subordinate—and so will you, Hammer. We'll be the lowest men on the ladder."

Hammer threw up his hands. "Will you listen to yourselves? You just said we're men of the Godless Clan. We follow our Kral's orders and we follow the law. None of us can marry without his consent—and we wouldn't be able to marry at all if not for him. He's doing us a giant favor by letting us marry these girls at all. I don't plan to throw that away so I can live the rest of my life alone. We don't even know if we'll make it back to his father's band. It's one year. Just one year before Vina comes of age. I won't do anything before then."

"Then you admit you want to leave," Ant pointed out. "You would leave if you had Vina. Is that what you're saying?"

Hammer hesitated. He really had no other reason to stay with Hangman—except for the obvious one.

"Our wives and children will be safer in a larger band," he went on. "We would do better to stay with Hangman even as his subordinates. We won't be able to defend ourselves as well on our own—but you already know that. You've seen what it's like wandering in this country without an established territory or a protected camp. I would rather raise a family in some protected location where other Godless can help me defend it. I don't want to take Vina into the wilderness alone. That would be disastrous."

"Would you leave if we found a protected place?" Scarecrow asked. "Would you be Kral to us in our own band?"

Hammer only had to think about it for a split second. "Yes, I would. If we found a place and we all had our wives, then yes, we would break away and form our own band. I don't think that would offend Hangman at all. I think he expects it."

"We all trust and admire Hangman," Pitch added. "None of us has a problem with him and we all accept his decisions, but that isn't the same as being our own band. We definitely don't want to make ourselves subordinate to someone we don't know and have never even met."

"We are our own band," Hammer told him. "We always have been and we always will be. No one understands this better than he does. Now come on. We have to catch up. We have at least another year to wait, so we better get comfortable with that."

Chapter 17

H angman squatted next to the fire while some of the women cooked the meat of a Stalkion that Red's men had hunted and killed. This was the first Stalkion the band had seen since the party left the mountains.

Hangman didn't fail to notice Hammer's band dropping back and disappearing on the way out of the gorge. He also didn't fail to notice the air of simmering tension and unease coming from Hammer's men when they returned to the band.

They usually stayed off in a cluster by themselves. No one thought anything about this, least of all Hangman. He accepted it as normal ever since Hammer's group had been young uninitiated boys.

Now they all separated and went to sit with their families, mothers, and sweethearts. Hammer sat with Lonion and the other uninitiated boys. Hangman would have considered that unusual on its own.

He couldn't explain it away by saying that Hammer had no one else to sit with, now that his mother and sisters were gone. Lonion was Hammer's only family.

Hammer could have joined Hangman's family. No one would have thought twice about that. Viking and Kuvik were already here as usual.

Hammer didn't even look at Hangman. Something was going on. All the events of the day came together in one complete picture. Hammer's men didn't want Hangman and the others to participate in that ambush at all. Did that idea come from Hammer?

Hangman always wondered which of these young men would be the first to challenge him as Kral. He didn't think it would be Hammer and Hangman still didn't think that.

Hammer would never challenge Hangman as Kral. Hammer admired Hangman too much.

Hammer would take his men and leave to form their own band. Hangman could definitely see Hammer and his men doing something like that.

They had all been on the ragged edge of doing exactly that since they first joined Hangman's band. They only needed one thing they couldn't get anywhere else. They needed wives.

Hangman didn't have a problem with Hammer's men taking their wives and forming their own band somewhere else—as long as they waited until the girls came of age. Then no one would be able to stop them.

Hangman didn't want to stop them—but he did have to stop anyone from challenging him. Hammer might not do it, but one of his men might. Hangman didn't worry about defeating any challenger from Hammer's band.

He cared more about defending the band. Killing a challenger would weaken the band. No one needed that right now—or ever.

He waited until everyone finished eating and the band slouched around the fires at their ease. Some of the men stood guard, but only half-heartedly. They paid more attention to everything going on inside the circle of firelight than outside it.

Some of the uninitiated boys went down to the nearby stream to get water. Hammer stood up, turned the other way, and started to cross the camp on his way to meet up with Vina's family.

Hangman got to his feet and intercepted Hammer before he got there. "Take a walk with me," Hangman told him.

Hammer stiffened instantly—so that confirmed it. He didn't protest. He corrected right away and followed Hangman out into the shadowy jungle.

"You did well today," Hangman began. "That ambush went perfectly."

Hammer stopped walking. "You know, don't you?"

"I know what?" Hangman asked.

Hammer chopped his hand through the air. "Don't pretend. You know the men have been speaking against you."

Hangman raised his eyebrows. "They have? Which ones have been speaking against me?"

"Not like that! I don't mean they would challenge you. They want to split off and form their own band."

"What's wrong with that?" Hangman asked. "Isn't that what you've all been planning from the beginning?"

"You know what I mean!" Hammer snapped. "They want to do it now. They want to take the girls and go now."

Now it was Hangman's turn to stiffen, but he only did it for a second. "Is that what you want?"

"Of course not! I don't want to marry Vina when she's underage! What do you take me for?"

"Take it easy, brother," Hangman murmured. "I respect your decision. I didn't bring you out here to confront you about that."

Hammer frowned at him. "You didn't?"

"No. I never doubted you."

"Why did you bring me out here, then?"

"I brought you here to find out if any of your men were speaking against me—I mean really speaking against me—as in they want to challenge me on your behalf."

Hammer's jaw dropped. "You can't be serious! You can't honestly suspect any of my men of that!"

"I didn't say I suspected them, but you sure were acting like they did. Saying they want to leave to form their own band isn't speaking against me. I have no problem with that. I've been waiting for the day when you did leave."

"We aren't leaving!" Hammer snapped. "I made that clear. I made it clear that I would stay."

"You made it clear that you would stay until Vina comes of age—until all the girls come of age. Am I right?"

Hammer looked away. "I don't see how it would work running a band with two Krals."

Hangman laughed. "You're right. It wouldn't."

His laughter jolted Hammer. He recoiled as though he'd been slapped. "How can you joke about this? This is not a laughing matter."

"I'm laughing because I'm relieved that none of your men want to challenge me."

"Of course they don't. They all respect you as Kral. They just...." He broke off.

"They just what? You might as well tell me what's really bothering them."

"If you're right that I'm Kral and we have our own band...."

"You do. You always have. You must know that. Your band has always been separate from mine."

"Then you understand why they want me to be their Kral—not you......" Hammer hesitated and then blurted out. "And you could imagine how they would feel about going under a Kral they don't know—someone they've never met—someone who would rule differently than you. We know you. We understand you and you understand us. We understand why you ruled that we have to wait for these girls—and you let us wait. You let us plan to marry these girls even though they're younger than we are."

"Yes, of course," Hangman replied. "Why wouldn't I?"

"Then you could understand that someone else might make a different ruling—that the girls had to go to men their own age. We wouldn't be able to marry them at all."

A heavy stone dropped into Hangman's stomach when he realized what Hammer meant. Now Hangman was the one to turn away.

"I'm sorry, Hangman," Hammer choked. "You've been so good to us....."

Hangman couldn't turn around. He couldn't even look at this young man—a man who staked his life and his friends' lives to keep this band alive these last four years—almost five years.

There never was a bigger stickler for the rules than Hangman's father, Shadow. No one knew that better than Hangman himself.

Shadow would never approve of the way Hangman bent the rules in this band. Shadow wouldn't listen to a word of excuse about how circumstance demanded that the band adapt and modify certain rules to fit their needs.

Hangman had been so single-mindedly focused on getting these people back to Shadow's band—or any Godless band.

Hangman didn't think anything of making himself subordinate to Shadow. Hangman had been subordinate to Shadow all his life.

Hangman didn't realize what that might mean to everyone else in his band. Red and his men all married older women—women far beyond the age of gathering. Things would play out differently for Hammer, his men, and the girls they planned to marry.

Hangman struggled to make himself heard, but he couldn't turn around. He couldn't make eye contact with Hammer—the man Hangman considered a brother.

"I don't suppose it means anything to you if I say I'll support you," Hangman husked.

"I don't know if I can trust that." Hammer's voice trembled. "I trust you, but how can I trust a man I've never met? You're the only Godless Kral I've ever known. You adapted your ways to take care of us. How can I trust that another Kral will do the same thing?"

Hangman shook his head. He already knew exactly what Shadow would say. He would go by the letter of the law—the law that said all young people had to go to the gathering.

Young people married others their own age. If they missed and didn't find someone in their own age group, they went back the following year. Girls kept going back until they married. If a boy missed a second time, he was out of luck for life.

Hammer and his men were already too old to go to the gathering. The girls wouldn't go until next year.

These young couples could only ever find happiness together if Hangman's band stayed away in the wilderness—and not just for another year, but for a long time.

They would have to stay away until they all got far too old for anyone to expect them to go to the gathering. That was the only way anyone would accept Hangman's ruling.

Leaving the band and forming their own—it was the only solution—the only solution Hammer's men could accept. It all made sense from their point of view.

"I'm sorry," Hammer murmured behind him. "I never wanted to betray you."

He sounded so broken that Hangman forced himself to turn around. "You aren't betraying me—not at all. None of you are. I support you. I absolutely do. Come back to my fire with me and eat with me and my family. We're brothers—always. If you and your men need to leave, then that's the way it will be. Nothing will ever come between us."

Hammer's features convulsed and his voice cracked. "Do you really mean that?"

"Of course." Hangman found himself squeezing the back of Hammer's neck. "We're brothers. I support you—and all your men. You'll find happiness. I know you will."

Chapter 18

Hangman led Hammer back to the camp. Neither of the men talked on the way.

Hangman's heart bled for Hammer and all the men of his band. They had been rock solid all these years. They had been as staunch, as powerful, and as enthusiastic as Hangman could ever have hoped for them to be.

They had all grown up into the most shining examples of what Godless men should be. They deserved to marry and raise families as much as anyone did.

Only a cruel trick of fate decreed that they wouldn't get to go to the gathering. They didn't deserve to live their lives alone because of that.

They found girls who wanted to marry them. They all waited for years. Why shouldn't they gain the reward for that? Hangman couldn't bring himself to deny that privilege. They had all earned it down to the last man.

He led Hammer back to the fire. Viking took a hunk of Stalkion meat off the spit, set the meat on a flat, clean rock, cut up the meat, and passed the food around to everyone.

Hangman sat down next to Mora. Hammer sat down next to Hangman. Kuvik and Cross sat on Mora's other side.

Zaedi and Thena scampered around playing near the fire. They bounced up and down. Zaedi made shooting, sizzling noises with his mouth and used a small, short stick to slash and chop like he was swinging a blade in battle.

"Be careful you don't fall into the fire, my son," Hangman told the boy.

"I'm being careful." Zaedi jumped into the air, spun around, and his foot landed on one of the stones that made up the fire circle.

He almost toppled into it, but Hammer shot out his hand, caught the boy, and pulled him back in time. Hammer pulled just a little too hard and Zaedi fell the other way. He pitched all the way over into Hammer's lap.

He smiled down at the boy, picked him up, and set him on his feet. "Don't attack me, little brother," Hammer told him. "I'm unarmed."

Zaedi brandished his stick at Hammer. "Defend yourself, Crusher! I'm a man of the Godless Clan!"

Everyone around the fire laughed—everyone except Hammer. He raised both arms, curved his fingers into claws, and bared his teeth in a monstrous snarl.

He heaved off the ground, hunched his back, and roared out loud while he stalked the boy down. Zaedi took one look at the Crusher, screamed, and ran for it. He charged around the fire, collided with Viking's leg, and huddled behind it to hide.

Viking laughed at him, patted him on the back, and left him there cowering and cringing in terror. "I'll protect you from the Crusher, little brother," Viking told the boy. "Something tells me he isn't as dangerous as he appears."

Hammer dropped his arms and sat back down. Hangman passed him a bowl of the meat that Mora handed to him.

Hammer took the bowl and put a piece of meat in his mouth. "I'm not, actually. Don't tell anyone."

"We already know, brother," Viking told him. "You aren't keeping any secrets from us."

Hammer grinned, but just then, Zaedi decided to try again. He came out from behind Viking's leg, stormed up to Hammer, brandished his stick blade again, and swiped it back and forth while he made swishing noises with his mouth.

He didn't come close to hitting Hammer. The boy just pretended to parry and thrust his blade at Hammer.

Hammer grabbed a stick of firewood that happened to be lying nearby, raised it in front of him, and used it to block and defend against Zaedi's attack. They sparred for a few minutes until Zaedi lost interest.

He stopped in the middle of their duel, sat down, and looked up at Hammer. "Tell me about your initiation, Hammer. Tell how you defeated the Blastidon."

"I can't do that, little brother," Hammer replied. "There are women and girls present. They aren't allowed to know the details of a man's initiation."

"Wildling told the details of his initiation—and Father has told me the details of his initiation—and Father has told me the details of Cross's initiation." Zaedi furrowed his brow. "Did you just make that up so you wouldn't have to tell me?"

Mora laughed. "Nice try, Hammer. You can't fool this one."

"Maybe I don't want to tell you because I'm embarrassed," Hammer explained. "Maybe I don't want you to know the details because I'm afraid you'll tell the girls in camp and they'll laugh at me."

Zaedi's eyes popped wide open and he gasped in astonishment. Then he burst out laughing and pointed in Hammer's face. "Did you make a fool of yourself at your initiation? Did you almost lose? Did you almost die?"

Hammer only smiled at the boy and caught Hangman's eye. "What I did at my initiation is none of your business."

"You fought a Blastidon, though, didn't you?" Zaedi insisted.

"Of course I did. Everyone knows that."

Just then, Thena decided to get involved in the conversation. She climbed out of Mora's lap, walked around the fire, and sat down in Hammer's lap. "What was it like to fight a Blastidon, Hammer?" she asked.

"Scary," Hammer replied.

"You were scared?!" Zaedi burst out laughing again. "I don't believe it."

"That's the point of the initiation," Hammer explained. "You aren't supposed to pick a creature you aren't scared of. That would make you a coward."

"I don't believe you were scared," Zaedi countered. "I think you're just saying that."

"I was. Ask your father. He'll tell you."

Zaedi turned to Hangman. "Is that true? Was he scared of the Blastidon?"

"Scared isn't the word I would use," Hangman replied. "I would say he was nervous—but he did think he might die—so I guess you could say he was scared."

"He was very brave," Viking chimed in. "I have rarely seen any man fight as bravely in his initiation."

"Definitely," Cross added.

"Only because I was so much older than most." Hammer turned back to Zaedi. "What do you think you'll choose to fight for your initiation?"

"Don't ask him that!" Mora exclaimed. "He's just a little boy."

"He's already thinking about it," Hangman interjected. "Asking him won't make him think about it any more than he already is. Let me see. He's already decided to fight a Crusher, a Blastidon, a Gorlock, a Shriker....."

"I did not!" Zaedi snapped. "I'm not going to fight any of those."

"What is it this week?" Hangman asked. "A Dushag?"

Zaedi made a face at him, but Thena interrupted again. "Did you get hurt in your initiation, Hammer? Did the Blastidon hurt you?"

"You know it didn't," Zaedi countered. "You saw him when he came back. He wasn't injured."

"I didn't get hurt—not in that way," Hammer replied.

"What other way is there?" Zaedi asked.

"He exhausted me," Hammer explained. "He drained me until I had nothing left. He almost won."

Zaedi gazed at him in worshipful awe. "I wish I could have been there."

Cross laughed again. "You are going to have a problem with this one, brother."

"I already do," Hangman agreed.

"I think it's time for both of you little ones to go to bed." Mora stood up. "Say goodnight to everyone."

Zaedi stood up and held out his hand to Hammer. "Let's call it a draw."

Hammer bit back a grin and shook the boy's hand. "Done. It was a draw."

Thena stood up and hugged Hammer. "Good night, Hammer."

"Good night, little flower."

"Good night, Hammer," Zaedi repeated.

"Good night, brother. Maybe we can spar again another day."

"I'll beat you next time." Zaedi made a few slashing movements and noises on his way to the shelter where Mora would bed down the children.

They hugged and said good night to Viking, Cross, Kuvik, and Hangman on their way inside. Mora shut the door, but everyone could still hear them talking through the walls.

"You have a beautiful family," Hammer remarked as soon as they left.

"You'll have one of your own one day soon, I'm sure," Hangman replied. "You'll make a good father. I can see that."

Hammer snorted. "They'll be too scared to play with the Crusher."

The other men laughed, but the subject killed their conversation. Hangman had a lot on his mind.

He never doubted for a single second that Hammer would marry Vina—and that all his men would marry the girls they loved.

All of them had been waiting far too long. They wouldn't accept any other outcome no matter the cost.

Chapter 19

M ora woke up before her children as usual. Hangman lay curled up on his side on the other side of Zaedi.

She pried herself out of bed, went outside, and found Kuvik squatting by the fire cooking some of the Stalkion meat from last night. Viking and Cross both slept nearby.

"Good morning," she murmured.

He cast a glance down at her body and then looked around grinning. "Where's the rest of you?"

She bit back laughter. "I feel light enough to float away on the breeze." She studied him. "Did you sleep?"

His smile evaporated and he stared down at his stick poking at the coals. "Not really."

She patted his shoulder. "Maybe the nightmares will go away in time."

He lowered his voice to a rasp. "Something tells me they will never go away."

She didn't know what to say to him. He always slept near her family when the band traveled anywhere. He never let himself get too far away from Hangman.

She, Hangman, Viking, and Cross were the only members of this band who knew about Kuvik's nightmares. He didn't talk about what they were. No one asked.

The four of them valued him too much as a comrade and a brother to ever tell anyone about them. If Kuvik ever told Hangman about his past, Hangman never shared the details with anyone. He kept Kuvik's secrets between them.

She squeezed his shoulder one last time. "The camp will be waking up soon. We should pack up."

"I'm ready to go," he told her. "Do you need help with anything?"

"Yeah, I need a wife."

He burst out laughing. It was one of the very few times she'd ever seen him laugh. "I'm sorry. I can't help you with that."

She laughed with him, but right then, they heard Maeno fussing inside. She went back in and then spent the next hour getting her children out of bed.

The noise woke up Hangman. He helped her deal with Zaedi and Thena while she put Maeno back inside his wrap.

They came out to find most of the camp up and moving around. Viking and Cross helped pack up the rest of the dried Stalkion meat.

The process of getting everyone moving for the day took ages. Then the band traveled at a crawl all day before they camped and did it all again the next day.

Every day felt like it lasted an eternity and yet they passed so fast that Mora barely noticed them changing from one to the next.

Every detail of her life demanded her total, undivided attention. Every instant of her children's care consumed every shred of her energy and focus.

She barely noticed anything else beyond the shades of their facial expressions, their body language, and all their little outbursts of need and emotion.

The band came to the edge of the jungle on the third day. No one in their band recognized this country.

They were in Godless territory, but they were still too far north. No one in their band had ever traveled here before. No one from Shadow's band ever traveled this far north and no one from Thunder's band ever traveled this far south.

Hangman halted on a high, blustery hilltop and surveyed the country lying even farther south. "We'll just have to keep traveling south," he decided. "We'll either find Shadow's old territory or we'll come to the Followers' territory—one or the other."

The party had to walk down that hill and cross some broken country with scattered patches of vegetation before they came to the next thick stretch of jungle.

One of the ancient cities stood in the middle of the open terrain. The same crumbling buildings raised their broken ruins to the sky.

The same broken wires hung from towers around the city. The same plants forced their way up through cracks in the pavement on the road leading into the city.

Mora didn't see any Crushers around, but that could change. The Godless usually avoided cities. They didn't go inside to scavenge the way the Followers did.

The Godless started down the other side of the hill. Mora didn't think about the journey anymore. This was just her life now.

Making it back to Shadow's territory or even rejoining Shadow's band—none of those things existed for her. They were all too far in the future for her to even think about. Everything right in front of her was so much more important.

She wasn't thinking about anything in particular when Zaedi took his hand out of hers and darted back to pick up something he spotted on the ground. Mora didn't see what it was.

She turned back to pull him along. She started to say, "Come on, Zaedi. We can't stop here...."

She stopped dead in her tracks and stared at a distant line of hilltops farther west.

Hangman happened to be behind her. He must have stopped on the hilltop to talk to some of his men. He came up behind her and saw her staring into the distance. "What's wrong?" he asked.

She could barely speak above a whisper. "Look, Hangman!"

He turned around. A line of people crossed the hills over there. The line formed a long string of black dots covering the hills for what looked like miles in both directions.

These weren't Renegades. These people shaved their heads except for tiny wisps of hair that they used to tie feathers and other decorations to their scalps.

The feathers twirled and wheeled in the breeze. They had a way of making each of those people look much bigger and more menacing than they would have otherwise.

All those people were men. They wore a different style of loincloth made out of long strips of hide wound and tied tightly around the man's legs and between them. The loincloths compressed everything as tightly as possible.

The men also painted their bodies, but not the way the Hungry Ghosts did. These men smeared their bodies with thick black lines of paint running in rows down their backs, faces, chests, thighs, and arms.

These people carried long spears tipped with long, iron heads. The men also each wore bandoliers of much smaller blades made up of short wooden handles tipped with the same long, iron spearheads.

"Who are they?" Hangman asked. "I've never seen them before,"

"Bounty Hunters!" Mora choked, grabbed Zaedi, and bellowed to those nearest her. "Run! Run for the city! Get into the buildings! Hurry! Everybody run!!"

She took off running, snatched Thena's hand, and when the two children didn't run fast enough, she scooped up both of them, one in each arm.

She held them tightly enough that they crushed Maeno. He started blaring, but she paid no attention. She ran for her life and kept yelling at everyone to do the same thing.

She told herself not to look back, but she wound up doing it anyway. The men dropped back, and the first time she looked, the Bounty Hunters broke out of their position and charged across the landscape to attack the band.

The Bounty Hunters let out a high, shrieking war cry as they came. The sound set Mora's hair on end and made her run faster. She stumbled and kept on running. Thena screamed out, "What's happening?!"

Mora couldn't answer. She would have liked to stop and help get the other women and children to safety, but she couldn't put her children in danger.

Viking followed her. He snatched up every fallen child and wound up carrying five of them in his beefy arms. Their mothers could run so much faster once he started carrying the children.

He took up the call and bellowed for everyone to run for the city. None of these people knew why, but it didn't matter as long as they got there in time.

The next time she looked back, the Bounty Hunters swooped down on the Godless men who stayed behind to defend the women's retreat. The men formed a matching line at an angle between the fleeing women and the oncoming enemy.

The two sides met in a clash of weapons that echoed in Mora's ears. She didn't give herself a chance to look behind her again.

Her lungs burned and her knees kept buckling, but she just had to keep running. Viking overtook her leading three women whose children he carried.

She stayed near him after that. They raced down the road into the city and into the nearest building.

"This way!" Mora yelled. "Follow me!"

She turned into the stairwell and charged up five floors before she couldn't climb any further. She burst into a hallway, stumbled down it, and finally turned off into a small room with a big wooden desk in the center.

She collapsed on her knees and dropped Zaedi and Thena onto the floor. The rest of the women staggered in. Viking put the children down. They rushed into their mothers' arms. Some of the mothers started crying and thanking Viking.

He looked around in confusion. "Now what do we do?"

Mora gulped to try to get her voice working and pointed behind her. "The window...." she husked. "The window....you should be able to see...."

He stood up, crossed to the window, and looked out. He didn't turn away and he didn't tell anyone what he saw out there. Mora didn't ask.

He finally whirled away from the window, growled, "Stay here," under his breath, and charged out of the room. His footsteps pounded back down the hall and he burst into the stairwell before all sound died away.

Only the women and children crying disturbed the silence. Mora stayed where she was on the floor so she wouldn't see what was happening outside.

She did her best to calm Maeno down. He settled again once she positioned him back in his wrap with no one sitting on top of him. He latched onto her breast and all was once again right with the world.

Zaedi and Thena huddled close to her. "Who are they, Mother?" Thena asked in a tiny voice.

"Bounty Hunters, my love." Mora heard her voice shaking. "They're marauders."

"Like the Renegade Clan?" Zaedi asked.

"No, not like the Renegade Clan."

"What do you know about them, Mora?" Aliva asked.

Mora made a strategic decision not to look up at anyone around her. She pretended to pick an invisible speck of dust out of Maeno's silky hair.

"They won't come into the city," she murmured. "Even if they do, we'll be able to defend this room. They'll only be able to come through that door. We'll be able to fight them off and kill them one or two at a time."

"What do they do?" Hicia asked. "What would they do if they captured us?"

Mora couldn't decide whether she should tell the women what the Bounty Hunters would do. The sound of the stairwell door bursting open stopped her from saying anything. Viking returned and brought all the other men with him—all but one.

They poured into the room and collapsed on the floor with the women and children. Half the men were bleeding, some of them badly.

They started applying leaf paste to their wounds. "We need Gooji juice," Hammer choked. "One of us has to go out into the jungle and get the sap."

"I'll go," Cross volunteered.

"We'll all go," Hangman decided. "They aren't there anymore. We can't stay here. The Crushers might come for us."

Mora looked around. "Where's Kuvik?"

Hangman looked away. "They took him."

Her heart stopped. "No!" she whispered.

"He stayed behind to defend us when we ran for it," Cross murmured. "They all piled in to subdue him. He bought us the time we needed to get away."

Mora gulped down a surge of despair. "No!" she quavered.

"What will they do to him?" Aliva asked again.

Mora spun around and almost lost her temper with the woman for asking too many questions. Mora barely fought herself under control enough to snarl the words through gritted teeth.

"They capture and enslave everyone—boys, girls, women, men—everyone. The Bounty Hunters don't care who they take. They treat all captives as slaves—and all the children of captured women as slaves. The Bounty Hunters sell their own daughters as slaves and drive captured men into forced labor. The boys who are young enough they train as warriors to go out marauding, stealing, and pillaging with the rest. Everyone else they keep beaten down so no one has the strength to resist or escape. They brutalize everyone, even their own." She forced herself to look down at the baby in her arms. "We won't see Kuvik again. We'll be lucky to get away from them—now that they know where we are."

"Why don't they come into the cities?" Hangman asked.

She shrugged. She couldn't look at him. "I don't know," she croaked. "I think it must be superstition or something like that. They have strange beliefs in demons and haunted places. Maybe they think the ancient cities are haunted by all the people who used to live here. I really don't know."

No one said anything for a long time. Most of the women here escaped from captivity in the Renegade Clan. Their captivity might not have been pleasant. It might have been nightmarish.

It couldn't possibly have been as horrific as it would have been with the Bounty Hunters. Mora wished she could bring herself to be more descriptive about what they would actually do if they captured the band.

The Bounty Hunters wouldn't put the men and boys to death. That would have been a mercy compared to what actually happened to them.

She didn't want to say all of that in front of the children even though she really should have told them, too. They needed to understand how important it was to cooperate in trying to escape from this enemy.

She struggled to contain her dread of getting caught by the Bounty Hunters, and in a little while, Hangman told everyone to get up and leave the building.

"We have to get back to the jungle," he ordered. "We can defend ourselves better there and we need to tend everyone's injuries."

Chapter 20

H eavy blows pounded Kuvik all over his body. He couldn't see a thing through the hide bag tied over his head.

He huddled on the ground and curled onto his side, but he couldn't protect himself with his arms tied behind his back and his ankles tied together.

The beating went on for a long time. The Bounty Hunters had already beaten him unconscious once. They started up again the minute he regained consciousness. They must have taken his movements as a sign. They couldn't see his face.

His last memory before they knocked him out was seeing the Godless men running toward the city. They made it far enough away to get inside the buildings before the Bounty Hunters caught up with them.

A few more blows landed on Kuvik's face and head. They stunned him and he swam out of consciousness for a minute—or it may have been longer. He woke up lying on a hard, flat, solid surface. It wasn't the ground. It wasn't stone, but it felt like it.

No one was beating him anymore and the bag no longer covered his face. He squinted through puffy, swollen, bruised eyelids at the building around him.

He lay on a smooth surface of what looked like polished black stone. Each piece had been cut into a perfect square and polished to a high, mirror shine.

The floor spread around him to the walls of a big room. This place didn't have any furniture in it—and no people.

His body ached all over, but his wrists and ankles hurt the worst where the rope cut into his skin. He wouldn't be able to loosen that rope or untie it.

He craned his aching neck around in a circle so he could see the rest of the building. Curved timber trusses help up the vaulted ceiling.

Massive double doors stood open at both ends of the room. The building looked like some kind of assembly hall, but he was the only person in here right now.

The doors gave him a view on both sides of more small, rustic houses lined up beyond this building. He was in some kind of village, but he didn't recognize what kind of village it was.

He didn't understand how the Bounty Hunters could have built such a sophisticated structure so quickly after invading this country.

Hangman, Red, and Viking all insisted that the band had been traveling through Godless country all this time. The Godless didn't build villages like this. The Godless had probably never even seen a village like this.

He made himself relax on the floor and not strain himself to see or do anything. The Bounty Hunters wouldn't leave him here for long.

They left him longer than he expected. The sky started to turn dusky shades of pale pastel outside. He fell asleep and woke up in broad daylight when someone kicked him in the stomach.

"Wake up, wretch!" a man's voice snapped. "No more lollygagging around!"

Kuvik jolted back to his senses in time to brace himself for another kick in the back. Four Bounty Hunters stood around him taking turns kicking, punching, and hitting him with sticks.

They avoided his head this time, thank goodness, but they didn't spare any other part of him. They even kicked his arms and legs.

He lay still and took it all. They kept shouting insults while they did it.

He sank into another semi-conscious stupor where he didn't feel anything. He remembered this from the nightmare of his earliest childhood before he got captured by the Hungry Ghosts.

The four men beating him still wore the same feathers in their hair. The feathers stuck out at odd angles and made the men looked like jungle creatures or some kind of horrible monster.

Kuvik had spent so many years thinking the Godless were evil monsters. That was before he got to know them.

Now he found the simple beauty of their appearance so comforting. They didn't fix themselves up to make themselves look ferocious. They hid their ferocity on the inside and let it out on the battlefield.

He understood a lot more about their ways now. They never marauded other people's territory. They never stole another Clan's women or put its men to the sword.

The Godless just lived their lives in pace. No one in Hangman's band ever once suggested that they go marauding another Clan's territory or resources. It never crossed the Godless' minds to do something like that.

They treated everyone well. That was the part Kuvik found the most incredible. In all the time he lived with them, he never saw any woman or man raise their hand against a child.

The only exception was when Cheina threw herself into the ants when she was wearing Raria in the wrap.

In almost five years of living with the Godless, none of them ever even raised their voices against their children. None of them ever deliberately inflicted any harm on their children.

None of the men ever struck or even spoke harshly to their wives. Kuvik didn't understand it when he first went to live with them. He didn't think it was real. He thought it must be a trick.

It took him over a year to fully believe they were as good as they appeared to be on the surface, but they were. He never saw any man force a woman to do anything. He never heard any of the men insult a woman or make her afraid that he might hurt her.

None of the Godless children ever had to worry about any adult in the band threatening them, harming them, or even reprimanding them.

The men went over the top to protect and care for their women and children—and for the women and children of all the other men.

Viking had a wife and children of his own somewhere, but he risked his life to protect every other woman and child in the band. They all did it.

Kuvik couldn't count the number of times Hangman had risked his life for the band. Hammer and his men grew up following that example. They grew up behaving the same way and they became the same kind of men.

Kuvik started to get emotional when he thought about them. God, he loved them! He wanted nothing but to get back to them, but he couldn't move right now.

His mind and body shut down, but he had to wake up and pay attention when the Bounty Hunters cut the ropes away from his wrists and ankles. He struggled to believe that was real, too.

They beat him so senseless that he couldn't form a coherent thought when they pulled him to his feet and shook him to make him stand up.

The Bounty Hunters slapped him more than once. "Pay attention. What are you—stupid?!" one of them barked. "Stand up straight! I'm talking to you!"

Kuvik's head swam. He swayed and the guy slapped him twice more. The guy slapped hard enough to stun Kuvik. He couldn't focus his eyes.

They yanked him out of the hall and into the village. He floundered to understand where he was.

The men shoved him into another building like the first except it was much smaller. The walls of these structures looked like they were made of stone or very tough wooden planks. Kuvik didn't recognize what kind of structure it was.

He didn't have time to think about it before his captors hurled him through the door. He stumbled and lost his balance.

He pitched across a wooden floor this time, tumbled, and sprawled at the feet of at least fifty people packed into a tiny room.

They all laughed at him and kicked him a few more times, but these people didn't kick nearly as hard as the men who just got finished with him.

He rolled onto his back and curled his arms and knees in front of him to protect himself. That was the moment when he saw a man sitting in a huge armchair to one side.

Kuvik's mind cleared enough to recognize that none of these people wore the kind of loincloths he remembered seeing on the men who captured him.

The man in the armchair wore some kind of pants and long robes over his bare chest. His clothes left his arms bare and the center of his chest exposed while the robes fell all the way to the floor

His robe seemed to be made up of hundreds of black, glossy feathers—the same kind of feathers the warriors wore in their hair.

This man wore feathers in his hair, too, but he didn't shave his head like the warriors did. He let his hair grow and tied the feathers straight into his hair.

He had lighter hair, eyes, and skin than the Godless—or any other Clan that Kuvik had ever seen. The Bounty Hunter warriors and all the people standing around had the same straight black hair, black eyes, and dark skin as every other Clan.

All the other people here wore clothes—a different kind of clothes from the Renegades. Kuvik didn't recognize what kind of clothes they were because he had never seen anything like them before.

The men wore pants made out of some glossy colored material and loose-fitting, flowing white shirts. The women wore poofy, brightly colored gowns hanging to the floor with their collars buttoned all the way up to their chins.

The warriors moved in and started kicking him again. The man in the chair laughed at Kuvik, too.

"You Godless filth!" the first warrior roared. "Where are your people hiding?! Tell us what you know or die as you deserve!"

He punctuated every word with a kick or a blow. The spectators had to pull back to give the warriors room to attack Kuvik.

"I'm not Godless!" Kuvik blurted out. "They....they captured me!"

"You're lying!" the same guy snapped. "You were with them! You fought to protect them!"

"Look at me!" Kuvik yelled out when another cruel blow landed on his leg. "I'm not Godless! I came from the Hungry Ghosts! The Godless captured me and held me as a prisoner!"

He didn't tell them that the Godless captured him and held him as a prisoner more than four years ago. He didn't tell them that the Godless released him and had been treating him as family ever since.

The same warrior barged forward, slammed his foot on Kuvik's chest, and smashed him down on the floor. The many beatings they'd already given him weakened him and made it impossible to fight back.

The second man stormed up from behind his big friend. The second man kicked Kuvik hard between the legs. Kuvik screamed out in agonizing, sickening pain, but it wasn't over yet.

The second man planted his foot there and crushed it into Kuvik's genitals. The pain blasted Kuvik out of his mind.

The spectators laughed themselves silly while he writhed and sobbed on the floor.

"Tell us where the Godless are hiding!" the first man bellowed over Kuvik's screams. "Tell us where they're going and where their camp is!"

All this pain went to Kuvik's head. He couldn't ignore it or shut it off anymore. He exploded out of himself and lost his temper in ways he never thought he would.

He reared off the floor against the guy's best efforts to hold him down, but their treatment sapped his strength to fight back.

"You son of a bitch!" he roared. "You're going to die for this!! I swear to God you'll pay! You bastards! Get the hell off me!!"

They didn't. The first man held him down while the second one stepped off, picked up his spear, and drove the blunt end of the shaft into Kuvik's genitals next.

The guy ground, twisted, and crushed the shaft between Kuvik's legs against his best efforts to break free. They overpowered him easily and all that pain blasted Kuvik out of his mind. He couldn't move, much less overcome these men.

The man in the chair waved his hand and both men backed off. They left Kuvik lying on the floor in a puddle of misery.

His own despair and desperation broke him all the way down. He couldn't cope with any of this. He needed to get out of here, but he couldn't even get up.

He fought down the urge to throw up right here on the floor, but the Bounty Hunters didn't give him a chance to. The first man kicked him over onto his back. "So you think the Godless will come here—to rescue a piece of shit like you?!"

Kuvik gulped down agonized moans. "They won't....I told you.....I'm not Godless.....they think I'm worthless.....they won't come for me....."

He really hoped the Godless didn't come for him. He wouldn't want Hangman to risk himself or any of his people to rescue Kuvik.

Hangman. Hangman was the one who gave Kuvik his life back. Hangman's kindness snapped Kuvik out of the trance in which the Hungry Ghosts kept him imprisoned all his life.

Hangman took Kuvik into his own family. Hangman made Kuvik his friend.

He would get back to Hangman's band. Kuvik had to get back there at all costs.

His life in the Godless band had been the only life he ever had—the only life worth living.

The man in the chair waved his hand at the warriors a second time. Two of them grabbed Kuvik and dragged him out of the building. He didn't see any of those people again.

The warriors hauled him through the village—and out of it. They passed through a stretch of normal jungle. At least they didn't transport Kuvik to some other unknown world.

They couldn't have. They couldn't have taken him very far away from the Godless—or at least the Godless' route south. He would be able to get back there....sometime.

The warriors entered a very different kind of village. This one looked more like a Godless village but with sturdier, more permanent houses built of bundles of thatch.

The warriors threw him into another large, nearly empty structure. A few low, bench-type shelves lined the edges of the walls to act as seats. That was the only furniture.

The warriors hurled Kuvik down on the floor and went back to beating and kicking him all over.

He curled into a ball and turned off his mind and body so he didn't feel a thing. He remembered this feeling—not just from his long-forgotten childhood, but from his early days in the Hungry Ghosts.

They didn't use beatings. They used other forms of torture to force people to join their ranks. They did it to Kuvik. They did it to his mother. They did it to dozens of other people the Hungry Ghosts captured while he was with them.

He turned off his senses to all of it, but somewhere in the back of his mind, a small voice told him not to.

The torture didn't turn him into a mindless slave. This did—this numbness.

This dull, lifeless, senseless distance between him and everything else—it didn't spare him from anything. It made him into a slave more effectively than anything else.

Chapter 21

Hammer glanced behind him toward the city getting farther away in the distance. The band had been safe there for a little while.

It would be cowardly to want to stay somewhere just to stay safe. Anyway, the band couldn't stay in that city—not without some way to hunt and protect themselves from other dangers.

Earthquake staggered at Hammer's side. Hammer tightened his grip on his friend and supported Earthquake on his shoulder to carry him out of town.

Hammer's men supported all their wounded comrades. Red's men and Hammer's band took casualties—some of them severe. Now the men had to get everyone to the jungle and find some Gooji sap on the double.

The women and children made it into the building without a scratch thanks to Mora's warning. None of the Godless would have known how to get away from the Bounty Hunters if not for her knowledge.

The band passed through the streets and made it to the road on the other side. The party had to pass through another open stretch of unprotected ground to the jungle beyond.

All the men kept turning around and scanning the surroundings. Now the men had another thing to check for on top of Renegades and creatures.

The Crushers still didn't come. They were the main creature threat in the cities.

The band walked exposed in the open for any Boultars or Ridgebeaks that might come down and attack from the air.

The band was back in Ridgebeak territory. Shrikers didn't live this far south of the mountains.

That hardly made Hammer feel better. This country still offered plenty of dangers, including human ones.

The Bounty Hunters posed the biggest risk. Mora seemed to think they lived in another inland part of the country and didn't travel this far east.

They were certainly traveling this far east now. They must be if they attacked the Godless inside their own territory.

The band traveled for two hours. The jungle didn't seem to be getting any closer. Hammer tried to hurry Earthquake along, but that only made Earthquake stumble more.

Hammer wound up carrying his friend most of the time, but Hammer didn't really care. Getting to the jungle was more important.

Earthquake had suffered a brutal spear cut across the abdomen. Hammer didn't let himself look at it.

Earthquake would probably pass out from loss of blood pretty soon. Then Hammer would throw Earthquake over his shoulder and carry him that way. They could travel faster and get to the jungle quicker.

Most of the wounded had the same problem. Cross and Lucky got off with minor injuries, but they still needed Gooji juice tonight.

The band would need to make a lot of Gooji juice tonight—which mean lighting a fire. That would cause problems. The band would have to camp on the ground and the light would attract the Bounty Hunters.

Hammer didn't let himself think that. He just had to get himself, Earthquake, and the rest of the band to the jungle. What happened after that would have to take care of itself.

He glanced behind him and the bottom fell out from under his world again when he saw another line of those black dots along the farthest hilltops.

The Bounty Hunters made their appearance on the same hilltops where Mora spotted them the first time. Hammer couldn't see the Bounty Hunters as clearly from here. He didn't need to. He would never mistake their appearance for anything else.

They lined up on the opposite side of the city, but the city wouldn't stop the Bounty Hunters from running around it and overtaking the Godless right here in the open.

"MOVE!!" he roared. "GET TO THE JUNGLE—NOW!!"

Everyone responded by sprinting ahead. Hammer couldn't take the time to support Earthquake while they both ran.

Hammer took off running his fastest and wound up dragging Earthquake's feet along the ground. Earthquake tried to run to keep up with him and only ended up falling.

His weight fell against Hammer's arms and shoulders. Hammer just kept running for the trees in front of him. He couldn't tell how far away they were.

The rest of the band burst into a run, too. The women and children outpaced everyone for a change. The children responded so much better, now that they understood what was at stake.

The women hardly had to carry anyone except the babies and smallest children who couldn't keep up.

Hangman, Viking, Cross, and a bunch of Red's men hung back, turned to face the city, and drew their weapons in readiness for the Bounty Hunter's second assault.

Hammer couldn't stand to run away. He yelled, "Keep going!" and let go of Earthquake.

Earthquake supported his own weight better than Hammer expected. Earthquake staggered and limped in a gut-wrenching lurch toward the jungle, but at least he stayed on his feet.

The Bounty Hunters charged down the hills and Hammer turned back to join the men. The Bounty Hunters' line swept across the grass, around the city, and kept heading south to intercept the Godless.

The distance played a trick on Hammer's eyes. The Bounty Hunters appeared to come a lot slower this time, but they passed the city and he got another good look at them as they got nearer.

At that moment, a woman's scream echoed out of the trees behind the men. Children yelled in there and the clang of steel and the thump of blows echoed to where the men stood.

Hangman caught Hammer's eye. Hangman jerked his head at Hammer. "Go see what's happening. Protect the band if you can."

Hammer split away. More screams and yells spiked from the silence inside the jungle.

He raced into the trees without a backward glance at what the Bounty Hunters were doing. Did they station another flank of their warriors inside the jungle to cut off the Godless retreat? It sounded that way.

He followed the sound of screams and blows. The road vanished into the undergrowth. The sound led him to the left.

He burst into a clearing and discovered six Bounty Hunters fighting four Godless women. The women tried to defend a bunch of children huddled against a fallen tree trunk.

Hammer took one look at the scene and attacked the Bounty Hunters from the side. The closest man broke away from fighting Choma to attack Hammer instead.

He struck hard and fast, cut the guy down, and started carving his way through the rest of the attackers. The women doubled down at his arrival. The Bounty Hunters couldn't fight everyone at once.

Their assault started to cave just as someone else attacked them from behind, chopped one of their heads off at the neck, and ran another through the back from behind. That left three.

Their bodies fell away and Hammer found himself staring at Vina standing right in front of him.

The fight between the remaining three Bounty Hunters and the four Godless women drew Hammer and Vina back to the task at hand.

They joined in and the six adults finished off the remaining attackers. Their bodies fell in a pile before anyone could catch their breath to look around.

Hammer stared at Vina. She shone with some kind of angelic light. "Are you all right?!" he gasped. "I heard women screaming. I was worried."

"It came from over there." She pointed behind her. "I don't know who it was."

He turned the other way. The four women pounced on the children and gathered their children in their arms.

The women didn't gather all the children. Hammer went over to them and discovered Zaedi and Thena in the group along with Wildling's two children, Astea and Loso, and Butch's two little sons, Kabi and Zakra.

Hammer squatted down in front of the children. "Where are your parents?" He turned to Zaedi. "Where's your mother? She wouldn't leave you here. I don't believe that."

"The Bounty Hunters came out of the jungle," one of the women choked. "Mora and the others stayed behind to fight them while we ran for cover. She told the children to come with us. She's over there somewhere."

She waved toward the same place Vina said she heard the screaming. Hammer couldn't look over there. Did the Bounty Hunters take Mora—or any of the men?

Another of the women grabbed Hammer's arm. She was Sida, Prodigy's wife. "We have to get back to Hangman's band!" she stammered. "My children—my children are with them! I have to get back to my children!"

"We're going to find the others as soon as we can. We have to keep going and get to safety right now. We'll meet up with the others as soon as we find them." He turned to evaluate the rest of the group. "We need to keep moving south. That's what your parents will do and that's what they would want us to do. Come on. Let's go."

He helped the children stand up. He wound up lifting Zaedi, Thena, and the other four parentless children to their feet.

They all crowded around him. He took Thena's hand and then he took Astea's hand. He couldn't hold everyone's hands.

The boys responded by holding onto his wrists or his shoulder bags or even the waistband of his loincloth. He really didn't care as long as they stayed with him.

He set off walking toward the south. He heard a few more sounds of conflict, but he didn't go over there to check it out. He didn't want to put any of these people in danger.

They would up having a problem pretty soon. Zakra and Loso were too small to keep up with the others. They slowed everyone down, especially Hammer.

The other women had to take care of and even carry their own children. They couldn't help him.

Vina moved in, bent down, and murmured something to Zakra before she picked him up. He latched onto her, wrapped his arms around her neck, and clung to her while she carried him. She picked up Loso next and he settled himself on her other side.

Kabi took hold of Vina's shoulder bag. That left Hammer with Zaedi and the two little girls.

Sida kept looking all around her for her children who weren't there. She didn't step in to help out with the children who didn't have any adults taking care of them.

The party made better headway after that. They worked their way deeper into the jungle. Hammer kept going until the sun started to go down.

The sound of combat faded long before that. He kept searching the surrounding terrain for any sign of someone from the Godless band.

He searched the surrounding jungle for any sign of the Bounty Hunters, too, but he didn't see anyone from either party.

He finally stopped everyone and told the women to climb up into the branches. That process took forever, too, because no one had any men around to help carry all these little children.

Zaedi and Kabi climbed on their own. Vina carried the two little boys. Sida didn't help. She didn't seem to be aware of anything outside herself.

Hammer carried the two girls into the branches and went back for Zaedi before he settled everyone into place for the night. "Stay here while I go look for the others. Do you have enough food?"

"We'll be fine," Vina told him. "Go—and be careful."

He would have liked to kiss her, but that could wait. He just touched her hand and launched himself at full speed racing through the treetops. He didn't waste time going down to the round.

He traveled all the way back to where he first entered the jungle and found the women fighting the Bounty Hunters. Then he backtracked to where Vina said she heard screaming. He didn't find anyone there—male or female, young or old.

He searched in widening concentric circles, but he still didn't find anyone or anything.

He returned to the tree line. No one battled out in the fields now. The Godless and the Bounty Hunters were all gone.

Chapter 22

Hammer returned to the women and children sitting in the canopy. Vina and the other women kept passing dried meat to the children.

They munched their food and watched Hammer slump on the branch in defeat. "I can't find them."

"Does that mean the Bounty Hunters took them?" Zaedi asked.

"I don't know what it means, little brother. All I know is that we can't let them take us. We have to keep traveling and I don't like traveling on the ground."

"How would we travel up here with so many little children?" one of the women asked.

Hammer let himself study them for the first time. Besides Sida, the other three were Ziuna, Golira, and Ena—Legacy's, Baron's, and Red's wives.

Hammer knew them all and he knew their children, but that somehow made this so much harder. Now he was responsible for all these women and children. Their lives rested in his hands and on his decision.

Traveling along the ground would be easier for them and probably quicker. Traveling through the treetops would be safer but infinitely more difficult. One of the children could slip and fall.

Zakra and Loso wouldn't be able to travel through the treetops at all—which meant Hammer and Vina would have to carry the boys—one boy to each of them.

Hammer didn't trust the others to travel through the treetops, either, especially not Thena and Astea. They would be able to when they got older, but not now.

Zaedi read Hammer's mind. "I can climb through the trees," Zaedi announced.

"Me, too," Kabi announced.

Hammer found himself smiling at both of them. "We might need you to. We'll see how it goes. I don't see any reason why we can't travel on the ground as long as the Bounty Hunters don't come back."

"What if they do come back?" Sida spoke up for the first time and her voice trembled. "What if we never meet up with Hangman's band?" She choked on the words and covered her mouth to stifle a sob.

"If we don't meet up with them, we just have to keep going," Hammer rummaged in his bag and pulled out some food for himself. "We can't give up."

"How would we find them if they did get taken by the Bounty Hunters?" Sida asked.

Hammer lost his patience with her, but he kept his voice in check so he wouldn't alarm the others. "We won't find them if they got taken by the Bounty Hunters. We won't go looking for them or even think about them if they got taken by the Bounty Hunters. We would all get taken if we did something as foolish as that. Our loved ones wouldn't want us to throw your lives away trying to find them, only to wind up as captives ourselves. Hangman, Cross, Viking, and Alien risked a lot to get us away from the Renegades. We won't throw that sacrifice back in their faces by deliberately getting ourselves caught all over again by a Clan that is even worse than the Renegades. We'll keep going. We'll do everything in our power to stay free, stay hidden, and to keep moving south to safe country. That's what they would want us to do. That's the only sensible thing to do."

She didn't open her mouth again. She looked away into the trees.

Hammer was starting to understand a completely different dimension of human nature—ever since his mother threw herself and his baby sister into the ants.

These women lost their minds. They didn't think clearly if they thought at all. They thought nothing of throwing their lives away—for nothing.

The men got extremely disturbed when the Hungry Ghosts killed themselves—and then again when Kuvik tried to starve himself to death.

Hammer was starting to understand this insanity much better now—or at least he recognized it when he saw it. Aster did it first. Then Cheina.

Now Sida was doing it. She became so mindlessly obsessed with finding her children. They might already be gone—lost to her forever. They might even be dead.

She would drive herself out of her mind thinking about them. She would throw her own life away trying to find them, save them, and maybe even bring them back to life. She would destroy what was left of her own life for the non-existent chance of getting back what she lost.

None of these people honored the gift Hangman and the others had given them. The Godless men gave Hammer and the other freed captives a chance they would never have gotten from anyone else.

Hammer considered it the greatest day of his life when Hangman, his brother, and his cousins came into that village and freed Hammer and the others. It was the start of a new life—a life beyond Hammer's wildest dreams.

He would never throw that away—not ever. He would spend the rest of his life honoring those men and living up to their example.

He would try his hardest to become as like them as he could. He would never squander his life on some vain hope with no chance of any payoff.

Now here he was and Hangman's words were coming true as never before. Hammer found himself Kral of his own little band of five women and a collection of children, some of whom didn't have parents at all.

This was what being Kral of his band meant—not being in charge—not having a family with Vina—not having other men look up to him. Any man of any Clan could do that.

Being Kral meant their lives rested on his decisions. He was responsible for all of them now whether he liked it or not. He was the one who would get them through this—and he sure as hell wouldn't take them back where they might get caught.

One thought haunted his mind. He might meet up with Hangman, Mora, Wildling, Butch, or their wives sometime or other. He might stumble on them tomorrow. He might not see them for a month or a year or even ten years.

When that happened—when that day finally came around—Hammer had to be able to show those people that he got their children through this. He had to show their children alive, healthy, thriving, strong, proud Godless living their best lives.

He had to face Red, Prodigy, Legacy, and Baron and show them that Hammer got their wives and children through it so they could reunite with their fathers and husbands on the other end.

He wouldn't be able to look those people in the eye if he didn't get their loved ones through this. He wouldn't be able to live with himself if he had to face those men with the news that he got their loved ones captured and sent into captivity under the Bounty Hunters. No way would he let that happen.

The sun started to sink and the jungle fell into shadow. The noises around the party changed.

Hammer pulled a bunch of vines out of the surrounding treetops and wove them between the branches to make a mat for the children to lie down. Vina sat next to them and stroked Loso's and Zakra's hair until they fell asleep.

The children fell asleep much more easily than Hammer expected them to. They usually bounced off the walls for hours before their parents had to force the children to lie down.

They acted much more subdued around Hammer, Vina, and these other adults, but Hammer didn't sense the children acting intimidated or even frightened by the situation.

The children just acted a lot more grown up. The circumstances sobered them. They all realized the danger and they acted accordingly.

Zaedi stared at Hammer for a long time before the boy shut his eyes and drifted off. He curled up next to his sister with his arms around her. They looked peaceful and heavenly like that.

Hammer and Vina stayed sitting up and awake when the four women went to sleep. Sida found herself a crook in a tree trunk apart from the group.

"I hope she comes to her senses by morning," he murmured once she drifted off.

"Be prepared for her not to," Vina replied in the same undertone. She kept stroking her fingertips through the little boys' hair.

"I know," Hammer replied. "I'm starting to see a pattern here."

Vina didn't contradict him. "You did very well with her— with all of them. I'm really glad I could be here to help you with this."

"I'm so grateful you're here—and thank you for helping me against the Bounty Hunters. You don't know how relieved I am that you're with me right now."

She burst into a beautiful smile and gazed down at the children lying near her. "It's almost like we're already together and these are our children."

"I wish that was true."

"It can be. It can be true for as long as we're alone with them. We can be a couple and these can be our children."

His heart leapt. He swiveled over onto her branch, sat down next to her, and leaned in close. "Does that mean you'll spend the night with me tonight?"

She laughed, blushed, and looked away. "You know I can't. We can't do anything in front of the children."

He felt his cheeks burning, but he couldn't keep away from her. He leaned his body all the way against her from the side. He still hadn't crossed any lines. "So....I can call you my wife?"

She giggled and turned bright red. "Aren't you already doing that in the privacy of your own mind?"

Now he was the one who laughed. "Who told you my secrets?"

"You did, silly." She glanced at him, but only for a second. She floated before his eyes—close enough to kiss—but he already knew he wouldn't.

He leaned close to her ear and whispered, "Wife."

She giggled again. "Stop it."

"You know you are," he murmured.

She only blushed at him. "Not yet."

"Of course you are. You are right now. You're mine. You'll never go with any other man. I would kill anyone who looked at you sideways."

"I'm sure no one will look at me sideways," she murmured.

"Of course they would. Plenty of men would love to get their hands on you if I didn't let them know to stay away from you."

"Who would do that?" she countered. "No one in our band is interested in me."

"That's because they all know you're mine."

She looked away, but he still saw her blushing. "You better behave yourself," she told him.

"I am behaving myself. Am I not behaving myself?"

"Not when you talk like that."

"You mean like this?" He leaned closer to her ear and whispered, "Wife," again.

She laughed. "You're bad. You deserve to be punished."

"How would you punish me in ways I'm not already being punished by having to wait for you like this?"

"Stop it. Now you're embarrassing me."

"Are you embarrassed to be my...." He whispered, "Wife," into her ear again.

"Of course I'm not embarrassed by that."

"What is embarrassing you, then?"

"You are. You're sneaking around. You're doing things you wouldn't do in front of Hangman."

"Do you really think he would object to me calling you....." He leaned in and whispered, "Wife," into her ear again."

"Of course he would object because I'm not your wife yet."

"Sure, you are. What are you if you aren't my wife?"

"I'm nothing. I'm your cousin."

He should have treated that as the joke it was, but he decided not to. "He told me he's certain I'll marry you and have a big, beautiful family with you."

She turned around and her eyes widened when she stared up at him. "He said that?!"

"Sure. He knows it's just a matter of time—and he knows I wouldn't let anything stand in the way of us being together. I'm telling you no other man will ever touch you. I wouldn't let it happen."

She hesitated. Her beauty shone through her eyes—and then she glanced down at his mouth like she wanted to kiss him.

He would have given anything to kiss her right then, but he didn't and she didn't. She looked away. "I didn't know he said that," she murmured.

"Did you think he objected to me wanting to marry you? He doesn't."

"You told me that before, but I can't help worrying."

"You have nothing to worry about."

"Everything always goes wrong....." Her voice cracked. "What if something goes wrong with this? What if something happens to you.....or to me......? Something is always happening...."

He couldn't stand that choked strain in her voice. He put his arm around her shoulders and hugged her against him. He could get away with that much, at least.

He didn't say anything because there was no answer for those fears. They haunted him and everyone else in this world.

He lived in constant dread that something would happen to her. He would have liked to speed up time so he could marry her now, but they wouldn't be sitting here talking like this and feeling this way about each other if he did.

Things would change enough when he married her. Everything would change. It was inevitable.

At least he loved her now while he had a chance. If he never saw tomorrow—or if the Fates took her away from him tomorrow—at least they had tonight.

They would spend tonight loving each other as much as if they had been married for fifty years. No one could take that away from them.

Chapter 23

K uvik swam back to consciousness when he heard voices nearby. They didn't yell insults at him. They didn't even talk in a normal tone of voice. He heard men whispering.

"They're heading south—always heading south," one of the voices breathed. "We should hit them again before they meet up with any other Godless."

"We scattered them last time," a second murmured. "The women and children will be unprotected now. We should go out as soon as possible and get them while we can. Why fight the men when we can just take the weaker ones without fighting?"

"We can't do anything until Uthor tells us to go," a third added. "We shouldn't even be talking about this without consulting him."

"He doesn't understand the situation," the second countered. "He's only making it harder for us and putting the Godless in a better position the longer he delays."

"Tell him, not me," the third returned. "I don't make these decisions."

"You know I'm right," the second pointed out. "Why don't you back me up when I make suggestions to him?"

"I know my place," the third replied. "You might try it sometime. You aren't making any friends always shooting your mouth off."

"The maggot is awake," the first told them. "He's stirring."

Kuvik tried to keep still, but he couldn't keep as still as when he was asleep. The three Bounty Hunters standing near him turned around and pounced on him.

He didn't realize until now that they could stand in one place and hold a civilized conversation with each other. They always seemed to be attacking something.

They switched back to their violent, ferocious tendencies the minute they saw him awake. He yelped in fear and pain when they ripped him off the ground.

They didn't give him a chance to protest or even to catch his balance. They shoved him, sent him staggering across the big empty room, and back outside.

This was a very different village from the first one. The people here all stumbled around in a dazed stupor. Most wore rags, scraps of hide tied around strategic parts of their bodies, and almost all of them showed the unmistakable signs of severe beatings.

Men, women, and children barely opened their puffy, swollen eyes when these people staggered from building to building. Each person carried a heavy bundle of some kind, an armload of firewood, or engaged in some other kind of heavy work.

Kuvik cringed when he saw himself reflected in these people. He must look like them—covered in bruises, bleeding from multiple cuts, and half out of his mind from too many blows to the head.

He didn't see anyone wearing the fancy clothes of the spectators who laughed at him in front of the crowd.

The Bounty Hunters who passed through this village all wore the same wrapped loincloths, feathers in their hair, and body paint smeared in diagonal parallel lines on all their limbs, chests, and backs.

The warriors behind him pushed him again and sent him sprawling into the dirt. He fell on his face and they came up behind him kicking him and bowling him over and over in the direction they wanted him to go.

He fell onto his chest again, raised his head just for a second, and saw another Bounty Hunter farther across the village. The man had cornered a woman and her young son against the wall of some house down there.

The guy raised a thick wooden baton and beat both the woman and her son senseless to the ground. The woman raised her arms over her head to protect herself. Her son huddled against her side, but she couldn't protect herself or him.

The guy kept hammering the woman until she buckled under the assault. Her arms sank and he went to town on her head and body. Her son got caught in the attack.

The guy didn't stop until he flattened both of them into an unconscious heap against the wall. They might both be dead.

Kuvik saw the whole incident in a split second. No one intervened. The other beaten prisoner-slaves stumbling around pretended not to see what was happening. They looked like they'd already suffered something similar themselves.

This must be normal here. This must be how the Bounty Hunters treated their captives—the way they were treating Kuvik right now.

They barely started kicking him before they hauled him to his feet again and shoved him forward. His mind shut down a little more. He distanced himself from all of this.

He went through years of this both in his home Clan and in the Hungry Ghosts. He was the one who made it normal. He slipped back into it now with no effort. His mind didn't understand the concept of resisting. This horror was all too familiar.

The Bounty Hunters pushed him into another big, open hall with no furniture. The same man with long hair and feather robes sat in his big fancy armchair along one of the longer walls.

Two hundred Bounty Hunters packed the hall. They were all the male warriors who attacked the Godless outside the city. Kuvik didn't see a single female here.

The Bounty Hunters all talked to each other and some of them laughed. Then Kuvik's captors brought him in and all the Bounty Hunters turned around and laughed at him.

The crowd parted and the men started cheering, yelling, and chanting something Kuvik didn't understand.

His captors threw him down on the floor in front of the armchair and started kicking him again. That man must be their leader—the man they said made the decisions about when and where to attack the Godless.

Uthor. They said his name was Uthor—and the Bounty Hunters planned to attack the Godless again. Hangman and the other men must be out there right now trying to defend their families from......from this.

Kuvik's mind shifted gears between the Godless band he knew and all those hollow-eyed stumbling slave-zombies outside.

The Bounty Hunters would turn the Godless into this. The Bounty Hunters wanted to turn all the Godless into these mindless, obedient beasts of burden.

Hangman. Viking. Cross. Mora. Hammer. Red. Wildling—all the people who had been kind to Kuvik and given him his life back.

They actually made him feel human for the first time in his life. They made him feel like he meant something to them—because he did.

That last conversation with Mora came back to haunt him. She knew and actually cared that he had nightmares about his past. She worked around the clock to take care of her family, but she asked about him.

She would have helped him if she could. She did help him. They all did.

The warriors who brought him to this hall flipped him over on his back. Two of them stood on his arms to hold him down.

Another stepped up on the center of Kuvik's chest and balanced there. All the surrounding men pointed, laughed, yelled instructions and encouragement, and grabbed each other when Kuvik yelled out in pain and distress because he couldn't breathe.

That one man had to hold onto his friends to keep his balance. Then another man came along and stepped up onto Kuvik's stomach. They added more men one at a time. They had to stand body to body so they could all fit on top of him.

Their weight crushed him into the floor. He howled in agony and fought for every precious breath of air. He couldn't even breathe well enough to yell out or cry or even sob.

They got tired of that game pretty soon. All the men got off and moved out of the way.

The men who had been standing on Kuvik's arms pulled him back to his feet. He could barely stand upright.

They shoved a spear into his hands. It was the same kind of weapon the Bounty Hunters used to attack the Godless.

All the other warriors moved out of the way. They backed off into a wide ring and flattened themselves against the walls.

Kuvik couldn't think clearly enough to realize what was going on—until a different group of men entered the hall.

They led a juvenile Crusher tied up with ropes. The creature bellowed and thrashed trying to free itself. Its efforts jerked the men inward. They barely stayed clear of the creature's jaws to avoid it snapping one of them in half.

Even a juvenile Crusher couldn't fit through the door to enter the hall. Four more warriors rushed over, grabbed the rope tied around the creature's neck, and used all their weight to haul the Crusher's head down.

Then the other men heaved to drag the creature into the hall. The Crusher roared in rage and frustration, but the Bounty Hunters sent more men over there to overpower the creature.

In the end, more than thirty men had to help each other force the creature under the doorframe.

Kuvik backed away when he saw what the Bounty Hunters were about to do. People behind him attacked him with their fists and drove him back onto the open floor in front of Uthor's chair.

Kuvik glanced around in wild panic. Hangman fought a fully grown Crusher when he was still an uninitiated boy. That didn't mean Kuvik could do it.

Hangman grew up Godless. He grew up fighting all kinds of creatures—and he was Hangman. He could do things like that and live to tell the tale.

Kuvik could never do anything like that. He didn't want to fight any Crusher, not even a juvenile.

The creature had to stoop not to hit its head on the roof beams. It roared in murderous fury at all the Bounty Hunters standing around.

The creature strutted forward much faster once they got it inside. The Crusher stormed into the hall looking for someone to attack.

The men steered it into the middle of the floor, positioned it in front of Kuvik, and let go of the ropes. The Crusher glared at everyone around it—and then saw Kuvik standing there holding the spear.

All the Bounty Hunters bolted. The men who had been restraining the Crusher charged back into the crowd to hide among their people.

The noise escalated to thunder when Kuvik faced off against the Crusher. The surrounding onlookers cheered, yelled, and even threw things at the Crusher to make it attack.

Kuvik thought fast. He knew all the stories about how the Godless took these creatures down. Hangman had told Kuvik countless times about how he killed a Crusher during his initiation, how Cross broke the Gorlock's foot during his, and how Wildling used ropes to bring down full-grown Shrikers.

Kuvik understood all of that rationally. Did he dare to try something like that here?

The Crusher took three pounding steps toward him. He circled to his right to keep out of the creature's way while he decided how to attack and kill this creature.

He didn't have to kill it—not completely. He only had to disable it. The feet were the obvious solution. The Crusher couldn't move without those.

The creature rushed him and he dove sideways, but his injuries slowed him down. His reaction time failed him. He barely made it to safety that time, but the Crusher only came after him again....and again.

He missed his timing the third time. The Crusher dove for him, snapped its massive jaws, and tried to bite him in half. He sprang clear, but his aching body didn't want to move fast.

The Crusher's armored head smashed into him and knocked him down. He rolled away from the creature, but it stalked after him no matter where he went.

He tumbled within range of all the surrounding Bounty Hunters. They kicked him back into the circle—right in front of the Crusher.

The creature dove one more time. He couldn't get up in time. He couldn't do anything.

He swung the spear forward without really knowing what he would be able to do with it. He didn't know how to fight with one of these spears, but it was his only weapon.

He barely got it into position before the Crusher lunged for him with its big, fanged mouth open to devour him. He stuck the spear up and aimed the long, iron head at the Crusher's face.

The creature thrust its head right down on top of the spear and the spearhead stabbed the creature in the eye.

The Crusher reared away bellowing and tossing its head in fury. Kuvik scrambled to his feet and aimed the spear at the Crusher again, but the creature went ballistic and didn't see him.

The Crusher stormed around the hall nearly trampling everyone in sight. The Bounty Hunters screamed in frightened laughter and tripped over each other to get out of the creature's way in time.

Kuvik knew what he had to do now. He stayed clear of the creature until it saw him standing there. The Crusher turned around to glare at him.

Blood and ooze poured from its ruined eye socket. The Crusher bared its teeth and snarled at him before it came after him again.

He dodged it a few more times. He didn't want to take the chance of letting it hit him again or knock him down. He had to choose his position.

He forgot to watch where he was going. The Bounty Hunters kept yelling and scampering out of his way whenever he came near them.

The Crusher stalked him down every time. He didn't realize where he was until he ran into one of the walls.

He tried one last time to get away, but the Crusher blocked him in. He backed against the wall—and realized in that moment that this was the best place for him to be.

The Crusher saw him trapped. All the Bounty Hunters laughed, hooted, and cheered now that they were going to see the Crusher eat Kuvik.

He tightened his grip on his spear. He had to make sure to do this right. He would get one chance before the creature destroyed him.

The Crusher growled low in its chest, dropped its head close to the floor, and lunged. Kuvik shifted the spear to his right hand, raised his arm, and angled the spearhead toward the Crusher's only good eye.

He didn't try to stab. The Crusher's own movements impaled the spear into the eye and drove the butt of the spear shaft all the way back against the wall.

The Crusher lunged with such force that its power shattered the spear shaft. It disintegrated in Kuvik's hand and the broken spear shaft buried itself in the Crusher's head.

The blinded creature reared upward, thrashed its head, and burst into a frenzy of stomping around the room in wild terror and fury.

It couldn't use its tiny arms to get the spear out. The splintered shaft stuck out of the creature's eye socket while the Crusher blundered straight into the crowd.

The Bounty Hunters screamed and ran for it, but so many of them jammed the hall that they wound up trampling each other.

All the remaining Bounty Hunters shoved and pushed and jostled to get out the doors fast enough. The hall emptied, but not before the Crusher maimed and squashed fifty people in the chaos

Kuvik watched from his place against the wall. No one even looked at him. Now was his chance. He had to find his way back to the Godless. He had to warn Hangman about the Bounty Hunters' plans.

Kuvik glanced in the other direction. None of the Bounty Hunters went that way to escape the Crusher. A clear path lay before him to the other entrance doors leading out of the hall.

The Crusher rampaged through the building, smashed into a different wall, and then turned in a different direction.

The creature blundered into all the Bounty Hunters trying to stampede their way out of the hall. No one looked sideways at Kuvik. They all completely forgot about him.

He whirled away and raced out the doors into the village. He didn't know where to go. He just had to get into the jungle and take it from there.

None of the prisoner-slaves noticed him, either. None of them even raised their eyes from their work.

Chapter 24

K uvik dove behind a house and hid so no one would see him. Another three houses stood between him and the dense trees. He could hide in there.

Crashes and screams echoed out of the hall—and then a powerful concussion hit the walls. Part of the roof collapsed.

He took his chance and dove for the next house. No one saw. No one cared. He sprinted from house to house and plunged headfirst into the undergrowth. He was free.

He rolled on the ground and flattened himself under a clump of bushes to listen. He made it. He could get away from here.

The Godless had taught him how to travel through the treetops. He could travel fast that way without anyone seeing him. He wouldn't make camp. He would keep heading south until he found the Godless and warned Hangman and the others.

He stayed where he was for another five minutes while he caught his breath and waited for his heart to stop pounding. He scanned the village for any sign of anyone coming after him. They didn't.

The noise and impacts coming from the hall escalated until an almighty boom rocked the building. The village fell silent and a few blood-stained Bounty Hunters stumbled out of the hall.

They collapsed on the ground or leaned against walls trying to calm down. The Crusher didn't storm around inside the building anymore. The Bounty Hunters must have killed the creature.

Kuvik waited a little longer. Those men went off somewhere. They didn't come back.

He pushed himself up onto his hands and knees. Then he rotated back to squat on his heels. He could get away now. The Bounty Hunters would never find him.

He got to his feet, but he stayed behind the bushes to keep out of sight. He didn't want anyone to see him or chase him.

He was just about to turn away when a high-pitched shriek made him turn around and look behind him.

His heart stopped all over again when a group of seven Bounty Hunters entered the village from its other side. They also led their prey tied up with ropes, but this wasn't a Crusher.

The ropes bound a young Godless girl wearing the usual loincloth and top stitched out of hides.

Her long black hair stuck to a mat of sweat and blood on her face and neck, but Kuvik saw her face as clear as day. It was Yoa, the girl who kept trying to get close to him in Hangman's band.

The Bounty Hunters yanked the ropes tied around her wrists, neck, waist, and arms. She screamed in pain every time they strangled her with the noose or jerked her forward.

They laughed at her and one or more of them kept stopping to kick her in the legs, backside, and even in the stomach.

They knocked her down more than once, dragged her to her feet, and hauled her struggling and screaming into the village.

More Bounty Hunters gathered from all over. They leered at her and laughed when one of her captors turned the rope around in his hands and whipped her with the tail end.

Kuvik ducked behind the bushes. The Bounty Hunters must be a lot closer to capturing the band if they got Yoa.

She sobbed in wretched panic. Her terrified eyes darted all over the place in search of anyone to help her.

The sight of her face twisted in misery and hopeless fear drove a knife into Kuvik's guts. He always liked her. He just never let himself get close to her.

He wanted her to marry a real Godless man—a man who could give her the future Kuvik couldn't.

He told her so a dozen times, but she just kept coming back. She never threw herself at him. That would be illegal. She just tried to be nice to him. She never tried to do anything more than talk to him.

He couldn't accept even that tiny scrap of kindness no matter how much he wanted to. He would have given anything just to feel worthy of her—or any Godless woman.

He never thought he would marry anyone. Then he found out what the Godless were really like. That on its own proved he could never marry one of them.

Their woman deserved Godless men—not some maggot from nowhere. He told Yoa that, too, but she always insisted he was as good as any Godless man. She said he *was* Godless—which was exactly what Hangman and the other men kept insisting.

He never believed them, but it would be a cold day in Hell before he walked off and left any Godless girl in the Bounty Hunters' hands.

He didn't have to wonder too hard about what they would do to her. Dozens of men gathered around all laughing and sticking their tongues out at her.

Her captors pulled her to a halt and the surrounding men moved in. Some of them already started to untie and unwind their loincloths.

Kuvik had to act fast. He darted out of the bushes and threw away the hard-won freedom he just won for himself.

He dashed from house to house until he got as close as possible to the Bounty Hunters and Yoa. They didn't see a thing except her.

She saw exactly what they planned to do to her. Her desperate gasps and sobs escalated to broken cries. She darted one way and then the other trying to break through the wall of men.

They grabbed her, pawed at her, groped her through her clothes, and some of them started to tear her clothes off. She screamed and burst into another hysterical fit of struggling. Kuvik had to act now.

He charged the men in the back of the crowd and plowed straight through them before their bulk knocked him over. He toppled onto the ground right there in front of all those Bounty Hunters.

He scrambled to turn himself over and crawl onto his hands and knees even though he knew it was too late.

His diversion worked. All the Bounty Hunters saw him and turned on him instead. Some of the men here had been inside the hall with Kuvik and the Crusher.

They recognized him instantly, grabbed him, and attacked him. He heard Yoa scream out his name one time before a brutal kick hit him in the head. He reeled in space for a second and came to his senses being dragged across the village again.

He heard Yoa sobbing in loud, wheezing gasps nearby. He had to get her out of here at all costs. He couldn't show his face in front of Hangman or the other men if he didn't save her.

The Bounty Hunters hauled him to another building of the same construction, tore the doors open, and shoved him into another gathering of a couple hundred Bounty Hunters.

These men didn't stand around talking. They sat on cushions drinking some red liquid out of skin water bags.

Some of the men reclined on their cushions. Kuvik took a second to recognize the glazed look in the Bounty Hunters' eyes.

He remembered this very vaguely from his childhood with his original Clan. The men of his Clan used to do something like this. They drank something that made their brains foggy.

Kuvik had been too young to remember anything else except that the drink also made them violent—especially toward their wives and children. That must be what made the Bounty Hunters act like this.

They dragged Kuvik in and threw him on the floor to one side of the room. Uthor's chair wasn't here, but Uthor was.

He sat on a bunch of cushions drinking with other men both his age and younger. Everyone laughed when the Bounty Hunters brought Kuvik in.

The men threw him on the floor and six of them surrounded him. They aimed spears at him and took turns jabbing him while he shrieked and writhed on the ground in front of them.

All the men laughed and tipped up their skins to drink. More men dragged Yoa in. They held her to one side and kept jerking her around on the ropes to stop her from doing anything or going anywhere.

A few different men approached her and grabbed different parts of her body. Some of them even licked between her cleavage or up her neck, but her constant struggling stopped them from going too far.

All the men found this incredibly funny. Their behavior drove her insane and she struggled harder every time one of them came near her.

She kept screaming Kuvik's name. He didn't dare to look at her or he might lose his mind, too. He couldn't stand to see her looking down at him with all that fear and hopeless concern pouring out of her dark eyes.

The men stabbed him again and again all over his body. Blood covered his arms and torso. Then they started whipping him with ropes tied into thick knots at the end.

Uthor sat off to one side watching and drinking with his comrades. The Bounty Hunters never found anything so amusing.

Kuvik's mind started to shut down again. He fought to stay alert so he could keep an eye on Yoa, but he wouldn't be able to help her. He found it harder and harder even to see straight.

He drifted in and out of consciousness more than once during that last beating. He roared in pain every time they hit him—and then one of them kicked him in the head again.

He tumbled over onto his side and lay still. The men left him lying there and went back to drinking with their friends.

He didn't believe for a second that his torment was over. They would come back. They would probably just keep tormenting him until they eventually killed him.

He barely stayed conscious enough to see Uthor wave to the men restraining Yoa. They dragged her sobbing and whimpering to another pile of cushions near Uthor's place.

One of his younger companions got to his feet, but the guy already wavered and stumbled. He could barely keep his eyes open.

The Bounty Hunters didn't take the ropes off Yoa. They left her tied up with all their tethers dangling from her body.

They pushed her down on the cushions and the young man staggered over there. He lost his balance when he tried to lower himself onto the cushions next to her.

She struggled again and tried to roll off the cushions so she could run away. The Bounty Hunters left her legs and ankles free. She could still walk and run as well as ever.

The guy grabbed her, hurled her back down on the cushions, tore her clothes the rest of the way off, pushed her bound hands above her head, and all the surrounding Bounty Hunters laughed when he rolled on top of her to pin her down.

She struggled and kicked, but her efforts only gave him the opening he needed to work his hips between her thighs. He crushed his chest against her to smother her down on the cushions. All the men laughed and drank again.

Kuvik gulped down hopeless despair. He couldn't help her. He was too late. He only got her caught and attacked the same way.

He turned away feeling sick—and then he noticed something. The guy didn't take his loincloth off. He lay there with his face buried in the cushion next to Yoa's head.

His weight held her down and stopped her from getting out from under him, but he didn't take his loincloth off. He didn't do anything. He just lay there. He didn't move again.

She looked around trying to figure out what was going on. All the Bounty Hunters laughed even louder. One of them grabbed the guy's shoulder and rolled him off her.

The guy flopped over on the cushions. He was out cold. The men laughed, prodded him, and even pried his eyelids open. He didn't come around. He even started snoring.

Yoa tried to turn over and sit up. Her movements attracted the Bounty Hunters' attention. They grabbed the ropes, bound her ankles together and her legs at the knees.

They trussed her up so she couldn't move. Then they all walked away and went back to drinking with their friends. They left her lying there, totally helpless, to wait for the guy to wake up.

Chapter 25

Kuvik woke up tied hand and foot in some pitch-dark corner of a cramped, dusty, stinking structure somewhere. He couldn't see enough to tell where he was.

His body ached all over. Even opening his eyes hurt. He tried once to tug at the ropes around his wrists, but his arms, shoulders, and body hurt too much.

He collapsed there whining and groaning in agony, but he had to get up. He had to help Yoa if she was even still alive.

He had to get her out of here and take her back to the Godless. He had to warn Hangman if it wasn't too late for that already, too.

Kuvik actually let himself sob in misery when he forced himself to sit up. He buckled there shaking and whimpering in pathetic defeat. How could he save anyone when he couldn't even get these ropes off his hands?

He glanced around in the darkness. He didn't recognize where he was, but he was definitely in some kind of structure. Thick, sturdy boards made up the walls. He must be back in the first village—the village with the people in fancy clothes.

This structure was too small to be a house. It was too small to be any kind of dwelling. It stank of rot and maybe dead bodies. Maybe he was the dead body.

He kicked himself over to the nearest wall and pressed his eye to a crack between the planks. He didn't remember any of the houses having cracks between the planks. They were all too solid for that.

Moonlight flooded the village outside. He was definitely in the first village—which meant Yoa was still back in the other village with the Bounty Hunters. They must live apart from all these fancy people.

He sank back against the wall, shut his eyes, and caught his breath while he thought over the problem of how to get himself and Yoa out of here.

Every passing minute fired his protective fury toward her. He couldn't let these monsters hurt her. He may have already let them hurt her, but he could at least stop her from becoming one of these beaten-down prisoner-slaves.

That's what she would become if she survived that long. The men might just use her to death and throw her body down the ravine. It wouldn't be the first time that happened to a captive woman.

Thinking that gave Kuvik all the energy he needed to keep going. His own pain became the fuel that drove him forward against impossible odds.

In that moment when he leaned back against the wall, he felt something sharp down on the floor. It wasn't metal. That would have been too easy.

The planks of this structure ended in a sharp edge where the crosscut saw tore the wood fibers at each stroke. The sharp edge pricked Kuvik's fingers. He started to recoil before he realized just how sharp that edge was.

It wasn't as good as a blade, but it would do the job. He leaned back again, but he couldn't angle his hands into the right position.

In the end, he lay down on his side so he could position that sharp edge against the ropes between his wrists.

Then he inflicted an even more brutal punishment on himself. He had to pry his shoulders back and put pressure on them in the most painful possible position so he could saw the rope along that edge.

He bit his tongue to stifle his own agonized bellows of agony and frustration, but he didn't stop. He broke down in tears of pain and helpless misery long before the rope fell off.

When it did, he sat up, buried his face in his hands, and let himself fall apart with all these torturous feelings welling up in him.

Getting captured by the Bounty Hunters and brought to this village—getting beaten, tortured, stabbed, brutalized, and forced to fight a Crusher—it all brought back so many painful memories.

Why did he even try to escape anymore? Why did he think he deserved to live? The Hungry Ghosts spent years imprinting on his mind that he was worthless and his life was a big mistake.

He already believed that before they captured him. It didn't take much for them to erase all doubt from his mind.

The Godless. The Godless were the ones who made him see another way. Hangman was the first person in Kuvik's life who ever said the words, *I want you to live, Kuvik.*

Hangman backed it up with action, too. He made it real by taking Kuvik in, including him in their family life, and standing up to defend Kuvik to all the other Godless.

Hangman was the one who made the others accept Kuvik. Then Hangman was the one who showed them that Kuvik really did deserve to live. He became an asset to their Clan instead of a liability.

Those four years of bliss—they made this whole experience so much more unbearably painful. He could have easily become one of the Bounty Hunters' mindless prisoner-slaves if not for his experience with the Godless.

He wished like anything he could burn those four years out of his mind. His ordeal would have been so much easier if he never remembered any other way.

He didn't care about himself. He wouldn't have minded becoming one of the Bounty Hunters' beasts of burden.

He couldn't and wouldn't let that happen to Yoa. He might deserve it, but she sure didn't.

Nothing Hangman, Mora, and the Godless did for Kuvik meant anything if he let that happen to Yoa. He had to save her for them and for all the Godless. He long ago gave up any idea of doing anything like that for himself.

He took his hands down, ran his arm across his damp face, and sniffed. He wiped the snot on his shoulder and pulled himself together to get this done.

It was the middle of the night. He wouldn't find a better time to sneak Yoa out of the village—wherever she was.

He twisted onto his other side, positioned his ankles against the sharp edge of the boards, and sawed his way through the ankle rope next.

He accomplished the same thing more quickly this time. He could put more pressure on the rope by using his legs.

The ropes fell off and he struggled to his feet. He really needed a weapon, but he would have to worry about that later.

He approached the door of this structure. He could touch the opposite walls of the building without even straightening his arms.

The door wasn't locked. The Bounty Hunters must have counted on the ropes to keep Kuvik restrained.

He slipped out into the village, sprinted through the trees, and found his way back to the hall where he left Yoa.

The doors stood open on both ends of the building. He hid behind the wall and peered in. All the Bounty Hunters lay asleep on their cushions. None of them moved except for their endless snoring.

Yoa still lay naked and tied up on the cushions where the men left her. The guy who tried to attack her lay asleep at her side. Kuvik didn't see her moving, either. Was she all right—or injured to the point of death?

He tiptoed into the building without making a sound. He didn't need to be careful. All that snoring masked any sound.

He plastered himself to the wall and inched closer to all the Bounty Hunters. None of them moved. Uthor and the others lay asleep nearby.

Yoa's head shot up when she saw someone moving toward her. Kuvik eased out of the shadows and laid his finger to his lips to tell her to be quiet.

Her lips twisted up in a miserable grimace of silent torment. Poor girl.

Kuvik inched toward her hardly daring to believe he might actually get away with this. He squatted behind her and started untying the ropes from around her wrists.

He pretended not to see her naked body right in front of him. He would have to do something about that. He should have covered her up right now, but he didn't have anything to cover her with.

Getting her out of here took a higher priority. She didn't make a sound even when the ropes pinched her.

He wrenched the knot loose and then untied her ankles. She turned over on her back so he could get to them. The moonlight lit up every inch of her exposed flesh.

He concentrated on his work, freed her, and pulled her to her feet. He held his fingers to his lips again to warn her to be quiet and steered her toward the wall where the shadows hid them.

He took hold of her hand before he realized what he was doing. It was too late now. She grabbed hold of him and he drew her down the wall toward the open entrance doors.

A steady tide of snoring came from the building behind them. None of those men woke up.

Kuvik pulled Yoa outside and they both took off running for the trees.

Chapter 26

K uvik pulled Yoa down into a patch of undergrowth. Moonlight dappled the canopy overhead and gave just enough light for him to see her.

"Are you okay?" he whispered. "Did any of those men touch you after that guy passed out?"

She shook her head and compressed her lips to hold back sobs. "You came back!" she husked. "I thought you were dead!"

"I'm not dead." He raised his hand and touched her forehead. "You're bleeding. We need to get you some leaf paste—but first I need to find you some clothes. Stay here. I'll be right back."

He started to stand up, but she grabbed his hand and pulled him down. "Kuvik..... don't leave me alone.... please...." Tears welled up in her eyes.

He rubbed her arms trying to comfort her. He had to stop himself from touching her any more than that.

"I can't let you walk around this jungle looking like this," he murmured. "You'll be able to hide here. No one will see you until I come back."

"Kuvik....." she choked on the words. "I thought....I was scared...."

Her eyes darted every which way. Her features convulsed in misery.

He threw caution to the wind, put his arms around her, and hugged her. "You're safe now," he murmured. "I'm going to take you back to the Godless. You'll be safe with the band. Now stay here. It wouldn't be seemly for me to spend any time with you like this."

He wanted to do something else to show her that everything would be okay—somehow. He kissed her on the forehead, told her again to stay here, and he slipped away into the jungle.

He didn't know where he would find some clothes for her. He didn't want to go back into the Bounty Hunters' village.

Yoa wouldn't be okay if he got himself recaptured. He had to come up with some other solution—and he absolutely refused to travel another step until he found her something.

He was just considering going out into the jungle and hunting some creature for its hide. He actually turned around to return to her when he heard footsteps in the jungle not far away.

His heart stopped when he heard men talking. Why did he think the Bounty Hunters didn't post guards to patrol the area—even at night?

He should have expected this. Now he didn't have a weapon to use against them.

He sprang into the canopy to hide and perched in the branches before two of them walked underneath him.

They stopped near his treetop hiding place, talked for a minute, and then one of them walked off somewhere. The second one stayed there fiddling with something in his hand. Kuvik didn't see what the thing was.

Kuvik's mind shifted gears. There Bounty Hunters carried spears. He didn't need a weapon to use against them. The Bounty Hunters brought the weapon to him.

He snuck through the branches, positioned himself directly above the guy, and dropped. Kuvik aimed his feet for the guy's head, kicked him hard across the temple, and they both went down.

Kuvik snatched the guy's spear, yanked it out of the Bounty Hunter's grasp, turned it around, and stabbed his victim through the neck.

The Bounty Hunter collapsed on the ground flailing his limbs and rasping in a death garble as Kuvik twisted the spearhead back and forth to do as much damage as possible to his victim's neck.

The sound brought the other Bounty Hunter running back. Kuvik heard the man's footsteps, yanked out the spear, and darted into the undergrowth to hide.

The second man charged his friend, went down on one knee when he saw his friend dead and bleeding on the ground, and Kuvik stepped out of the shadows to impale the second man through the back of the skull.

This wasn't the Godless way, but it sure did the job. Kuvik took both their spears—and realized in another moment of clarity that they did him another enormous favor.

He untied and removed their loincloths, took them back to Yoa, and crouched in the bushes to hand them over. "These should work for now. I'll turn around so I don't see you."

She spread the fabric out, stared at it in astonishment when she realized what it was, and then raised her haunted eyes to his face. He couldn't look at her.

He turned his back to her and heard her rustling around back there. He didn't care what she looked like as long as she covered herself up.

She said, "You can turn around now."

He turned around. She had wound one of the fabric strips around her chest with two lengths crossed her shoulders to make a top. She did the same thing with the second strip to make a loincloth. The fabric covered everything.

"Thank you, Kuvik," she whispered. "You're too kind."

"We might need to wait until morning before we can find some leaves to make the paste. Let's put some distance between us and the Bounty Hunters. We'll cover as much territory as we can before morning." He held out one of the spears. "Take this in case we meet any more of them."

She took the spear and looked at it. "I don't know how to use this."

"What weapons did you learn how to use in the band?"

She shrugged. "Knives, kukris, and axes, mostly."

He nodded, took the spear back from her, and used the spearhead of his own weapon to cut the thong around her spearhead.

The head came off and he handed it back to her. "There. You can hold it here and use it as a blade. I wouldn't feel right about you going armed."

She hefted the spearhead in one hand and then stuck it in her waistband. She was as ready as she would ever be.

She followed when he climbed into the canopy and they took off at high speed toward the east. He didn't know where the Bounty Hunters' village was or where the Godless were, but he and Yoa couldn't stay here.

They traveled the rest of the night and well into the morning before his energy failed. He buckled in the branches and his shoulders slumped. "I can't go on," he panted. "I have to rest."

Yoa squatted down next to him. He sensed her studying him extra closely. He couldn't summon the energy even to look up at her.

She left him alone and climbed down to the jungle floor. He shouldn't have let her go alone, but he didn't trust himself to climb down there without falling.

She returned in a little while with a handful of leaves and a smooth stone from some stream. She used the stone to grind a hollow in the branch next to him and started pulverizing the leaves into paste.

"You shouldn't ...." he murmured. "You need it...."

"Will you stop that?!" Her voice choked. "You should see yourself."

He looked away and shut his eyes. He could just imagine what he looked like.

He hadn't done anything about his own injuries since he left the Bounty Hunters' village. Pain exhausted him more than anything.

He needed Gooji juice as much as leaf paste. He definitely wouldn't be able to climb down to go searching for that. He wouldn't light a fire on the ground anyway. It would only give away their position.

She worked in silence until she made a good portion of leaf paste. Then she dabbed up some with her finger and smeared it on one of the cuts on his arm.

He winced and jerked away from her. "Aargh! Don't touch me!" he blurted out before he thought to stop himself.

"So it's okay for you to help me but not for me to help you?" She snorted. "I'm sure you would let Hangman put leaf paste on your cuts if he was here."

"That's him! He's a man."

"I'm sure he's no more capable of doing it than I am." She picked up another blob of paste and spread it on one of the spear wounds on his leg.

He kicked out as much in pain as from shock that she was actually touching him. "Stop it!" he snapped. "I'll do it myself."

She glared at him. "What is your problem with me—apart from everything you keep saying about how you aren't ready to initiate or anything like that?"

"Leave me alone!" He turned side on so he wouldn't have to deal with her. "It's none of your business."

"It's my business if you collapse on the way back to the band." She scooped up another drop of paste and spread it on a gash across his back.

He couldn't fight her off anymore. He needed her care too much.

He shut his eyes and tried to stop himself from feeling her touching him. He really wanted her to take care of him. That was the worst part. It felt unimaginably good to have someone actually care to tend his wounds.

She spread the paste on multiple sites on his back, shoulders, and sides. He gulped down the insatiable need to feel anything for her.

She finally finished and laid her hand on his arm—on one of the uninjured spots. "Turn around," she murmured.

He turned around. He kept his head and eyes down while she put the leaf paste on his arms, chest, stomach, and legs. She had to push up the cuffs of his shorts so she could get to the cuts higher up his thighs.

Every touch of her hand burned him to the core. His guts twisted in knots. He didn't understand what he felt for her except for the irresistible need to run away from this feeling.

She finally murmured, "Look at me."

He dragged his eyes up and found her staring into his soul from inches away. She raised her hand and spread the paste across his forehead and down his cheek. Then she put it on his neck.

He felt something break when he looked into her eyes overflowing with care and heartfelt gratitude. She always looked at him like that, even before she got captured.

She held his gaze for a long time after she finished tending all his wounds. "You need Gooji juice," she eventually murmured. "You could get an infection if you don't drink some."

"We can't." He tore his eyes away. "We can't light a fire."

"There's another way we can do it. Stay here."

Now he was the one to grab her hand and hold her back. "Don't go down to the ground again. It's too dangerous."

"I won't," she told him. "I can do everything in the canopy. You'll see." She nodded at the tree behind him. "Get some rest. You need it."

She wandered off into the canopy. He couldn't bring himself to argue or interfere with her plans. She was right. He would probably die if he didn't get some Gooji juice pretty soon.

She came back with a thick section of a hefty tree limb. He didn't ask where she got it. She rested it in the corner of a branch, left again, and came back with a handful of tinder.

She used one of the sticks to drill into the wood, created an ember, and added tinder to start a fire inside the hollow.

She blew on it, built it up into a bed of coals inside the hollow, and put some good-sized stones in there to heat up.

She left the limb section there for Kuvik to tend while she went out looking for Gooji sap.

He must have fallen asleep with his head resting on his arms. He woke up toward dusk and saw her using two more sticks to lower the hot rocks into the hollow of another limb section.

The water sizzled and she left it to cool while she came over to him. "Here. Eat this." She scooped a handful of nuts into his hands.

"Where did you get these?" he asked.

"We know a bunch of trees in the jungle that are good for food, but they don't produce all year round. It's quicker and easier to hunt the creatures. They're always around."

He put the nuts in his mouth. "Thank you....for all of this."

She made a face. "I'm the one who should be thanking you."

"You are thanking me. No one has ever taken care of me like the Godless have."

She kept working for a second to peel the husks off the nuts. She didn't answer right away before she looked up, locked eyes on him, and said, "You are Godless, Kuvik."

He started to shake his head and turn away.

"Why do you keep denying it?" she blurted out. "All the men say so! It isn't like you have to keep denying it because you don't want me."

Those words stung him worse than anything. "How can you say I don't want you?!" he countered. "Do you know what I would give to be Godless—to live even for one day the way they do—to be one fraction as good as they are?"

"You are Godless, Kuvik!" she shrieked and tears sprang to her eyes. She yelled out way too loudly. "Stop saying you aren't! You would have told me long ago if you really wanted to marry me! Hammer and Vina have loved each other since they were children! You would know by now if you felt that way about me! Just say you don't want me! Stop blaming it on the Godless!"

His stomach turned when he realized what she was saying. She actually thought that. She thought he held back because of her—so he wouldn't have to marry a woman he didn't want.

He really would have liked to flee from her—from how he felt about her.

He would have given anything—maybe even his own life—just to feel worthy of her attention and affection. He couldn't imagine any better woman that he could marry.

He would have to completely reevaluate his whole idea of himself if he even considered marrying her—or any other Godless woman—or even considering himself Godless enough to look sideways at her.

He couldn't look at her with those tears pouring down her cheeks. She was crying because of him—because she loved him and wanted to marry him. She thought he didn't love her back.

He forced himself to lower his voice even more. He kicked himself for hurting her even unintentionally. "I couldn't marry you, sweet girl," he murmured. "You're underage."

"You don't have to rub my face in it," she choked.

He took another wild leap and slipped his hand into hers. "I'll take you back to Hangman's band. You'll grow up and marry a strong, brave, dedicated Godless man. You'll be happy then. Just let me take care of you until then. Will you let me do that? Will you let me take care of you until you meet the right Godless man that you will marry?"

She looked up at him with her eyes swimming with tears. He couldn't read her expression.

His heart cracked with so much tenderness for her. He just wanted what was best for her. He wasn't it.

He could think of a lot of men she would be better off marrying. She would be better off marrying any of Hammer's men—or anyone else.

She deserved the best. He could only preserve her like this until she found it. Then she would realize what she really needed.

She would move on from this childish infatuation with Kuvik. She would move on with a real man—a man who could take care of her the right way and give her the life she deserved.

He squeezed her hand one more time. "Will you let me do that?"

She nodded and tears streaked down her cheeks when she lowered her eyes to their joined hands.

He would have liked to put his arms around her and hug her again. A million thoughts came into his head about holding her to make her feel better—and kissing her on the forehead—and a lot of other things he shouldn't be thinking about her.

Holding hands with her like this—it felt right. It felt just far enough without going too far.

He didn't want to give her the wrong idea. She could do so much better than him.

She would go to the gathering if and when Hangman took the band back to Shadow. Kuvik's one duty was to make sure she got to the gathering with her dignity intact. Then the natural order of things could go on as if the Bounty Hunters had never captured her.

She would probably settle on one of Hammer's men before that. She would go to the gathering for a few minutes, she and her chosen husband would sit down together, and they never had to leave their own family band.

Kuvik would never go to the gathering. He was already too old.

He would live alone according to the law. He would dedicate himself to protecting the band and the Clan—the way he was doing it right now.

Chapter 27

Kuvik roused out of a sound sleep. He felt better, now that leaf paste covered all his cuts.

Yoa touched his arm. "Here. Drink this." She pressed a wooden cylinder into his hand. It felt like the thick branch of a tree.

She clasped one hand on the back of his neck and steered his hand to bring the container to his mouth. He tipped it up and she helped him dump the Gooji juice down his throat.

He immediately felt better, but he couldn't keep his eyes open. He let his head collapse back onto his arms.

He felt her touching him, but he lacked the strength even to mention it. She refilled the container and helped him drink two more doses of the juice before she let him sink back into sleep.

He woke up in darkness when she squeezed his shoulder again. "Kuvik, wake up!" she whispered.

He dragged his head up and tried to open his eyes. "What's wrong?" he asked.

"Be quiet!" she whispered. "There are Bounty Hunters on the jungle floor below us! They're searching for us!"

His head shot up and his lethargy evaporated in a split second. All his senses snapped to high alert.

He heard the Bounty Hunters the minute she said those words. Men's voices rang through the night from directly below these trees.

He pivoted into a squat and grabbed his spear. He'd been sleeping with it lying across his lap just in case something like this happened.

Yoa's many doses of Gooji juice helped a lot. His body still ached, but nowhere nearly as bad as it did before.

The moonlight coming through the canopy showed him a party of fifteen Bounty Hunters directly below him.

"We know they're here," one of them told the others. "We found the girl's footprints down by the stream."

"How would we find them in the dark?" another asked. "They could be hiding anywhere."

"We'll just have to come back in daylight and search for them then," the first decided. "We'll move on and go after the Godless instead. We already know where they are."

Kuvik turned to whisper to Yoa. "Travel through the branches and keep heading east. I'll catch up with you."

"What about you?"

"Don't worry about me! Just go! Please, Yoa! I'll be all right. I'll catch up with you. See if you can find Hangman and warn him that the Bounty Hunters are coming after the band. Go, Yoa!"

He pushed her away. He didn't want her around right now. She would be safe in the branches as long as she didn't go down to the ground.

She gave him one pained look and vanished into the shadowy canopy. She made no sound. She knew how to travel by stealth.

He headed off in a different direction, balanced through the branches, and hunted around until he attracted the attention of a Krakelow hunting in the darkness.

The creature detected him prowling around and came after him. He raced through the branches until it picked up enough speed to close the gap between them.

He circled and dropped right into the middle of the Bounty Hunters' group. They no longer stood in the same place. They were already walking away toward the east to ambush the Godless.

He plummeted out of the canopy, landed in a crouch between all those men, and they spun around to attack him.

The Krakelow landed on them a second later. He spun his spear around to finish off as many of the Bounty Hunters as he could.

That was the moment when he heard a high-pitched female voice scream out his name in the distance. It came from the east.

He launched himself into the canopy just in time to avoid the Krakelow's thrashing coils. He streaked through the treetops and came upon Yoa struggling against five Bounty Hunters.

The jungle ended just a few feet away. She had to descend to the ground to continue traveling east. The Bounty Hunters ambushed her there.

Kuvik didn't have time to attract the attention of any other creature to do his fighting for him. He didn't want them to do his fighting for him.

He dropped on top of one of the Bounty Hunters and Kuvik drove his spear down into the guy's chest through the gap behind his collarbone. Kuvik twisted the spearhead to make sure he really killed the guy.

The body hit the ground and the other four Bounty Hunters let go of Yoa to come after Kuvik instead.

He ripped his spear out of the dead man's body, but Kuvik didn't have time to turn the weapon around to use it the right way.

He swung without thinking and snapped the shaft across the side of one of the Bounty Hunters' necks. The shaft splintered and shattered—and so did the guy's neck. That left three men still standing.

They piled in and raised their spears to stab him to death. He tucked and rolled away to give himself just a minute of space to decide how to defend himself.

In that moment, Yoa pulled the spearhead from her waistband and stabbed one of the Bounty Hunters in the back. The guy fell with the blade head sticking out of his ribs.

The other two glanced around to see what was going on—and Kuvik struck without mercy.

His fight against the Crusher made him deadly and determined never to let the Bounty Hunters retake him—or to let the Bounty Hunters take anyone else if he could stop them.

He stabbed his spear through one man's head. The skull cracked and the bones clamped around Kuvik's weapon. He couldn't withdraw it in time.

The second man thrust his spear at Kuvik. Kuvik still had his hands wrapped around his own weapon. He veered in time to avoid the thrust and nailed his elbow into his enemy's face.

The Bounty Hunter's head snapped back and his eyelids fluttered for a second. Kuvik yanked the spear out of the guy's hands, whipped it around, and stabbed.

Kuvik looked around in search of the next enemy to come after him. There was none, but more Bounty Hunters would come pretty soon.

He turned to Yoa and once again made a strategic decision not to see all the emotion and gratitude flooding from her deep, soft eyes.

She only felt that way because he was taking care of her and protecting her. She felt that gratitude that he was taking her back to her real husband—the man who would really make her happy.

He took a few steps toward her to tell her to come with him toward the east. He still had to find the city where he got separated from the Godless. Then he would be able to travel south from there and hopefully meet up with Hangman's band in Shadow's territory.

Kuvik put out his hand to Yoa. He realized in that moment that he was about to take her hand—as if they were sweethearts or something.

He stopped dead in his tracks when he heard rustling in the nearby jungle. Hangman and the other men had taught Kuvik what that sound meant.

He gulped when he saw an army of ants come marching out of the jungle behind him. They headed for the tree line. They would pass this spot and keep going out into the open country.

Did that open country lead to the city where Kuvik wanted to go? He had to let the ants pass first.

He lunged for Yoa, grabbed her with one arm around her waist, and launched into the treetops carrying her with him. He put her on a branch at a safe height above the ground.

The ants marched to the edge of the trees and discovered the dead Bounty Hunters lying there. The ants swarmed all over the bodies and started devouring them down to the bone.

The bodies imploded. The food checked the ants' migration for a few minutes at least before they finally moved on.

They left not a single trace of the Bounty Hunters, not even a bloodstain. The ants also ate the Bounty Hunters' loincloths, their hair, and the feathers tied in their hair.

The ants devoured the Bounty Hunters' spear shafts and left the iron spearheads lying there on the ground.

Kuvik waited for the ants to leave. Then he scouted the area to make sure no other parties of Bounty Hunters came around to overtake him and Yoa.

He jumped down to the ground and waved to her. "You can come down now. It's all clear."

She climbed down next to him and squinted across the countryside to the east. "How will we find the band?"

He pointed to a line of low hills farther to the southeast. "I was thinking we could climb those hills. We should be able to see the city from there. Then we can pick up the trail of the Godless heading south."

He bent down and picked up the extra spearheads. "You better take these. We might need them."

He divided them up—three for her and four for himself. He didn't think he would need that many, but it would be better to have too many than not enough.

Chapter 28

Hammer paused to listen to the jungle sounds ahead of him. He picked up the sounds of a dozen creatures moving around, but none of them put him in danger.

Kabi came up next to Hammer and furrowed his brow. "What are you doing?"

"I'm listening, little brother. I'm listening to hear if there are any Bounty Hunters in the area or if any creatures are threatening us."

"How do you do that?" Kabi asked.

Hammer squatted down next to the boy and raised his forefinger. "Do you hear that scratching noise?"

Kabi nodded.

"That's the sound of a mother Gurlg. She has chicks with her.... .four of them. Do you hear that buzzing sound? That's the mother Gurlg signaling her chicks to peck up whatever she found for them." He laughed. "Did you hear that squeak? One of the chicks got bitten by an Abnormit. The mother wants the chicks to eat it, but they didn't act fast enough."

Zaedi came over to them. "I want to learn, Hammer."

"Use your ears, little brother. Listen. Do you hear that husky sound in the branches? A Krakelow is up there."

"Is it coming for us?" Kabi asked.

"No, little brother. Listen more closely. It's moving away from us. The Krakelow doesn't even know we're here."

The four women approached them from behind. "Why are we stopping?" Sida asked. "Is something dangerous ahead?"

"A Gurlg is ahead," Kabi announced.

Hammer laughed again and faced the women. "I'm going up into the canopy. I need to make sure no one is......" He stopped mid-sentence when he heard another sound.

"What's wrong, Hammer?" Zaedi asked.

He pushed the children away. "Keep heading south. I have to check something. Don't stop. Go on. Get moving. You boys take care of the women and younger children."

Vina's eyes locked on him from a few feet away. Her expression asked a million questions—and then his hands flew to his blades when he heard someone coming toward him very fast through the canopy.

He sprang into the branches as fast as he could, took a position directly above the women and children, and braced himself for the worst.

He almost collapsed in relief when he recognized Kuvik coming toward him. Kuvik flew through the trees as fast as any naturally born Godless.

"You scared the crap out of me, brother!" Hammer gasped. "Don't come up on me so fast!"

Kuvik slowed and peered down through the branches at the women and children on the ground. "Is it just you? I thought you were with the others."

"I don't know where they are. I've been searching for them for four....." Hammer cut himself off. "You look awful, man."

Kuvik made a face. "You should see the other guys."

Hammer opened his mouth to say something, but he stopped again when he saw Yoa catching up with Kuvik. She looked as beautiful as ever—except that she wasn't wearing the same clothes stitched out of hides,

She wore some lengths of white fabric wrapped around her body. Hammer didn't see anything else about her that he would consider out of the ordinary.

Hammer frowned at her and then at Kuvik. "How is Yoa with you if you don't know where the others are?"

Now it was Kuvik who opened his mouth to answer before he stopped himself. He glanced at Yoa and she glanced at him. Volumes of information passed between them in that glance.

Hammer wasn't the only member of their band who noticed Yoa trying to get close to Kuvik. Hammer wasn't the only member of their band to notice him pushing her away just as he pushed away all the men's suggestions about him initiating into their Clan.

That one glance told a different story. Things were different between Kuvik and Yoa now. Hammer didn't know how things were different, but they were.

Kuvik compressed his lips and faced Hammer. "Yoa got captured by the Bounty Hunters," he murmured. "I got captured by the Bounty Hunters. That's why I look like this. They brought her in while I was there.....I got her out.....but the Bounty Hunters are moving against Hangman's band. The Bounty Hunters know where you are. They'll send out more men until they capture all of you. We just ambushed some of them in the jungle over there..." He waved behind him.

Hammer gaped at Kuvik in shock. Hammer already knew Kuvik got taken by the Bounty Hunters. That explained why he looked so bad—but Yoa?

What did they do to her? Was that where she lost her clothes?

Kuvik didn't explain and Hammer didn't ask. "Where are they coming from?" Hammer asked. "Where do you say you ambushed some of them—and where are they coming at us from?"

Kuvik waved behind him. "I'll have to show you. Climb up with me."

Kuvik clambered higher into the canopy. Hammer followed him until the two men perched on top of the highest branches. They sat on a bed of leaves where they could survey the countryside for miles around.

Yoa tagged after them. Her eyes told Hammer more than he ever wanted to know about whatever was going on between her and Kuvik.

Kuvik cared way too much about Godless law ever to lay a finger on an underage girl no matter how much she claimed to love him. Hammer didn't worry about that.

Whatever this was between them developed beyond anyone's expectations. It all happened in a few days. Getting out of danger and Kuvik rescuing her from a hellish fate was bound to do that to anyone.

She stayed close to him no matter what, but she stayed out of his conversation with Hammer. Hammer read so much meaning in her dark eyes. She would become even more single-mindedly attached to Kuvik because of this—if she wasn't already.

What was there to stop him from marrying her? He kept repeating endlessly that he wasn't Godless, but everyone knew he really was.

All he had to do was initiate. He could do that in a short afternoon. Then he could marry Yoa and live happily ever after.

He deserved her and she deserved him. Hammer couldn't think of a couple who deserved each other more. Kuvik deserved a good woman who worshiped the ground he walked on. Who better than Yoa?

She deserved a staunch, powerful, caring Godless man who would do anything for his Clan, band, family, and friends. Who would that be if not Kuvik? No one was stauncher, more powerful, and more dedicated than he was.

He didn't notice Hammer's attention to Kuvik or Yoa. Kuvik perched in the branches and pointed at a patch of jungle on the distant horizon.

"They come from over there. They have a village there—or it might be two villages. I don't understand their society, but they're over there. They take captives over there and the raiding parties come from there. They have a leader who makes the decisions. The Bounty Hunters are coming after Hangman's band. The Bounty Hunters know you're all in this area. They know you're scattered and they know you're heading south. They'll keep coming until they take everyone."

"So....you didn't see any of our other people in that village? The Bounty Hunters didn't bring in anyone else?"

Kuvik shook his head. "Not that I saw—but I didn't see everything. Things were pretty chaotic—and I might have been unconscious for quite a lot of it....." He looked away into the distance.

Hammer couldn't help but squeeze his shoulder. "You made it out—and you got Yoa out. You're a hero."

"What do you want to do about them?" Kuvik turned to confront Hammer. "You're Kral now."

Hammer snorted. "Hardly. I'm Kral to a bunch of women and children. That's all."

"You're more Kral than I am. You should decide."

"We're brothers—and you're older than I am," Hammer insisted. "We should decide together."

Kuvik shook his head. "No, you should. I told you what's happening. Hangman said you were Kral of your band. He isn't here. That leaves you."

Hammer pursed his lips. "Fine. If that's the way you want to do it, then I say we go over there and ambush a whole lot more of them. I say we send Vina, Yoa, and the other women farther south while you and I sneak back into the jungle over there and eliminate as many of the enemy as we can track down."

Kuvik only nodded. "I agree. It's a good plan."

Hammer's eyes fell out of their sockets. "Is that what you were going to say?"

Kuvik shrugged. "Something like that."

"Well, why didn't you say so? You hear me and the men making suggestions to Hangman all the time. Why didn't you tell me your idea?"

"I'm not Godless. I couldn't make a suggestion like that."

Hammer scoffed in his face. "Fine. You aren't Godless, but you're my only subordinate. I demand that you make suggestions to help me come up with ways to make my decisions."

Kuvik burst into a brilliant grin. "If you insist."

"I insist. Now come on. We have to get these women and children somewhere safe before we leave them alone."

The two men climbed down. Kuvik and Yoa confirmed all of Hammer's suspicions by sharing another meaningful glance when he climbed down to her level.

Then she stayed near him again on the way to the ground.

Vina hugged Yoa when the two girls met up. Then all the women hugged Yoa, too. They made a big fuss over her getting taken by the Bounty Hunters.

"I'm all right," she murmured. "Kuvik rescued me before anything bad could happen."

Hammer interjected before the conversation went any further. "Kuvik and I are going to go see if any more Bounty Hunters are sneaking up on the rest of the band. We'll take you all a little farther south, find a sheltered place where you can camp in the branches, and then we'll leave you alone for a while." He glanced at Vina. "Can you handle that?"

"We'll be fine. Do whatever you have to do."

The party set off. Hammer became aware of how slowly they were traveling, now that Kuvik was here to see them inching along the ground at a snail's pace.

Yoa picked up Thena and then squatted down so Kabi could ride piggyback. "No fair!" Zaedi exclaimed. "Now I'm the only one who has to walk."

"I'll carry you, little brother," Kuvik told him.

Zaedi turned around. Kuvik picked him up, hoisted him in his arms, and sat Zaedi on his shoulders.

"No fair!" Kabi exclaimed. "I want to ride like that!"

"Forget it," Yoa told him. "Ask Hammer. Maybe he can carry you."

"I just told you Kuvik and I will be going scouting soon." Hammer turned to Zaedi. "You and Kabi will be the men in charge after we leave. I'm making you two responsible for defending the women and children in our absence. Understand?"

That sparked another round of discussion. Zaedi and Kabi discussed how they were going to patrol the area and which weapons they would use to fight which creatures.

Hammer kept going for another hour, but he still didn't see anything to threaten the party. He, Kuvik, Vina, and Yoa carried the children up into the canopy and then helped the other women carry their children up there.

Hammer squatted down next to Vina once everyone got settled. "You should be all right here. Don't go down to the ground and don't move unless you absolutely have to."

"I understand. We'll be here when you come back."

He let his eyes dart toward Sida. She hadn't stopped staring off into the distance since he joined their party. "Keep an eye on things, will you, please?" he murmured.

Vina nodded. "I will—although I don't know what I would be able to do if something did happen."

"It helps to know you're watching. I appreciate it."

She smiled at him. Her eyes communicated so much understanding. He didn't have to explain anything to her.

He stood up in time to see Kuvik easing closer to Yoa. He looked deep into her eyes and murmured, "Are you going to be okay here?"

She nodded. She didn't break eye contact even once. "Be careful, okay?"

"I will." He squeezed her hand just for a split second before he turned away. They sure were acting like sweethearts.

Hammer and Kuvik set off through the trees moving fast. Hammer didn't have to wait for Kuvik. His injuries didn't slow him down any.

They traveled all the way back to the edge of the jungle where Hammer got separated from the rest of the Godless.

Hammer settled on a branch where he could see the countryside in front of him. Kuvik squatted next to him.

"We have to cross this open area to get there," Hammer remarked. "The Bounty Hunters will see us coming."

"Another stretch of jungle connects the two—down there." Kuvik pointed farther south. "We can travel through the trees unseen and then double back north. I'll show you where I ambushed the Bounty Hunters."

"You ambushed them?!" Hammer countered. "You said before that 'we' ambushed them—meaning you and Yoa."

Kuvik looked away and shrugged. "Okay. I ambushed them."

Hammer chose his next words with care. "You and Yoa....I'm happy for you. You make a good couple."

"Not at all," Kuvik insisted. "There's nothing going on between us. I just helped her. That's all."

"She would be good for you. She's a nice girl—and beautiful."

"I'm sure she'll make some Godless man a good wife someday."

Hammer let the subject drop. He could think of one Godless man who would make a perfect husband for Yoa. He was sitting right here on this branch.

One of these days, Kuvik would wake up and realize that he had been Godless all these years. His initiation would be nothing but a formality—like Hammer's had been.

Then Yoa would make a perfect wife for Kuvik. She had been loving him long enough. She loved him and waited for him as faithfully as Vina waited for Hammer.

Chapter 29

Hammer and Kuvik raced through the branches back to the spot where Kuvik rescued Yoa from the Bounty Hunters—the last time.

Kuvik sat down in the branches and pointed down at the spot. "That's the place. The Bounty Hunters ambushed Yoa there before she went out into the open."

"What did you do with the bodies?" Hammer asked. "How did you conceal their deaths?"

"The ants got them," Kuvik replied.

Hammer squinted across the open countryside at the jungle in the distance. The two men could see the same spot where they had been sitting just a short time earlier.

Then Hammer turned to peer into the jungle. "Do you think the Bounty Hunters are using this spot as a staging area? Do you think they gather here before they strike out across these fields?"

"That was my thought," Kuvik replied. "They aren't jungle people like we are. They prefer to attack on open ground—as we've seen. I wouldn't be surprised if they avoid the jungle entirely and wait for the band to come out into open country south of here."

"The Bounty Hunters don't avoid the jungle entirely."

Kuvik's head shot up. "They don't?"

"No, brother. That's how I found these women. They were locked up in a struggle against the Bounty Hunters in that jungle over there. The Bounty Hunters either followed them inside or ambushed them there. I'd say it was an ambush."

Kuvik looked away. His features fell and his heart sank. "Oh," he mumbled.

"This information of yours is going to be a game-changer." Hammer patted his shoulder. "You can lead us to their village. That's going to be important. Come on. Let's take a look around and see if we can find any of them."

The two men worked their way farther west and then split up to cover more ground.

Kuvik scoured the jungle for any sign of the Bounty Hunters. He would have traveled all the way back to their village to find their raiding parties.

He wouldn't have gone *into* the village. He would have stayed out of sight in the treetops, but he didn't have to. He found a raiding party of thirty Bounty Hunters heading east toward their staging point.

Kuvik liked that idea. He had been wondering if they might be using that spot. It sure was nice to hear someone as respected as Hammer confirm the idea.

Kuvik stayed high in the canopy where the raiding party wouldn't see him following them. He tracked them for a while before they stopped somewhere in the dense jungle.

He was just making up his mind to go get Hammer when Hammer came out of the jungle to catch up with Kuvik. The two men joined up on the same branch and observed the Bounty Hunters on the ground below.

They brought some of their slaves with them this time. Two were men loaded down with heavy bundles of weapons and other equipment tied to their backs. The other two slaves were women equally burdened with enormous bundles.

The four slaves staggered under the weight and let their bundles drop the minute the Bounty Hunters stopped walking.

The Bounty Hunters went after the four slaves, beat them with sticks, and made them keep working to build a fire and construct shelters for the Bounty Hunters to sleep in once night fell.

The slaves hustled to obey, but the Bounty Hunters didn't just leave the slaves to do their work unmolested. The Bounty Hunters kept attacking the slaves at random times for no reason. One of the men knelt down and started to construct the fire so he could light it.

The Bounty Hunters stood off to one side talking about something. They didn't pay any attention to the slaves until one Bounty Hunter happened to turn around, hurled his stick at the man in front of him, and clubbed the slave across the side of the head.

The Bounty Hunter didn't even stand up when he did it. He struck out and immediately turned back to finish his conversation with his comrades.

The blow knocked the slave out. He toppled into the dirt and lay there insensible. The other man came over and started constructing the fire in his place, but the second man stayed on the other side of the circle to keep out of range.

The other three slaves worked without stopping until the sun went down. The second man built the fire, went hunting, came back with a small Gurlg chick, and roasted it on the spit to serve to the Bounty Hunters.

They didn't acknowledge his efforts all evening. They didn't share the food with the women or with the man who caught the chick. The slaves didn't eat at all.

The Bounty Hunters brought out skins of whatever that red drink was. They drank all the way through their meal. It made them loud and sloppy.

They started grabbing at the two female slaves and laughed when the women struggled. Their efforts encouraged the men.

The Bounty Hunters eventually dragged the two women off to their shelters and vanished inside leaving only the one conscious male slave outside.

He knelt down next to his comrade and examined the guy's head, but the first man didn't wake up, not even when the second man rolled his friend onto his back, lifted his eyelids, and peered into his eyes.

Kuvik felt Hammer seething in barely suppressed rage as the evening wore on. Now Hammer knew what the Bounty Hunters were like.

The two men didn't look at each other until after the second man curled up on the ground by the fire and went to sleep.

Hammer glanced over at Kuvik. Hammer's eyes asked a million questions about how to eliminate these Bounty Hunters.

Kuvik didn't want to harm the slaves, especially not the women inside those huts. Their lives were already bad enough. Killing them wouldn't help.

Kuvik motioned for Hammer to follow him. Kuvik broke off some branches from the canopy, wrapped them with a certain vine he knew, and the two men descended to the ground.

Kuvik snuck past the sleeping men, handed one of his branches to Hammer, and the two men stuck their branches into the fire.

Chemicals in the vines ignited and flared the branches into blazing torches. Hammer spun one way and Kuvik spun the other way. The two men strode through the camp setting every shelter on fire. The flames licked up the walls made of dry thatch.

Hammer tossed his torch back into the fire and drew his blades to wait for the inevitable confrontation. It came sooner rather than later.

The second male slave woke up first and yelled out in alarm. His voice woke up his formerly unconscious friend. Then one of the women screamed inside the hut.

That woke up everyone else. Yells, bellows, and more screams echoed through the camp.

The door of one of the huts burst open. The Bounty Hunters staggered out followed by the woman they took in there with them.

Hammer was waiting for them. He raised his blade and cut down three of them before any of them even thought to draw a weapon.

Kuvik pushed the two male slaves away into the jungle and stationed himself where he would be able to intercept more Bounty Hunters coming out of the other two huts.

The Bounty Hunters pushed the woman out first. Kuvik raised his spear and checked himself to avoid hitting the woman.

That moment of pause gave the Bounty Hunters the time they needed to see exactly what was going on. They just forgot to bring their weapons with them when they evacuated their huts.

They scrambled to recover in time. They had all the weapons they needed tied up in the slaves' bundles. None of the Bounty Hunters could get to them in time.

Hammer and Kuvik stormed through the camp killing every Bounty Hunter in sight. The slaves bolted and didn't look back.

Kuvik tried not to notice them heading back toward the west. He really hoped they didn't go back to the Bounty Hunter village.

They weren't his problem anymore. He felt no guilt whatsoever when he and Hammer wiped out the Bounty Hunters to the last man.

The two men retreated and watched the flames reduce the huts to ash. Kuvik lost interest once he made sure the fire wouldn't spread.

He went over to the bundles and untied some of the weapons. Most of them were spears, but he found plenty of blades.

Jewels encrusted some of their blades and handles. "Whoa!" Hammer exclaimed. "The Bounty Hunters must have stolen these from other Clans."

"These look like Renegade make." Kuvik pulled out some of the rectangular blades that Hammer's men liked. "You should take these."

Hammer pulled out two good-sized kukris. These were made of metal, too, with matching polished horn handgrips.

"You should take these," Hammer told him. "They suit you."

Kuvik turned bright red. "If you insist."

Hammer clapped him on the shoulder. "I insist. Hangman is going to be so jealous."

"Not likely," Kuvik muttered. "His weapons are so fine."

"Do you think he would lower himself to using something that wasn't?" Hammer pushed the blades into Kuvik's hands. "Take them as a souvenir that you escaped the Bounty Hunters and came back to kill ten times more of them."

Hammer didn't give Kuvik a chance to protest. Hammer swung up into the branches. Kuvik stared down at the kukris in his hands. He never dreamed he would ever get a chance to use weapons like this—much less own them and call them his own.

Hammer insisted, though, so Kuvik took them and set off to follow Hammer back through the jungle.

Chapter 30

Hangman climbed a tall tree and swayed in the branches where he could see for miles to the south. He didn't see anything dangerous out there, but that was an illusion.

This whole country seethed with threats. The unseen threats posed a much greater danger than the ones he could see.

He had developed a pathological hatred of open countryside where his band had to walk out in the open. The band was just asking for trouble every time they left the jungle.

Staying in the jungle was asking for trouble, too. He had to make a decision one way or the other.

He only had to glance to the southwest to make up his mind. The Jagged Points raised their rugged peaks to the sky down there. He would have recognized those mountains anywhere.

They flanked Shadow's territory. Hangman was getting close—very close. He couldn't stop now. He had to keep going.

His worst fear haunted him that he would make it all the way back there and find Shadow's band gone. They could have vanished off the face of the Earth the way Thunder's band vanished from the mountains where Red and his party left their relatives.

Then Hangman would never see Shadow, Katha, or his brothers again—not to mention all the cousins he left behind.

Shadow and Katha might have given Hangman and Mora up for dead long ago.

Hangman's younger brothers Jarun and Landus would have initiated by now—if they were still alive at all. Hangman wouldn't even recognize his brothers when he saw them again.

He tried not to think about that. He just had to make it back to Shadow's territory. If Shadow's band wasn't there, then Hangman would move his people into Shadow's old camps. Hangman knew that country. He knew where his people could find safety.

He climbed down from the tree and returned to the band—what was left of it. He sat down next to Mora, but she didn't look up, not even when he squeezed the back of her neck and petted her hair and cheek.

She pretended to straighten out something with Maeno's wrap. He blinked up at her and didn't stop nursing when she touched him.

Hangman didn't say anything and neither did Mora. Maeno was the only child they had left. They hadn't seen Zaedi or Thena in almost a week. They were almost certainly dead out there somewhere or captured by the Bounty Hunters.

Hangman and Mora weren't the only ones struggling to cope with the loss of loved ones and family members.

Wildling and his wife had lost both their children and so had Butch. The two couples kept falling into each other's arms at random times to comfort each other. Prodigy struggled to take care of his children after his wife Sida disappeared.

Red, Legacy, and Baron came off the worst. The three men lost their wives and all their children. The three men didn't look at or talk to anyone, not even their comrades.

None of the three men would make eye contact when Hangman and the others discussed where to travel and how to protect the band.

The three men fought and participated as well as ever. They just didn't engage or interact with anyone. All three had completely switched off from life.

Hangman didn't try to correct their behavior. No one interrupted their grief. Hangman had his own struggles to cope with after losing Zaedi and Thena.

Hangman had come to view Zaedi as his heir—his oldest son. Hangman had invested so much in the boy even though he was still so young.

Zaedi turned out to be such a ferocious little warrior. There never was a son of the Godless Clan born more enthusiastic and busting to take on the whole world. Hangman had resigned himself to struggle to rein in Zaedi's energy and natural drive to fight and conquer.

At the same time, Hangman saw himself reflected in his son. Hangman wanted nothing more than to cut the chains that held Zaedi down, set him loose on the world, and stand back and watch the madness ensue.

Hangman wanted to give Zaedi all the freedom and encouragement he needed to become the powerful, deadly warrior he was born to be.

Hangman wanted to see Zaedi rampaging through the jungle on an unstoppable mission to master this world the way Hangman did when he was younger.

None of that would happen now. Zaedi wouldn't grow up to be a powerful, deadly Godless warrior. Zaedi wasn't Hangman's oldest son anymore. He wasn't Hangman's son at all.

Maeno would become all those things. Hangman remembered only too clearly how helpless and dependent Zaedi had been as a baby. He grew up, started walking, and then he started fighting all his imaginary enemies in preparation for the day when he would face real ones.

Maeno would grow up and become a little terror running around camp slashing things with a stick. He would become as dangerous and unstoppable as Zaedi ever would have been.

Hangman knew all that in his heart of hearts, but he couldn't help but grieve over the son he lost—the son he would never see grow up.

He would never see Thena grow up, either. She would never go to the gathering or become a wife and mother. She would never find a sweetheart in this band and settle down to raise her family with Hangman and Mora as the loving grandparents.

Hangman kept all those feelings hidden from everyone, especially Mora. She had a hard enough time coping with the loss. She paid extra attention to Maeno. She wouldn't let Hangman come near her. She kept saying she wasn't ready to move on.

He didn't push it, but he would eventually. He would have to pull her out of this eventually—and he would need to pull himself out of it by having more children.

He really felt sorry for Red, Wildling, Butch, Legacy, and Baron, but Hangman didn't show that, either. He insisted that they participate in all the band's movements and defense. He couldn't let them fall off the edge of a cliff.

They participated. Butch and Wildling kept getting tears in their eyes at random times. No one commented on this or mentioned that it should be otherwise.

The other three just weren't here anymore in anything other than body. They sat alone every evening. They didn't talk even to each other. They completely shut down.

No one had seen Hammer, Vina, or Yoa, either. Hammer's loss completely demoralized his men. They lost all their fire and became docile and resigned to staying under Hangman's leadership possibly forever.

Hangman couldn't wait any longer. He went through the band, called all the men, and ordered the women to get moving. Everyone knew they had to cross open country today. Everyone knew what that meant.

The women armed themselves and quite a few of the older children did, too. The men surrounded the band in a ring of weapons and kept a sharp eye on the surroundings.

The party left the jungle and started heading across country. Another road led to another city in the far distance. Nothing but wide open fields stood between the band and the city.

Hangman glanced up at the sky for Boultars and Ridgebeaks. He didn't see any—which racked his nerves even more.

He didn't like that rim of dark jungle to the west. Anything could be hiding in there waiting to leap out and attack the party. It was the perfect hiding place.

The party kept pushing forward without incident for two hours. Hangman squinted toward the Jagged Points and then farther east from there.

Shadow said he would take his band farther east into Godless territory. He could find fortified valleys and protected areas where the band could defend itself better.

Hangman would keep traveling until he found Shadow's. His family was still out there. His gut told him so.

He started to drift off into his memories when a shout startled him to high alert. He spun around and his hands flew to his kukris.

His worst nightmare came true when a bunch of people charged out of the jungle to the west exactly the way he just feared they would. They broke cover and raced across the grasslands to intercept Hangman's band.

He took a second to realize that these people weren't Bounty Hunters or Renegades. Almost all those people were women—and children.

They made it halfway before Hangman recognized Kuvik. His bald head and tattered, cut-off shorts gave him away.

Then Hangman's mind clicked and he recognized Hammer—and all the children.

Chapter 31

Mora screamed and took off running across the field. Prodigy, Legacy, Red, Baron, Butch, and Wildling all did the same thing.

Hangman got there a second later. He fell on his knees and couldn't stop the tears from pouring down his cheeks when he saw his children alive.

All the men attacked their wives and children. Everyone sobbed their eyes out when they hugged their lost loved ones.

Hangman crushed Zaedi in his arms. Hangman had to force himself to pry his arms away from the boy.

Zaedi just stood there in a daze trying to understand everything that was happening. Thena screamed and wailed in loud sobs. She wouldn't let go of Mora to save her life.

All the families stood there holding onto each other and bawling their eyes out for a long time. Hammer, Vina, Kuvik, and Yoa stood off to one side—until Hammer's men moved in.

Another celebration broke out on the side as they all surrounded him, touched him, hugged him, and some of them even kissed him on the cheek or the hair.

They wouldn't stop smiling and beaming at him. They grabbed him, jostled him, and bombarded him with questions.

The women and girls surrounded Vina and Yoa. No one could get a word out until someone finally got Yoa to admit where she'd been and what happened to her.

Dead silence fell over the band when everyone heard about Kuvik rescuing her. Hangman only noticed now how injured Kuvik was, but he kept smiling at everyone.

"Kuvik says the Bounty Hunter village is in the jungle to the west—over there." Hammer pointed to the northwest.

"It is there," Kuvik insisted. "Yoa and I came from there."

"We should go back and carry out a strike on them," Hammer suggested.

"Let's get to the city," Hangman interjected. "We can discuss it there from a protected place. Then we'll venture out once we know everyone is safe."

The party moved off heading south again. The men didn't stay on guard as much as they should have. They were all too busy hugging and kissing their wives and children.

Hangman found it impossible not to do the same thing. Mora cried all the way south. Thena absolutely would not let go of her mother. Thena bawled all the way south, too.

Mora kept petting and kissing both children in between broken sobs of relief and gratitude. Hangman put his arm around her and kissed her, too. He couldn't remember ever feeling this happy and relieved.

That nightmare world he'd just been living in—it would continue to live in his memory in dread that something really bad happened to his children and he never got them back.

Hammer and Vina held hands in sight of everyone. Hangman was too grateful to Hammer to intervene. He and Vina earned the right to hold hands today of all days.

Yoa walked next to Kuvik. They did not hold hands, but the energy between them couldn't have been more obvious. They were as together as any couple here as far as Hangman was concerned.

Hangman saw absolutely no reason why Kuvik shouldn't marry into the Godless Clan. He was Godless. He could initiate whenever he wanted to. Then he just had to wait a few months for Yoa to come of age. Nothing could be simpler.

Hangman refused to think about all the objections Hammer raised—like the fact that Yoa would have to go to the gathering and take a husband her own age.

Hangman succeeded in bringing this band far enough south. They were entering Shadow's territory. This band could make it to the gathering—which meant this band was now subject to all the laws governing gatherings and marriages.

Returning to this territory meant Kuvik could never marry Yoa—just as Hammer could never marry Vina. All the same problems still waited out there to strike and rob these people of their hard-earned happiness.

Hangman put that off until another day. Today was too beautiful and blessed to let any of that bother him—or anyone else.

The party traveled for half an hour before Wildling lifted up Loso in his arms and carried the little boy like that. Wildling kept diving in and kissing the boy on the neck.

Wildling turned around, shot Hangman a wild grin of pure ecstasy—and all the color drained from Wildling's face when his eyes darted behind Hangman to the jungle the party just came from.

Hangman's stomach dropped. He had been seeing that expression way too often these last few days.

Wildling practically dropped Loso in his haste to draw his weapons. "Here they come!" Wildling bellowed. "Everyone get to the city! Hurry! RUN!!"

No one asked any questions. The women broke into a dead run for the city. All the children ran, too.

The single girls scooped up children right and left and staggered under the extra weight. No one even turned around to see what Wildling was looking at. No one had to ask.

Hangman spun away, drew his kukris, and the rest of the men and uninitiated boys pulled into line. The men kept walking backward to stay as close to the women as possible, but the men couldn't keep up.

The Bounty Hunters emerged from the jungle to the northwest—the side where Hammer and Kuvik said the Bounty Hunters kept their village.

The Bounty Hunters formed up in a long line of their own. "At least they didn't bring as many men this time," Lucky remarked.

"Kuvik has been eliminating them for us," Hammer replied.

Hangman glanced over at Kuvik. He looked half-dead from so many injuries, but he seemed to have grown even in just the week since the Bounty Hunters captured him.

He stood taller, narrowed his eyes more dangerously, and he held two matched metal kukris in his hands. Hangman had never seen weapons so fine in his life.

They were bigger than Hangman's kukris and smaller than Alien's, but still imposing enough.

Their weight made Kuvik flex his muscles tighter than he ever did with Renegade weapons. His chest, back, and shoulders swelled to make him look much more intimidating. Hangman wouldn't want to face the guy in combat.

Hangman didn't even want to know what happened to Kuvik and Yoa in Bounty Hunter country. Hangman would never ask and Kuvik would never tell. Hangman didn't question that for an instant. Kuvik would take that story to his grave.

Yoa might know and that was how it should be. Hangman didn't blame her for sticking close to him after the way she said Kuvik rescued her.

Hangman had to face front when a high-pitched yell broke out from the Bounty Hunter ranks. They rushed onto the field to attack the Godless.

The men stood their ground and didn't retreat. The Bounty Hunters had to run a long way to get here.

That moment gave Hangman the chance he needed to see the women and children vanishing inside the city. They were safe. Now the men could concentrate on the fight at hand.

A charge of fury went through the Godless. The men had their families back. The men had something to protect now. Every man braced himself to go down swinging. The Bounty Hunters wouldn't break through this line—not today.

Hangman had Zaedi and Thena back. No one would go near them, especially not these demons from Hell.

Mora and Maeno were back there. The Bounty Hunters wouldn't set foot in the city today. Over Hangman's dead body, maybe. He would take plenty of them down with him before he let that happen.

The Godless line braced for the collision as the Bounty Hunters got closer. Hangman's attention zeroed down to the smallest detail of his enemy's faces. These were just men. He could kill them—and he would kill them.

All his doubts evaporated in that moment. The Godless would win. They would drive the Bounty Hunters back and force them to leave their dead on this field.

The Bounty Hunters knew it, too, in that moment of crystal clarity. The same charge of realization ran through their ranks. They knew they were going to lose.

That instant passed in a breath of wind and the Bounty Hunters closed the gap. They smashed into the Godless with shrieks and clangs of weapons against weapons.

The Godless understood the Bounty Hunters' fighting style now. They favored spears for some reason. The Bounty Hunters tried to stab, blocked blade cuts with their spear shafts, and used every evasive maneuver to try to work their spears inside a man's fighting radius.

The Godless had fought the Bounty Hunters enough times to learn all those tricks. Hangman slashed his blade and smashed the Bounty Hunters' spear shafts to destroy the Bounty Hunters' advantage.

He even slammed his blades against the spearheads themselves. He aimed for the leather thongs that bound the spearhead to the shaft. He had gotten really good at hitting these thongs, cut the heads away from the shafts, and rendered the weapons useless.

Kuvik's new blades became welded to his arms as extensions of his limbs. He inflicted brutal damage on the Bounty Hunters' weapons and then started on the Bounty Hunters themselves.

The Godless took no prisoners, hacked their way into the Bounty Hunter ranks, and spared no one who happened into range.

Hangman went into a killing trance. He sheltered his family behind him. He fought to protect them. No stinking Bounty Hunter would go near his family—never in a million years—not as long as he was still alive.

His men fought with a kind of bloodthirsty ferocity he'd never seen before. It infected him. The Godless slaughtered their way through the Bounty Hunter ranks until the last straggling survivors broke and ran for it.

Chapter 32

Mora shot to her feet when she heard footsteps coming up the stairs of one of the city's tall buildings. She collapsed in relief when Hangman walked in with the men and uninitiated boys. "Are they gone?" she choked.

"They're gone—for now." Hangman looked around. The women and children had taken refuge in another upstairs room in one of the few intact buildings. "We might as well stay here for tonight. We can talk about what to do next. The Crushers won't see us if we stay below the windows."

He and Mora sat down with their children. Mora couldn't stop stroking Zaedi and Thena. They were back. She got her family back.

All the families sat together. The men held their children on their laps and the women rested their heads on their husbands' shoulders.

Kuvik sat down next to Hangman. Mora found herself smiling at Kuvik. He smiled back, but it wasn't his usual smile. He looked different—and not because of all the cuts and bruises all over him.

"Are you okay, Kuvik?" she asked. "I have some leftover Gooji sap. We could make you some juice."

"I've already had plenty. Thank you, though. Yoa made it for me. She wouldn't leave me alone until I drank it—all of it."

He said it casually and accepted the food that Hangman offered him. Kuvik didn't show the slightest embarrassment or unease when he mentioned Yoa taking care of him.

The injuries to his face and body showed the unmistakable signs of daily leaf paste applications. She must have been keeping a close eye on him and treating him every day that they had been separated from the band.

She didn't sit next to him now. She returned to her family the way she used to before she got captured.

Hammer came over to sit near Hangman's family, too. Hammer and Lonion shared the meal with Hangman, Mora, Viking, Cross, and the children.

Vina returned to her family, too. No one mentioned the two couples spending all that time alone together.

Zaedi came right over and confronted Hammer. "Defend yourself, vile jungle monster!" Zaedi demanded. "I plan to kill you and take you home to feed you to my family."

Hammer shot out a hand and made a fake dive to catch Zaedi by the wrist. Zaedi dodged but not fast enough for Hammer to miss him.

Hammer deliberately snatched at empty air a few inches from Zaedi's arm. Zaedi tried to grab Hammer's and missed for real.

Then Hammer shot out a hand and grabbed Zaedi by the leg. Hammer's fingers clamped his leg and he yanked the boy off his feet.

Zaedi landed on his seat and tried to kick Hammer's hand away. Hammer let go on purpose and went back to making fake grabs.

Thena came over and leaned her weight against Hammer's shoulder. "What are you this time, Hammer?"

"He's a Krakelow," Zaedi explained. "He's always a Krakelow."

"I'm a Dushag this time," Hammer corrected.

"Are you sure you aren't a Cursed Sand monster?" Kuvik interjected.

Hammer laughed. "Good one. Okay, I'm a Cursed Sand monster tonight."

"Do you know this game, Kuvik?" Mora asked.

"He's been playing it with them for three days," Kuvik replied. "These children can't wait to die."

"They need practice," Hammer countered.

"They need practice dying?" Cross asked. "That doesn't sound like a very fun game."

"They're the ones who always ask me to play," Hammer replied and made another grab for Zaedi's arm this time.

The boy dodged, but the move turned out to be another fake. Hammer changed direction at the last second, lunged forward, seized the boy around the middle, and pulled him in fast.

Zaedi screamed. "Save me! Save me from the Cursed Sand!"

"Nothing can save you now! Ha ha ha!" Hammer lifted the boy by one arm and one leg, buried his face in the boy's stomach, and made grunting, rooting, and snarling noises like he was devouring Zaedi alive.

The boy screeched and called out for anyone to save him. The other adults laughed.

Hammer finally put Zaedi down. The boy charged away and hid behind Viking where no one could even see him.

"Now you've done it," Hangman told Hammer.

"Maybe he'll leave me alone for a while," Hammer replied. "He and Kabi wouldn't stop interrogating me all week."

Hangman laughed again. "Thank you so much for taking such good care of them. I can see they were in the best possible hands."

Hammer turned red and glanced over at Mora. "Maybe second best."

"We're forever in your debt, Hammer," Mora exclaimed. "You're a part of our family forever now."

He looked away. "I just did what any reasonable person would do. I didn't do anything special."

"Tell me more about this village where the Bounty Hunters stay," Hangman asked.

Hammer glanced over at Kuvik. Kuvik looked down at the ground. "What do you want to know?"

"What is it like?" Hangman asked. "What are they like?"

Kuvik gulped and stared off in the other direction. "Do you really want to know?"

"Yes," Hangman replied. "Mora has her ideas, but everything she knows she learned from books and secondhand stories. You're the only one here who has actually seen them in the flesh."

"I'm not the only one," Kuvik murmured. "Yoa has seen them."

"You're here with us now, I mean," Hangman insisted. "Just tell us what you saw."

Kuvik heaved an almighty sigh, puffed out his cheeks, and squared his shoulders, but anyone could see his heart wasn't in it. Everyone fell silent to listen. The pressure must have been immense.

It took him a long time to work up the courage to speak. He couldn't keep the tremor out of his voice when he did finally start talking.

"They beat everyone from the minute they walk into the village," he husked. "All the captives are walking around covered in bruises. The Bounty Hunters keep everyone constantly beaten down and the Bounty Hunters can attack and beat anyone whenever the Bounty Hunters feel like it. They keep the captives working all the time carrying heavy burdens and doing all the work around the village. The Bounty Hunters can take any woman they want whenever they want. They attack and beat anyone even to the point of death for no reason."

Dead silence answered him. Hangman turned to stare into the fire. Even the children fell silent when they heard how bad it was.

"The Bounty Hunters drink a lot," Kuvik went on.

"What do you mean?" Cross asked. "What do they drink?"

"I'm not sure what it is. It's some kind of liquid. It dulls their senses, but it also makes them violent and cruel...."

"It's alcohol," Mora murmured. "It's called alcohol. It makes your brain fuzzy and it disconnects you from understanding any consequences from your actions. It makes you impulsive and indifferent that you might be making a mistake or hurting anyone."

"Yes," Kuvik agreed. "My people used to drink it a lot." He looked away. "The Bounty Hunters are like my people in a lot of ways."

"Is that what happened to Yoa?" Viking asked. "She doesn't look beaten to me—not like you are."

Kuvik cast his eyes to the ground. "No. They didn't beat her."

Mora cringed at those words. No one asked what the Bounty Hunters did to Yoa.

"They....." Kuvik had to pause and rally his courage a second time before he could go on. "They tortured me. I can only guess they do it to everyone. They made sport of it—and then they set me against a Crusher to fight it while everyone laughed and cheered. They knew exactly what to do and how to do it. They must do it all the time. It's their way of enjoying themselves, I guess—and then they all laughed and watched when one of them tried to force himself on Yoa. He would have, but he drank too much and passed out."

Hammer broke the silence by turning to Hangman. "We have to hit their village. Kuvik can show us where it is. We can carry out a surprise attack and wipe them out—or most of them."

"We wouldn't be able to wipe out a whole Clan," Kuvik pointed out.

"We could reduce their numbers—by a lot," Hammer countered and turned back to Hangman. "Listen to reason for once. These fiends will keep coming after us. They already know we're out here with women and girls. The Bounty Hunters won't stop for anything—but they might think twice if we cut down their ranks. We would at least stand a better chance when they do come out for us."

Hangman didn't look up from the flames. "I was thinking the same thing, actually. I think we should leave the women and children here—in this city. Maybe even in this building. They'll be safer than out in the countryside. They can stay hidden from the Crushers. Other scavengers won't come up this far."

"They won't," Mora told him. "We can go downstairs and hunt around for food if we need to. We can do it at night when no Crushers or any Clans are around. I know where to look to find supplies."

Hangman looked up and made eye contact with both Hammer and Kuvik. "You're right. This is the best way. We can't let these marauders keep coming after us—not without striking back. We have too much to lose."

Chapter 33

Hangman sensed Kuvik getting tense and jumpy when the Godless men settled in the jungle canopy. It was still the middle of the afternoon.

"How close are we?" Hangman asked him.

Kuvik nodded toward the trees east of their hiding place. "Only a few miles. We can get there in a couple of minutes."

"How do you think we should do this? Give us your ideas."

Kuvik wouldn't look at him. "I think we should wait until later in the night—maybe very late at night—after all the men are asleep from drinking too much. They won't wake up. They'll sleep through everything."

"I don't like it. It sounds cowardly, but you're the expert here. We'll do it your way."

Kuvik started rocking on the branch. He didn't seem aware of anyone around him. "I would set fire to the building—or whichever one has the most men in it. We'll need to be careful we don't kill any of the captives."

"How will we do that?" Hangman asked.

"We can go into the other houses and kill the Bounty Hunters. We'll have to take the captives with us."

Hangman didn't answer. He didn't plan on that—but it made sense. He couldn't leave those people behind for any surviving Bounty Hunters to re-enslave them.

None of the other men objected to setting fire to a building while the occupants were asleep and out of their minds on some drink. Viking, Cross, and Red would have been the first to object if anyone was going to.

This band had already crossed too many lines. Why not this one?

What difference did it make what lines the band crossed as long as the men protected their families? Killing Bounty Hunters one way was as good as any other.

Hangman didn't raise any other objection, either. He committed himself to doing this Kuvik's way. He knew best what the men would be facing in there.

He also knew what kind of numbers the Bounty Hunters had. Hangman and his men wouldn't likely be able to defeat anyone in open battle with so few on the Godless side.

This called for another stealth maneuver of brains over brawn. The stakes demanded total victory. Defeat was no longer an option.

The men passed around the food they brought with them. A few people slept as the afternoon wore on. The sun started to go down. No one moved or spoke. Most of the men just relaxed and waited for Kuvik to give the word.

Hangman cast his mind back to Shadow's band. Hangman had been thinking about Shadow more and more—and all the other relatives Hangman left behind. That time seemed like decades ago.

None of those people would recognize him as Kral of his band. He *wouldn't* be Kral as soon as he met back up with Shadow.

Then again, Shadow might be dead. Then Fang would become Kral—unless Fang was dead, too—which meant Viking would be Kral—except that Viking wasn't there.

Hangman didn't know who would be Kral in that case. Who would Shadow or Fang hand off to if they didn't have an heir to hand off to?

Feather and Banjo were Midnight's sons—the only two initiated men from any of Midnight's brothers. Hangman didn't see Feather or Banjo becoming Kral. Neither of them had the authority to command anyone, especially not other men.

One of Shadow's men would probably challenge to become Kral. Then he would fight any other challengers. Devil, Breaker, or Grizzly might challenge.

They were the sons of Midnight's daughter Neia and her husband Cosmos and had the balls to do something like that. Then again, Cosmos himself might challenge.

Anyone could become Kral if it came to a challenge. Hangman had no way to know who he would meet when he got back to his father's territory.

Hangman might meet up with a Kral who flatly refused to take any of Hangman's people into the band—including Hangman himself. The new Kral could turn the band away. Then what would Hangman do?

He decided during that long, boring, nerve-racking wait that he would ask his men what to do. A Kral shouldn't ask his men. A real Kral would just decide and tell them what to do.

This band no longer functioned that way. It never really did function that way. Hammer's band—Red's men—Viking—Cross—even the uninitiated boys had all earned the right to make up their own minds about what they did and where they went.

They might decide to travel all the way back north to Thunder's mountain country and take up residence in the valley again. Hangman wouldn't argue with that. No one else lived in that country and he could think of worse places to live.

The band would be able to defend the valley, now that Aster wasn't around to signal the Renegades where and when to strike the band.

Hangman rested his head on his arms, shut his eyes, and drifted into a fantasy about the valley. It had been a paradise before the Renegades came along.

He might have had his own reasons to travel south to find his family—the same reason Red and his men had to travel all the way north to find theirs.

Hangman must have drifted off. He startled awake when someone laid a hand on his shoulder. He jolted upright to find Kuvik's eyes burning into Hangman from out of the dark. Kuvik didn't say a word.

All the men got to their feet, straightened out their weapons, and headed off through the canopy. The party traveled more slowly. No one ran. They moved slowly, fluidly, silently, and undetected.

Kuvik went in front and led the way to another rim of trees overlooking what looked like a small town. No one moved around between the sturdy, plank houses. The whole place slept in peaceful silence.

The moon shone on steepled rooves. Hardly any light glimmered from any of the windows. Kuvik pointed to an enormous structure on the other side of the village. Another stand of jungle surrounded the village on the far side.

That big building marked the end of the village. Kuvik had already explained numerous times that there was a second village—or maybe part of the same village—on the other side of those trees.

The Godless had to hit both parts of the village and finish off everyone. Kuvik didn't understand much about the difference between the two villages, but he was adamant that the Godless should wipe out all the Bounty Hunters from both villages.

He also made it clear that the Bounty Hunter leader ruled both villages. This man called Uthor was the one ordering the Bounty Hunters to go after the Godless.

Uthor could be in either village. Kuvik became murderously determined that the Godless not leave either village until the men killed Uthor for good. Kuvik didn't care if he killed anyone else as long as he got Uthor.

Hangman paused there at the edge of the trees. Kuvik had drawn diagrams of both villages and pointed out every significant part he thought the party should destroy.

Seeing the village in real life changed things. Hangman couldn't explain how.

Kuvik retreated into the canopy and came back with a makeshift torch. He nodded to Hangman, dropped to the ground alone, and entered the village on silent footsteps.

He stopped at the entrance of the big gathering hall. Hangman couldn't tell what Kuvik saw in there. He went very still and quiet staring through the door. Was something wrong?

He shook himself in a minute, turned aside, and dropped on one knee there. He rummaged in his shoulder bag, pulled something out, and set his torch alight.

The flames reared up and cast his face in a haunted glow. He looked so much deadlier like this.

The flash of those flames set off everyone else in the band. The men dropped out of the canopy, swarmed the village, and spread out among the houses with every weapon drawn.

Kuvik stormed through the building touching his torch to planks, bundles of thatch, and anything wooden he could find.

He started with the big gathering hall, ran his torch along the walls, and touched it to the eaves under the roof.

He split away and hustled from house to house setting them all on fire. The flames consumed the gathering hall in seconds, raced up the walls, and engulfed the roof. No one came out of there.

Hangman cast his eye over the rest of the buildings in the village. Any second now....

A door burst open on his right. Flickering yellow-orange flames glowed on the other side of the main room.

A man and a woman charged outside followed by three children. Hangman raised his kukris—and then saw bruises all over the prisoners.

The man actually wore a rough loincloth made out of hides. It was an identical loincloth Hangman had seen every Godless man wearing all his life.

The woman wore tattered rags over her emaciated limbs covered in black bruises. The children weren't much better off.

Hangman froze with his weapons raised to strike—and then three Bounty Hunters rushed from the house behind the captive family.

He dove in, swung, and took down one of the Bounty Hunters right there on the doorstep. Neither of the other two brought a single weapon. They raised their arms to protect themselves.

Hangman showed no mercy. Attacks and battles broke out all over the village as more Bounty Hunters emerged to escape the flames. The Godless attacked and leveled every enemy the minute they appeared.

Hangman raced from house to house. He had to pause multiple times to avoid cutting down all the captives. He never dreamed there would be so many.

They crowded out of the burning houses all mixed up with the Bounty Hunters. None of these people expected an attack like this.

The sounds of combat erupted behind Hangman's back, but he couldn't even look around him. His men rampaged through the village killing anywhere and everywhere.

Hangman came to the last house. The door stood open. A bunch of dead Bounty Hunters lay sprawled on the doorstep.

He turned around......and came to a stop. His arms sank to his sides still holding his blood-stained kukris.

A few hundred captives stood around in the center of the village. They huddled together holding onto each other and watching all those houses go up in flames.

Hangman didn't see any Bounty Hunters still standing.

Kuvik raced up to him. "We need to get to the other village before someone warns them that we're here!" He spun backward and raised his voice to call out. "We're here to get all of you out—but we need your help to finish off the other village! Come with us, put an end to these Bounty Hunters—and then you can all go home!"

Those words electrified the captives. They all burst into excited talk, rushed away, and came back with hand tools and a few weapons.

Kuvik rushed to the front of the crowd and called them all to follow him. The captives raced after him into the trees on their way to the other village.

Hangman and his men hung back. Hangman wasn't sure if he should go with these captives. He didn't really want to see what they did over there to their former captors.

He exchanged glances with Cross and Viking. The men followed at a distance.

Kuvik and the freed captives had already set fire to the second village by the time Hangman and his men got there. The captives went from house to house.

The former captives knew exactly who to kill and who to keep alive. They worked methodically through the village putting an end to everyone who held them as prisoners.

The party reassembled in the center of the second village. "You're all free to go home to your own Clans!" Kuvik announced. "If any of you doesn't have a place to go, you can come with us to Godless country. You'll be welcome there and you have my word no one will harm you."

Murmuring broke out among the former prisoners. Kuvik wandered over to Hangman while they waited for everyone to decide what to do.

"Are you sure about this?" Hangman murmured out the side of his mouth. "There are way too many people here. We wouldn't be able to take all of them."

The former captives answered him by splitting up their group. People started to drift away. Men and women met up with each other and rejoined with their children.

Families departed. Individual people and couples split off and vanished into the trees going one way or the other.

Twenty people stayed behind when it was all said and done. They were an equal mix of men, women, and children. None of them connected up with each other. They were all totally unrelated.

They all looked so pathetically injured and starving that Hangman couldn't bring himself to leave any of these people behind.

He just said, "Let's go," and led everyone into the jungle.

Chapter 34

Kuvik went from one freed captive to another. They huddled under the trees out in the jungle. None of them could travel through the treetops. All the Godless prisoners left on their own.

Kuvik didn't recognize which Clans these people belonged to. None of them retained any sign of their former connections or origins.

They all wore rags and many of their injuries had suppurated or become so infected that these people probably wouldn't survive.

Cross went from person to person applying leaf paste to all their injuries. Red and his men built a fire in the center of their camp and boiled up batch after batch of Gooji juice to treat everyone.

Some of his men went hunting and cooked meat over the same fire to give these people a decent meal before they had to trek across country to meet back up with the rest of Hangman's band.

Kuvik made it back to the other side of the group where Hangman stood watching. "I'm starting to think you might have been right about this, Hangman," Kuvik murmured. "I don't know if any of these people can travel."

"They will be able to," Hangman replied. "Don't worry about them."

Kuvik looked up. "You don't regret bringing them?"

"Not at all. They'll be fine. They just need help. That's all."

"How can you be sure?"

"They'll be more bloodthirsty than any of us when it comes to fighting the Bounty Hunters. These people will help defend us and themselves. They'll be assets to our Clan. I'm certain of it."

Almost as if his words made it happen, Hammer and his men came out of the trees just then. They carried armloads of weapons taken from the Bounty Hunters' village.

The men lowered everything into piles next to the fire. "This is all we could find, but this should be enough," Hammer announced. "We brought a mix of weapons so everyone can get what they want. We didn't think anyone wanted to use spears."

"We don't want spears," Hangman decided. "Regular weapons are better. We saw that in the last battle."

He stepped out into the middle of the camp and turned around to face everyone.

"More Bounty Hunters will come after us as soon as we leave here," he told them. "They'll follow us, attack us, and try to retake you all. They'll also try to retake us, our wives, and our children. All of you need to be ready to fight to defend yourselves and our band. You all need to drink your Gooji juice, get something to eat, and then arm yourselves to be ready to move out. We have a long way to go and we can expect the Bounty Hunters to come after us."

Hammer came over to him. "I have an idea, Hangman."

Hangman bit back a grin. "Another one?"

"The Bounty Hunters know where we are—or where we were. They know where we're going. I suggest we divert and take a different route to your father's territory. We shouldn't go back to the main road. We should cut straight south from here. We'll enter your father's territory farther west, but then we can turn east and find our way back to where you want to go. The Bounty Hunters will look for us along our old route. They won't find us because we won't be there."

Hangman raised his eyes. "All right. Good idea. Take your men, go back to the building, and bring all the women and children here. We won't be ready to move for a while anyway. We have some time before we need to worry about any Bounty Hunters coming for us."

Hammer only nodded and he and his men took off through the canopy. The former captives watched them go. "That's incredible," one of the men breathed. "How do they do it?"

"They learned," Hangman told him. "None of them were born knowing how to do it. Those men came to live with us when they were fourteen—and Kuvik here came to us when he was much older. He learned.....didn't you, Kuvik?"

Kuvik nodded. All the captives turned around to stare at him. "You were a captive in the village, too, weren't you?" one of the women breathed. "I remember seeing you there."

"Yes, I was." Kuvik fought his voice under control. "That's how I knew where to come back to get rid of these bastards."

"Teach us how to travel through the branches like that," the same man insisted.

"I will, but I won't do it tonight," Hangman replied. "You all need to regain your strength and recover from your injuries. Get some food into your stomachs first."

"Where will we go after this?" one of the young boys asked. "We have nowhere to go."

"Our band is traveling south to my father's territory," Hangman replied. "We'll have to avoid the Bounty Hunters and fight them when we can't avoid them—and all our other enemies—but that's nothing every other Clan doesn't have to deal with. At least you're free now."

Red went around with another dose of Gooji juice just then. None of the freed captives talked much after that.

They took Hangman at his word, ate a lot, and drank a lot of Gooji juice. Red and his men had to work in shifts to gather enough sap, boil enough juice, and hunt and cook enough food for everyone.

The captives crashed hard as soon as they got some food in their stomachs. The Gooji juice also knocked them out while their bodies recovered from all their injuries.

Kuvik scaled into the canopy and patrolled the area while he waited for the captives to wake up.

Hammer returned with the women and children on the second morning. The women and girls took over taking care of the freed captives, feeding everyone, brewing gallons of Gooji juice, and filling the new people in on how the band did things according to Godless law.

Two men and two women left when they heard about how the Godless lived and the rules of initiation, gathering, and everything else.

These four people didn't explain why they left and no one asked. Kuvik didn't feel any inclination to keep them around. He didn't want anyone around who didn't express as much enthusiasm as he felt for the Godless.

How could anyone complain about the Godless after what these people just suffered at the Bounty Hunters' hands? These people thought they could go it alone and pick and choose which Clan was the best.

The Godless didn't mistreat anyone. They didn't force themselves on helpless women and girls. Kuvik didn't need to know anything else about them to know they were the best Clan.

The band moved out on the third morning. The party headed due south from the Bounty Hunter's village.

The men scouted far and wide for any sign of pursuit, but no one pursued. Kuvik took the opportunity of one of these scouting runs to return to the Bounty Hunter village alone. He descended to the ground and walked right into the village. It was completely deserted.

The gathering hall had burned to the ground with all the Bounty Hunters asleep inside it. A bunch of charred human bones stuck out of the mountain of ash and charcoal.

Kuvik felt absolutely no remorse when he stood next to the pile and stared down at bare skulls and a few feet poking into view. Good riddance.

Most of the other houses had burned down, too. Nothing remained of the second village where all the fancy people lived. Nothing moved here. No one lived here.

He really wished he could go through the whole Bounty Hunter Clan and burn it all to the ground, but he didn't even know where to look for them.

He would kill any of them that showed their faces to him in the future. He wouldn't spare a single one of them—but he would get as many of their captives free as he could.

He caught up with the band and traveled with them for a while. The freed boys and young men practiced climbing trees and traveling through the canopy when their strength started to return.

The youngest children still had to travel on the ground, but Hangman always camped in the trees.

He sent parties of men out to hunt, cook the food on the ground, and dry the meat for traveling rations. He didn't let anyone else stay on the ground overnight.

The party traveled for another week before they crested the top of a tall mountain and faced the east.

Mora gasped. "This is it!"

"This is what?" Red asked.

"This is the Ashtaw Valley!" She pointed at the herds in the distance. "We came here before—to domesticate the Ashtaws."

"What does, 'domesticate,' mean?" Hammer asked.

"It means we tried to tame them—so we could ride them into battle against the Renegade Clan." Her face fell. "We didn't get to it, though."

"That sounds amazing!" Hammer exclaimed. "Could we do it?"

"It would take years—or at least a lot more time than we have to give to the project." Hangman turned sideways. "We'll deviate around the valley. We're too close to Shadow's territory. We should be there in a few days. We can't stop now."

He headed off down the ridge heading east. Mora, Hammer, and some of Hammer's men lingered. Mora stared down at the creatures for a few more minutes before she sighed and followed Hangman away.

Hammer stayed the longest. He frowned at the Ashtaws in the distance. The Godless couldn't even really see the creatures from here. Their enormous herds made a darker kind of cloud across the distant valley floor.

Hammer finally tore himself away and the whole party moved off. They followed the ridgeline around the valley to its eastern side where Hangman said they could descend into the jungle nearest Shadow's territory.

Chapter 35

Hangman squatted on a high rock and stared toward the east. He had to stop himself from racing down the mountains and rushing back to Shadow's territory right this very minute.

He had to sit and wait for the women and young children to get ready to move. They stopped and rested a lot and they always stayed a long time when they did.

Hangman always had to restrain himself from hurrying them away, but it got so much worse the closer he came to his father's territory.

The women and children needed more rest than the men. The children needed tending. Some needed to be carried while they slept during the middle of the day.

Hangman could have left his men to guard the band while he traveled forward to Shadow's territory. Hangman could have at least checked to see if Shadow's band was still in the area.

He just couldn't bring himself to leave Mora and the children. He didn't want to let them out of his sight unless he absolutely had to.

He found it impossible not to study the eastern horizon—as if he could see his family from here. He wouldn't see them. They might not even be there.

Kuvik came over and squatted down next to Hangman just then. Hangman forced himself to look away from the eastern horizon. "Did you circle the valley on the northern side?" Hangman asked.

"I just came back from there—and Hammer's band is over there scouting the route behind us."

Hangman nodded. His eyes already started to migrate eastward again. "We should get the women and children down into the jungle. We're far enough east now. We can leave the valley."

"Hangman....." Kuvik faltered. "I want to initiate into the Clan."

Hangman's head snapped around. He stared at his friend. "You do? That's wonderful!"

Kuvik looked away. "I might not be ready, but I want to."

"That's perfect, brother," Hangman exclaimed. "We'll do it tomorrow morning as soon as we get down into the jungle. We can't do it here on these heights."

Kuvik only nodded.

"I'm proud of you," Hangman told him. "You deserve this."

Kuvik gulped. "I know Yoa won't come of age for another three months, but I want to marry her. I need your permission."

Hangman opened his mouth—and stopped. What could he say? What *should* he say?

The band would go back under Shadow if Hangman had his way. Yoa would go to the gathering either way. The band was too far south not to take her.

Hangman didn't get a chance to answer before Hammer and his men came running up the slopes behind the band. Hammer charged over to Hangman. "Bounty Hunters....." Hammer panted. "Coming down from the north."

Hangman shot to his feet. "Are they coming from the village?"

Hammer shook his head. "They're coming from the north-west—too far away from the village. They weren't following us until they found our tracks. They didn't know we were here. They were just traveling—but they're following our trail now."

Hangman spun around. "Everybody get down into the jungle—now! You women and children move out! Split up into your teams!"

Everyone got up at his word. No one complained or stayed behind.

Eight men had joined the band after the strike against the Bounty Hunters. Those eight acted as guards over the women and children while the Godless men defended the band's retreat.

Hangman turned back to his men. "Where are the Bounty Hunters?"

Hammer waved behind him. "At the head of the valley. They're climbing up to where we first spotted the Ashtaws."

Mora came up to them just then. "We should use the Ashtaws against them. It would tip the advantage in our favor. It will be the quickest way to win a decisive victory against them."

"We don't have time to domesticate the Ashtaws now," Hangman told her. "We only have a few hours at the most."

"We don't have to domesticate them," she insisted. "We only have to steer them to attack the Bounty Hunters in our place."

"How would we do that?" Hammer asked.

"We can use the head harnesses I told you about before—the ones that cover the Ashtaws' eyes."

"We would never get a harness on their head!" Lucky exclaimed. "Their heads are too high off the ground!"

"We can use Fogpo leaves to lure their heads close to the ground. Then we can put the harnesses on and mount the creatures to ride on their backs."

"You aren't riding on an Ashtaw's back," Hangman snapped. "You aren't going anywhere near them."

She only smiled at him. "You know what I mean."

"We would have to work fast," Viking pointed out. "We don't have much time."

"How would we mount them?" Prodigy asked. "We would need ladders or something to get up there."

"You can use the trees," Mora replied. "The women and I will use Fogpo leaves to draw the Ashtaws under the trees. We'll put the harnesses on the creatures' heads. Then you can climb down the trees and get on the creatures' backs. You'll take the ropes and ride the Ashtaws against the Bounty Hunters."

Hangman scowled at her. "I don't like this."

She raised both hands. "It's just an idea. It would drive the Bounty Hunters off and stop them from following us."

"If it worked, you mean," Red corrected.

"All right. We'll do it," Hangman decided. He pointed at Mora. "Get down in the jungle with the women and start constructing the head harnesses. We'll gather as much Fogpo as we can. Then you and the women will have to lure the creatures to the tree line. Red, you take your men to the north and keep an eye on the Bounty Hunters. Send us back messages when they come within range."

Mora raced away. "This is insanity," Viking murmured.

"I think it's a great idea," Hammer exclaimed. "This is the perfect way to defeat the Bounty Hunters."

"It's a fantasy," Viking countered. "It can't possibly work."

"Not at all," Hammer insisted. "It might take a little longer. We might not be able to do everything now in the next couple of hours, but it would work better if we had the time to put into it."

"We don't have the time to put into it." Hangman turned away. "Get down to the jungle and gather as much Fogpo as you can find. Bring it up here so the women can use it when they're ready."

Everyone got to work. Hangman helped the men cut and gather dozens of Fogpo branches. Then he went down to the jungle to check on the women.

The children helped out cutting vines and leaves from the undergrowth. The women cut up extra pieces of hide and even their own traveling shoulder bags to make the head harnesses for the Ashtaws.

"How many Ashtaws will we want to capture?" Mora asked him.

"However many harnesses you can make in the time before the Bounty Hunters get here."

"We'll make ten," she decided. "That should be enough and it won't take too long.

He watched her direct the other women. She came up with a design with two long ropes threaded through the harness. The ropes had to be extra long to reach from an adult Ashtaw's head down to its back.

The ropes opened or closed flaps that covered the creatures' eyes. She claimed that would steer the Ashtaw in whichever direction it could see.

Hangman started to have a bad feeling about this. It was far from a perfect system. This method of steering the creatures didn't control how much they would turn in any direction nor did it control their speed.

The rest of the band couldn't be more enthusiastic, especially Hammer. He got all involved in designing and improving the harnesses. He wouldn't stop talking to Mora about how it worked and how to maneuver the creatures.

Hangman got another powerful sense that he wouldn't be able to stop Hammer from doing anything he really wanted to do.

Any other Kral would have brought Hammer to heel a long time ago. Any other Karl would have taken steps to stop Hammer from developing his own authority and his own independent faction within Hangman's band.

Hangman couldn't bring himself to regret any of this—especially not Hammer's independence. Hangman felt nothing but pride when he saw Hammer and his men acting on their own, making their own decisions, and even moving away from the rest of Hangman's people.

Hammer would make a good Kral. At least Hangman knew he would be able to hand off the band to a qualified leader if anything happened to him.

Hammer and his men got so excited about riding the Ashtaws that Hangman wouldn't have to do it. The band didn't have enough men.

The women constructed the harnesses much more quickly than Hangman expected. Then Hammer and his men held a discussion about who would ride the creatures.

They selected Hammer, Cross, Kuvik, and half of Hammer's men for the first trial run. "We might all fall off on our first attempt," Hammer remarked. "We would need time to practice."

"You might not have time," Hangman pointed out. "None of us has time. Let's go see how these things work before the Bounty Hunters get here."

Chapter 36

Mora and a bunch of the women went with the men to the rim of the valley. The Ashtaws grazed directly below this peak.

"You and your men should go down there and climb into the trees," she told Hammer. "We'll lead the Ashtaws to you, harness them, and you can climb down onto their backs."

"How will you give us the ropes?" he asked. "The creatures are bound to raise their heads as soon as they feel the harnesses on them. We'll be too high for you to hand us the ropes—and the creatures could stomp around and run for it. You would have to get out of the way so they don't trample you."

She found herself smiling at him. His enthusiasm for this project became infectious. She really hoped it worked.

"I have an idea," Vina interjected. "You men could carry the harnesses into the trees with you and let them hang by the ropes. Then we can slip the harnesses over the creatures' heads and you would already be holding the ropes in your hands when you climb down."

Hammer nodded. "That could work. We would need to time it so we get on the creatures' backs at exactly the same time when you harness them. They'll likely get agitated from both."

"Let's try it," Mora told him. "We're likely to experience some setbacks. We can see what happens and perfect our technique."

"We'll have to perfect it quickly," Kuvik interrupted. "Here comes Legacy."

Legacy reported to Hangman on the Bounty Hunters' position. They were still working their way around the valley covering all the territory Hangman's band traveled over to get here.

Hangman didn't tell everyone that the Bounty Hunters were close enough to threaten the party. The Godless still had some time.

Hammer and his men took the harnesses down to the trees. Mora and the women picked up the Fogpo branches and set off down the hill toward the Ashtaw herd.

"I sure hope you're right about this, Mora," Vina breathed.

"I've done it a million times. Getting the Ashtaws to follow us is the easy part. The men have the hard job in actually trying to ride these creatures."

The women fell silent when they got near the enormous herbivores. The Ashtaws raised their heads.

Then came the inevitable moment when the Ashtaws realized the women were carrying Fogpo branches. A bunch of Ashtaws turned around and lumbered toward the women.

"Turn around!" Mora ordered. "Head back to the jungle! Walk slowly! Don't run! Stay calm!"

"How can we stay calm?!" Vina squeaked. "They're huge!"

"Don't look at them," Mora ordered. "Face front and pretend the Ashtaws aren't there."

The Ashtaws' heavy pounding footsteps made them impossible to ignore. The women kept whimpering in terror, but they stayed calm and walked up the hill, topped the rise, and headed down the other side.

The Ashtaws darted their heads down to snatch mouthfuls of Fogpo leaves. Some of the creatures did this forcefully enough to actually rip whole branches out of the women's hands.

The women resupplied themselves at the top of the ridge. Far too many Ashtaws followed them all the way down to the jungle.

Mora spotted the harnesses dangling from the branches. She and the other women headed that way, stopped there, and dropped the Fogpo branches on the ground.

The Ashtaws acted exactly the way Mora expected. They lowered their giant heads to munch the leaves. She snatched the nearest harness and yanked it over the creature's head. Her actions interfered with its meal.

The Ashtaw jerked its head back the way Hammer knew it would. The creature snorted and tried to shake the harness off just as Cross dropped out of the canopy and landed on the creature's back.

The creature rumbled deep in its chest, reared away, and tried to shake Cross off, but he stayed on. He pulled one of the ropes and the creature veered to the right.

Mora had to dive out from under the creature's giant feet. It stamped down hard, wheeled, and took off in the direction he steered it.

The other women followed the same procedure. The men landed on the Ashtaws' backs, took the reins, and all the creatures charged back out into the open.

The men scrambled to steer the creatures where they wanted to go. Chaos ensued for a second and Kuvik's mount charged up the slope heading back toward the valley. Mora couldn't tell if he steered it that way or not.

Some of the men had better success than others. Cross's mount seemed the most cooperative. The creature kept charging forward and suddenly stopping, but it always ran where he wanted it to go.

Hammer's mount ran around and around in circles. It always seemed to go in the opposite direction from where he tried to steer it.

The Ashtaws blundered around in the open for a minute—until all the Ashtaws saw Kuvik's mount running back up the slope to the valley.

The men struggled to control their mounts. The whole project looked like it would descend into chaos, and at that moment, all the Ashtaws took off to follow that one enormous female back to the valley they knew so well.

Mora and the other women raced after them. Mora didn't know what she would be able to do to salvage the situation. She mostly just wanted to be on hand to help any of the men if they fell off and injured themselves.

The mounted Ashtaws made it to the top of the ridgeline. Mora stopped short and her breath caught when she saw Red and the other scouts racing up the ridgeline coming from the northern side of the valley.

They would only be coming back in a group like that for one reason. No one had to ask. The Bounty Hunters followed them also running fast. The Bounty Hunters closed the gap.

Red spotted the Ashtaws ahead—and then he saw the women. He yelled to his men and they all diverted down into the valley. Mora and the women dropped back, but she just couldn't bring herself to leave.

Hammer's mount made it up the ridgeline and he saw the Bounty Hunters pursuing Red's party down the hill toward the herd. Hammer yanked one of his reins, called to the other riders, and his mount actually obeyed him for once.

The Ashtaw swerved hard to the left. The creature didn't stop thundering over the countryside to rejoin the herd.

All the men signaled their mounts to go that way and the Ashtaws copied Hammer's mount. They all charged to the left and picked up speed as they pounded down the hill into the valley.

The Bounty Hunters didn't notice anything until they made it halfway down the slope toward the herd. The noise attracted the rest of the Ashtaws and they all looked up.

Mora and the other women struggled to the top of the rise and hid behind the hillside to watch. The mounts plowed into the Bounty Hunters and trampled most of them. A few ran for it.

Hammer tried to steer his mount back around to go after the survivors, but the noise triggered a stampede in the rest of the herd.

Four men got caught in the rush. Their mounts wouldn't divert no matter what the men did. All the grazing Ashtaws broke into a run. Those four plunged into the middle of the herd. Mora lost sight of them.

Hammer's mount wheeled when he signaled it to go. Then it skidded to a halt and floundered to understand what was going on. It heard its comrades running away, but the harness stopped the creature from seeing anything.

Cross's mount behaved perfectly. So did Scarecrow's and so did Ant's. The three of them barreled back up the valley and went after the rest of the Bounty Hunters. Scarecrow's mount didn't stop when it got near the enemy.

He dove off, rolled on the grass, and sprang to his feet in front of the Bounty Hunters. He engaged with them, but Cross's mount got there before the fight could escalate.

He steered his mount right and left in a perfectly coordinated attack pattern. His Ashtaw trampled Scarecrow's adversaries and then Cross went after the others.

He tracked them all down until he finished them all—but he and Ant were the only two of the original ten riders still sitting on their mounts.

Hammer and other men jumped off when their mounts ran out of control to rejoin the herd. The four men whose mounts ran off into the stampede didn't come out of it.

The men rejoined. Hammer ordered Cross and Ant to dismount. Their Ashtaws just stood there in docile silence. They didn't stampede.

The men eventually hiked back out of the valley and rejoined the women on the ridge. Kuvik, Lucky, Pitch, and Omen were all gone.

Hammer turned back to cast one last look down at the herd. "Well, it worked," he murmured. "We better go report to Hangman."

He hesitated just long enough for Pitch and Lucky to come into view down there. They walked along the high slope inside the valley—out of the Ashtaws' path.

Hammer waited there for the twins to join him. "Where are the others? Where are Omen and Kuvik?"

"We didn't see them," Pitch replied. "We didn't even see each other until it was all over."

The group waited a little longer. Neither Omen nor Kuvik reappeared.

Hammer sighed. "We better go."

Chapter 37

Hammer cringed when he saw Omen standing in the Godless camp when the party returned to the jungle. Omen stood there talking to Hangman and Viking. Omen must have returned by another route.

Yoa noticed the group first. "Where's Kuvik?!" Her voice started rising. "Where's Kuvik, Hammer?!"

"I don't know," he mumbled. "The herd stampeded....."

She rushed from man to man and then from woman to woman as the party rejoined the rest of the band. "Where's Kuvik?! Where's Kuvik?! What happened to him?!"

"His mount ran out of control when the herd stampeded," Mora told her. "Pitch and Lucky got caught in the same stampede......"

Yoa barely heard her. Yoa kept barging from one person to the next, grabbing them, and demanding to know where Kuvik was. Everyone could see he wasn't here.

Hammer and his men went over to Hangman, but Omen must already have told Hangman what happened.

Yoa rushed over to them before Hammer had a chance to say a word. "We have to go out and find him!" she blurted out. "We have to find him!"

"I'll go," Hammer offered. "We'll go search for him. He can't be too far away."

"I'm going with you!" Yoa snapped. "We have to find him!"

"No, we can't," Hangman countered. "The Bounty Hunters could have sent out another party. The band has to stay together."

"But...we have to!" she blurted out. "We can't just leave him out there! He could be hurt—or lost—or anything!"

Hangman locked his eyes on her, but he didn't reprimand her. He lowered his voice to a soft murmur. "It's too dangerous, Yoa. Kuvik has been hurt and lost before and still found his way back to us. He wouldn't want us to risk the whole band to go looking for him. He wouldn't want me to let *you* risk yourself to go looking for him. We have to keep moving east. We might find Shadow's band and join forces. Then we'll stand a better chance against the Bounty Hunters. If it works, we can come back another time and look for him. Come on. Let's get out of here."

"He was going to initiate!" She broke down sobbing. "He was going to initiate!"

Hangman took a step forward, put his arm around her, and gave her one quick squeeze before he turned away.

He waved at Hammer. "Take your men out there, scout the north side of the valley, and make sure no other parties of Bounty Hunters are moving in on us. Keep your eyes open for any sign of Kuvik, but don't deviate to go looking for him. That could leave the whole band unprotected."

He turned away and gave orders to the rest of the band. Yoa stood there wailing and wringing her hands until her mother came over to get her. She took Yoa back to their family.

Yoa didn't stop crying even after the band moved out. Hammer retreated and took his men back to the ridge. They didn't see any sign of Bounty Hunters—not here, anyway.

The Godless men didn't see any sign of Kuvik, either. "It seems a shame not to go looking for him," Scarecrow remarked. "He's such a good man."

"He's tough," Hammer replied. "Hangman is right. Kuvik has suffered worse than this and still come back. The Ashtaws wouldn't have carried him too far away. He'll probably catch up with us in a few days."

"Did you know he planned to initiate?" Ant asked.

"This is the first I've heard of it," Hammer replied.

"I bet you anything Yoa had something to do with it," Pitch suggested. "He probably wants to get married when the time comes."

Hammer didn't answer. His mind immediately switched back to Vina. Yoa would come of age first, but Vina and the other girls would catch up pretty soon. Then they would go to the gathering and leave Hammer and his men out in the cold.

He made up his mind to the same resolution he'd made a hundred times before. He would see what happened when Hangman took the band back to Shadow's territory.

Shadow's band might not be there—or Shadow might be agreeable to Hammer and his men marrying these girls.

That would never happen. Hammer already knew that. These young couples developed in isolation from any Clan. None of them would have gotten together if they had met anywhere near a gathering.

He told his men to get moving. They circled the valley and then traveled all the way back over the territory to where they had first discovered the Bounty Hunters approaching. The men didn't find anything there.

They didn't catch up with Hangman and the others until close to sunset. The women and children begged him to stop, but he wouldn't let them until they emerged from the jungle into a clearing—a big clearing.

The party stopped there and everyone looked around. Blackened circles marked different spots around the area. Plants and seedling trees sprouted between a few charred posts sticking out of the ground. The jungle was already starting to encroach and grow back.

"What is this place?" Red asked.

"This is Shadow's long camp," Mora murmured. She walked over to one of the burned-down piles of charcoal. "Our house was here. Shadow lived over there with his wife."

She bent over and picked up a fragment of metal from the cold, dead embers. A rectangular corner of a Renegade blade shone in the sun. "They must have attacked again," she murmured.

No one else moved for a second. Shadow's band wasn't here.

Hangman shook himself sooner than anyone expected. "Keep heading east," he ordered. "We'll camp in the jungle. We can fall back fortified valleys farther east. We can take refuge there even if Shadow's band isn't there."

No one argued or complained or asked for it to be different. The band filed into the jungle east of the long camp. They didn't stop for another mile. A heavy silence hung over Hangman all evening. He didn't say a word to anyone, not even Mora or his children.

The others organized the camp and assigned themselves to watches to keep track of the surrounding terrain.

Hammer took charge of his men so Hangman didn't have to. He must have prepared himself for something like this—ever since Red and his men found Thunder's band gone.

It could happen to anyone. That was the risk of leaving one's family even for a day. Nothing could guarantee that they would be there when you came back for them.

Red and the others would never find out what happened to their families. The men had all given up on that a long time ago.

Everyone spoke in low murmurs so they didn't disturb Hangman. Hammer and his men left to patrol the area. They ranged farther afield than they normally would have.

Hammer split his men, sent some of them all the way back to the Ashtaw Valley, and sent another group westward to check out the situation in Renegade territory closer to the mountains Hangman called the Jagged Points.

Both patrols came back at dawn and reported that both the Bounty Hunters and the Renegade Clan were moving eastward.

Hammer returned to the band, but he didn't tell Hangman about what the men found out. Hammer sat near Hangman's family and shared their food. He didn't say anything until morning.

Hangman woke up first and went back to brooding while he stared into the distance. Hammer didn't disturb him. Hammer braced himself to take over defending the band against its enemies.

Hangman startled him out of his senses by jolting to life, turning around, and asking, "What's the position west of here? What are the scouts finding out there?"

"The Bounty Hunters and the Renegades are both moving against us—but they aren't together," Hammer replied. "The Bounty Hunters are north of the valley moving on the same southeast line as the last group. The Renegades are west and south of the valley. We don't know yet if they know about each other, but they both know about us."

Hangman nodded. He bounced back much more easily than Hammer feared. "I've been thinking you're right about the creatures. They're our best chance to defeat our enemies, especially if the Renegades and the Bounty Hunters are working together—or if we have to fight them both."

Hammer's head shot up. "You want to use the creatures?! That's great."

"You and your men are the most enthusiastic about domesticating them. You should do that."

Hammer had a hard time hiding his excitement. "Okay. We can do that."

"You saw how Mora constructed those harnesses. Maybe you could consult with her about how to improve the design so you have more control over the creatures. She originally had the idea to capture some young ones, tame them, and raise them up so they're easier to handle. All of that will take time. We probably won't have time before we need to use the creatures against our enemies—but anything will be better than nothing."

"Um....okay. I can do all that." Hammer studied the side of Hangman's face. "Are you going to be okay?"

"I'm fine. I'll take the women and children to our protected lands farther east. I'm the only one who knows how to find them."

"That means my men and I will stay at the valley." Hammer thought fast.

His first thought was to keep Vina and the other girls with him just in case Shadow really was in the east country and got any crazy ideas about keeping the girls there. Hammer couldn't come right out and say that, though.

"I'll drop off the women and children where we know they'll be safe—either with Shadow's band or somewhere they'll be protected,"

Hangman went on. "Then the rest of the men and I will come back and join you. Our plan will be to hold both Clans at the valley so they don't penetrate any deeper into Godless country."

"Okay. I understand." Hammer hesitated. "I'll take the men out there now. We'll meet you back there."

Hangman nodded. "Get started on the creatures now—but talk to Mora first. Get her ideas. Then you'll be able to implement them depending on how the creatures behave."

Hammer tracked down Mora. She spent an hour drawing pictures in the dust of what she called, 'bridles'. They were a different kind of head harness with a bar that fit inside the creature's mouth.

"That's how you control the speed and direction," she told him. "You pull back on the reins to make the creature slow down or stop. Then you pull their head from one side to the other to make them go that way—but you have to train them to do what you want."

"How do you get them to speed up or go?" he asked.

She laughed. "The ancients used to kick the creature with their heels. That might work with an Ashtaw—or you could also use a small rope to whip their sides."

"Wouldn't that send them running out of control? The pain would startle them."

"The Ashtaws' skin is so thick I don't think they would even feel it—or you could train them so you only had to give them a light flick to signal them to speed up. You're going to have to improvise and make it up as you go along. We don't know anything about these creatures. No one has ever domesticated them before. It's going to take a lot of trial and error before you get a herd of mounts you can actually use in battle—and don't forget you're going to have to actually train them for combat. Riding them around is one thing. You'll have to train them to stay calm when an enemy attacks you and probably attacks your mount, too."

Hammer furrowed his brow and scratched the back of his neck. "It's a lot more complicated than I realized."

"You're going to be great. Just think how much more powerful we'll be when we use these creatures against our enemies."

"That's what I am thinking about."

She patted him on the shoulder. "You better get out there and get started. You know where to find me if you need any more information."

He stopped at the edge of the jungle and looked back at Vina for longer than he should have before he left the band and took his men west to the valley.

This Ashtaw project better not be a way to separate him from her—or any of his men from their sweethearts.

Hammer didn't suspect Hangman of trying to separate them, but Hammer didn't like where this was going. He might have to take drastic action if it ended badly.

Chapter 38

The Godless men crouched in the treetops and looked down over a different valley. This one sat behind the Ashtaw Valley to the west.

This was technically Renegade country, but the Godless men could clearly see the Bounty Hunters moving in on a party of Renegades in the middle of the valley.

"Those Bounty Hunters don't care who they steal from, do they?" Wildling remarked. "No one is safe from them."

"This could work in our favor," Hangman remarked.

"How do you figure?" Hammer asked.

"They'll be fighting each other pretty soon. Then the Renegades will find out that Bounty Hunters are in the area. The Renegades will try to counterattack against the Bounty Hunters."

"That won't make them forget about us," Viking pointed out. "They could decide to join forces against us."

"Then we'll have to make sure they don't. They won't fight each other forever. Then we'll come around and attack both of them. We'll make each Clan think the other is attacking them. We'll distract them with each other. That will stop them from coming after us."

"How do you want to do that?" Hammer asked.

"I want you and your men to go back to the valley the way we planned. Use Fogpo leaves to capture as many young Ashtaws as you can handle. They don't have to be big—just big enough to carry your weight. We'll start training them young so they get used to it. They'll understand as they get older that they have to keep doing it."

"What do you want me to do with them once I capture them?"

"Take them down into the eastern jungle and keep them there—or better yet, take them back to our camps in the east. You can follow the track left by the women and children. Mora and the other women can help you tame the creatures. They'll be able to start training them even when you aren't there."

Hammer's heart leapt. He already knew Hangman wasn't trying to keep him away from Vina.

A clash of weapons broke out in the distance. All the men faced front to watch the battle between the Renegade Clan and the Bounty Hunters.

The Renegade Clan took the early upper hand. The Bounty Hunters insisted on using their spears. They left the Bounty Hunters at a disadvantage when it came to close combat.

The Renegade Clan's superior metal weapons cut straight through the spear shafts, severed the spearheads from their shafts, and disarmed the Bounty Hunters.

That didn't stop them or slow them down. They brought their prisoner-slaves with them carrying bundles of weapons.

The Bounty Hunters fell back closer to the Godless' hiding place, rearmed with stolen blades, and forced their captives to fight on their side.

"We should fall back, too," Hangman decided. "We don't want them to get too close to us."

The Godless fell back, but not fast enough. They took off through the canopy, but the battle overran their position in no time.

"Keep going!" Hangman whispered to Hammer. "Get those creatures out of the valley before these men get there!"

Hammer and his band streaked away. Hammer didn't like leaving Hangman and the others in danger, but the chance to tame these creatures overpowered every other consideration.

The men raced through the canopy. It took them a long time to circle the valley back to the eastern jungle.

"Half of you get started gathering as much Fogo as you can carry," he told his men. "The other half of you start weaving as much rope as possible. We're going to need a lot of both."

He didn't stand around to give any other orders. He went to work with the others cutting Fogpo and stacking the branches behind the valley rim.

He copied everything Mora did last time. She had the right idea about starting with what the band already knew and modifying it depending on what worked and how well.

The men also amassed a giant pile of Fogpo branches inside the jungle itself to feed the young Ashtaws once the men caught them. Mora's stories about keeping her young Ashtaw calm with a steady supply of food made the most sense to Hammer.

It took a few hours for the men to braid enough rope even to approach the valley rim. The herd was back. "Kuvik isn't here," Stray murmured.

"We aren't here to worry about him," Hammer ordered. "Take your ropes and your Fogpo. Concentrate on the young ones—anything big enough to carry your weight. Distract them with food, rope them, and lead them away from the herd. We'll get as many as we can."

The men coiled their ropes and hung them from their waistbands so the Ashtaws wouldn't notice anything out of the ordinary.

Each man took a branch and carried it down to the valley floor. The Ashtaws were starting to understand that people coming from that direction meant food.

The Ashtaws broke away from the herd and came forward long before the men got there. Hammer got occupied feeding a huge female Ashtaw who devoured his branch in no time.

She had two young at foot—a newborn juvenile as tall as Hammer and another older juvenile from last year. The older one towered almost to his mother's shoulder. He was way too big.

The two juveniles bumped Hammer out of the way trying to horn in on their mother's feast. Hammer slipped his rope off his waistband, unwound the noose, and slipped it over the little one's head before the creature noticed what was happening.

The three Ashtaws kept eating while Hammer picked up the rope and tightened his grip on it. Now came the hard part.

He took a few steps forward to head back up the valley toward the jungle. The rest of his men also led young Ashtaws on the end of their ropes. The men captured ten Ashtaws. That was a pretty good haul for the men's first attempt.

Hammer only made it ten feet before a commotion broke out on the ridgetop farther north.

He looked up and saw Hangman's party in battle against a mixture of Bounty Hunters and Renegades. They all fought each other.

The noise startled the Ashtaws. The mother Ashtaw turned away and lumbered back toward the herd. Her two young ones tried to copy her.

The little Ashtaw yanked the rope nearly out of Hammer's hands. He held on and the little Ashtaw squawked when it couldn't rejoin its mother right away.

Hammer reacted by thrusting the Fogpo leaves in the creature's face. The leaves distracted the little one for a second.

Hammer started walking again. He kept the branch close enough to the creature's face to keep it moving at the same pace. He only hoped the leaves lasted long enough for him to get the little creature over the ridge.

The other men did the same thing. They separated their captured Ashtaws from the herd and started working their way back toward the jungle.

Another clang of metal on metal alarmed the Ashtaws even more. The large adults started to stampede again in the other direction.

The little Ashtaw tried to turn around. The leaves no longer worked to cover up the fact that the creature's mother was running off in the opposite direction.

Hammer tried to tighten his grip on the rope, but even an Ashtaw this small overpowered him easily. The creature started to turn around to walk away from the ridge.

He sprang in front of it, around the creature's other side, and leaned all his weight against the creature's neck to make it run in the right direction.

The Ashtaw panicked and took off running its fastest. Only Hammer's efforts kept the creature running toward the ridge instead of breaking away.

He had to run along next to the creature to keep up with its speed, but it outpaced him pretty soon. He stumbled and went down hard, but he didn't let go of the rope.

He held on, fell on his face, and the Ashtaw kept charging away in the other direction. It dragged him a long way down the valley while the rest of the herd trampled off in the other direction.

The creature finally came to a halt far up the valley from where it started. No other Ashtaws were around. The creature shook its head to get the rope off. When that didn't work, the little Ashtaw looked around, didn't see its mother, and lowered its head to graze.

Hammer dragged himself to his feet feeling bruises all over his body, but at least he still had the little creature. He coiled up the rope and eased over to the creature.

The Ashtaw raised its head still munching a mouthful of grass. The Ashtaw must have remembered him feeding it. The creature didn't run away or even startle when he stopped next to its head and then touched its neck.

Its long neck bobbed the head back and forth above him. The creature's shoulder came up to his chest. He could easily have vaulted onto this creature's back. He didn't need to climb into the trees to mount it.

He would have to save that for another day. He turned around—and froze when he saw Hangman and the other men still locked in battle against the two enemy Clans.

Hammer's men were just leading their captured Ashtaws over the ridge and picking up fresh branches to lure the creatures into the jungle.

Hammer tugged the rope. "Come on, little brother. Let's go."

The Ashtaw followed him willingly. This was working so much better than Hammer realized—all except the part about Hangman having to fight the other two Clans.

Hammer planned to take the Ashtaws to the pile of Fogpo, restrain the creatures there, and then bring his men back out here to help Hangman.

Hammer met up with his men at the ridge just as Hangman, the other men and uninitiated boys, the Bounty Hunters, and the Renegades came around the rocks into view.

Everyone fought everyone else. Godless fought Renegades and Bounty Hunters. Bounty Hunters fought Godless and Renegades. Renegades fought Godless and Bounty Hunters.

Every fighter in the battle had to double-check his target before he attacked someone. The three Clans' clothing and appearance gave them away as friend or foe to whoever might be about to attack.

Hammer braced himself to drop the rope and maybe let the little Ashtaw run away so he could help defend his comrades. At that moment, another party of fighters leapt out of the surrounding rocks and landed in the center of the battle.

Hammer actually did drop the rope, seized his weapon, and sprang forward before he realized that the new party was another group of Godless men. They threw themselves into the battle fighting every Renegade and Bounty Hunter.

The Renegades and Bounty Hunters still had to fight each other. The new Godless swung the battle in their favor and eventually forced all the Renegades and Bounty Hunters to flee.

Chapter 39

R ed, Prodigy, and Carnage charged after the fleeing Renegades
and Bounty Hunters, but the new Godless standing in front
of Hangman consumed all his attention.

He turned around still holding his kukris. Dead Renegades and
Bounty Hunters lay all over the ground.

Cross charged the newcomers and threw his arms around an older
man with long, greying hair. "Father!"

Shadow pushed his son back and beamed at him with shining eyes.
"My son! Look how you've grown up!" Shadow turned to Viking and
hugged him, too. "Nephew! You're alive! I never thought I would see
you again."

Viking's voice broke. "We lost Alien, Uncle. I'm sorry."

"Never mind." Shadow turned to survey the rest of Hangman's
party. Shadow didn't know any of them.

Then his eyes locked on Hangman. A jet of fire stabbed Hangman
in the guts. His father was here. His family was alive after all.

The two men collided in a crushing hug. Hangman felt himself
starting to get emotional when he smelled his father's hair. It was the
smell of decades of his childhood just praying for the day when he
could go out hunting with his father and become a man in this Clan.

Tears stood in Shadow's eyes when he pushed Hangman back and gripped his shoulders. Shadow compressed his lips to hold back emotion.

Hangman couldn't say a word. He never really let himself believe he would see his father again.

"Is everyone alive?" Hangman finally choked. "Is Mother alive?"

"They're mostly all alive. We lost a few others." Shadow waved behind him. That's when Hangman noticed his cousins standing in the group.

Feather, Banjo, Devil, Breaker, and Grizzly all surrounded Hangman, Cross, and Viking. The cousins couldn't stop laughing in relief, hugging each other, and touching each other to make sure they were all real.

Hangman froze when he came face to face with a tall, well-built young man at the far end of the line. For a split second, Hangman mistook the guy for one of Hammer's men—but he wasn't one of Hammer's men. It was Hangman's younger brother Landus—the next youngest after Cross.

"His name is Bantam now," Feather murmured. "He's a proud man of the Godless Clan."

Hangman held out his hand to shake Bantam's hand. "I'm proud of you. I wish I could have been there." He pulled his brother into a hug and then everyone started talking at once.

Hangman introduced everyone in Shadow's party to Red, his men, and the uninitiated boys. Hangman told the story about rescuing Mora from the Renegades, freeing the captive women and children, and meeting Red and his men in the jungle near the ammunition dump.

Hammer and the others wandered over leading their captive juvenile Ashtaws while everyone talked. The little creatures munched the Fogpo leaves the men held out for them.

"What are you doing this far west—and this far south?" Hangman asked his father. "We came over here tracking the Bounty Hunters. They've been following us all the way south."

"That's why we're here," Shadow replied. "We came tracking the Renegades and found out about the Bounty Hunters pretty quick. We realized we better hold them here—and then we saw you."

"Where is the band camping nowadays? We went back to the long camp, but you weren't there. We feared the worst."

"We haven't lived there in a long time. We moved east to the gorges after you left. The long camp was too far west—too close to Renegade incursions. We have to travel farther out of our territory to engage with them, but at least our families are safe."

"That's what we were hoping. We want to join up with your band and take our families to the gorges, too. We've been traveling for too long."

Shadow nodded and turned aside to survey the rest of Hangman's men. "You have a good band here. They all look strong and determined."

He went through the group assessing each man with a practiced eye. He stopped in front of Hammer and the others. "What are you doing with these creatures?" Shadow demanded. "Let them go. We don't have time to mess around with them."

"We aren't going to let them go," Hammer fired back. "Do you know what it cost us to catch these creatures?"

"I don't care about that," Shadow snapped. "I said let them go. We have to withdraw from the area and these creatures are a waste of time...."

"No, they aren't," Hammer insisted. "We've already used them once against the Bounty Hunters. We saved our band with these creatures. It would be foolish to let them go now. All we have to do is....."

Shadow lowered his voice to a snarl that got everyone else's attention. "Did you just hear me tell you what to do, boy? You won't go anywhere near my family unless you accept me as your Kral. Now let the creatures go and don't make me tell you again."

Hammer's features closed up in a wall of granite. Hangman didn't spend the last five years watching this man grow up without understanding what that look meant.

Hangman raced over there and held out his hand to Shadow. "F ather....please....This is Hammer....and these are his men. He runs his own band. He has his own authority and makes his own decisions. You can't just order him around like an uninitiated boy."

"He is an uninitiated boy if he doesn't know enough to obey his Kral." Shadow spun around to glare at Hangman next. "Have you been acting as Kral of this band?"

"Hammer and I are joint Krals....."

"There is no such thing as joint Krals. Who's in charge—you or him? It doesn't matter because I'm the only Kral in this territory." Shadow turned back to glare at Hammer. "Let the creatures go right now or take your men out of my territory. I'll take it as an act of war if you set foot in my territory again."

Hangman turned to Hammer, but Hangman didn't have the heart to tell Hammer what to do. They had covered far too much ground together for that.

Hangman read the same truth in Hammer's eyes—the truth both men had been living with for the last four years. Vina and the other girls were back there in the gorges. Hammer could only get them by reentering Shadow's territory.

All of Hammer's men stood behind him watching and waiting to see what he would do. Hangman pleaded with his eyes for Hammer to let the creatures go, but Hangman couldn't make Hammer do anything. Hangman learned that a long time ago.

Hangman cringed when Hammer finally compressed his lips and pulled the rope off the creature's head. He pushed the creature's head away, waved his arms, and yelled out, "Yaa!!" to startle the creature into running off down the hill.

All his men copied him. The creatures galloped away into the valley. They were the only Ashtaws here now, but the others would come back pretty soon.

These young ones would rejoin their mothers and go back to their tranquil life as if none of this had ever happened.

Shadow didn't stick around to rub his victory in Hammer's face. Shadow turned away. "All of you pull back to the gorges. We'll decide how to come after these invaders, now that we have more men."

He stormed through the ranks flashing his eyes at everyone, returned to the rocks where he and his party first appeared, and climbed down them toward the northern side of the valley.

He struck off through the jungle heading back toward where the long camp used to be.

"You said you sent your women and children forward," Shadow barked over his shoulder. "Where are they?"

"I sent them east, but none of them knows the way to the gorges," Hangman replied. "Mora is with them, but she doesn't know the way, either."

"We'll track them and catch up with them. Maybe Katha and the other women will find them once they get close."

Hangman didn't reply. His ears became hyper-tuned to the silence behind him.

The party of men simmered with tension back there. He didn't have to turn around to see exactly what was happening or who it came from.

Every man in Hangman's band looked up to Hammer. This band staked their lives on Hammer and his men. Hangman respected Hammer too much to order him around like a child.

Red brought his band under Hangman from the very first day, but Hangman wouldn't have told any of them what to do like children, either.

Hangman wouldn't have objected one bit if Red wanted to keep his band separate from Hangman's. Hangman expected it.

He still found it impossible to believe that Red and his men even wanted to subordinate themselves to him. Hangman didn't blame Hammer and his men for wanting to stay independent. Hangman encouraged it even more than Hammer wanted it.

Things wouldn't go well between Hammer and Shadow if Shadow tried to flex that authority over Hammer. Hangman didn't expect the two men to come to loggerheads this soon, but he didn't see how they could avoid the inevitable break.

Hammer had a right to be proud of his authority and his men's support. He earned it a thousand times.

Why should he give it up—so some stranger could tell him what to do and humiliate him in front of his men? Hangman knew Hammer too well not to know how that would end.

Chapter 40

M ora turned a corner between high stone walls in the Godless country's eastern gorges. She held Zaedi and Thena by their hands, carried Maeno in his wrap, and glanced behind her to make sure the other women and children stayed with her.

Four older children from the Bounty Hunter's village usually stayed near her, too. One girl about ten years old held onto the strap of Mora's shoulder bag.

The other three were boys between eleven and thirteen. They didn't hold onto her. They just followed her everywhere she went.

None of the four had parents. The adults who left the Bounty Hunter's village to join Hangman's band didn't take any interest or offer any care to the children who escaped with them.

Mora had invited these four children to sit with her and share her food when they first joined Hangman's band. Now the four of them wouldn't leave no matter what she did.

They tried to help her with her work. They tried to play with Zaedi and Thena, too, to keep them occupied so Mora wouldn't have to do so much.

The four children didn't really know how to play. They didn't know how to talk to children. They were hardly children themselves.

The Godless children made these four extremely uncomfortable—probably because the four of them understood that they weren't normal children. They grew up in captivity doing slave labor. They didn't have childhoods.

Mora didn't ask what happened to the girl. No one asked and the girl didn't say. Mora tried to be extra kind to all four children. She really wished Kuvik was still here. He would have known how to deal with these children.

Kuvik wasn't here. The children seemed to need to be near her more than anything, so she let them. She gave them work to do whenever she could. She did her best to keep them occupied.

The adults who escaped from the Bounty Hunters seemed to have the same problem. They didn't know how to act around normal people. These adults seemed to have forgotten what their lives were like before their captivity.

Some couldn't remember the circumstances of their capture or even the details of how they'd been living or what happened to them in the Bounty Hunters' village.

Three of these people had completely blocked out everything that happened between the time of their capture and when the Godless rescued them and brought them to Hangman's band. Some of these people couldn't even remember which Clans they belonged to.

Everyone in the band tried to accommodate the new arrivals, get them involved in life, and give them plenty to do. That was all anyone could do for them.

Mora faced front. She really wished Hangman and the other men would come back. She didn't know where she should take these people. How far east should she go?

She turned another corner in the sandy stone walls—and stopped dead in her tracks when she came face to face with a bunch of Godless women. They squatted by a small stream washing hides in the water and refilling their water gourds.

"Katha!" Mora gasped. "Rila.....Niea....."

Katha got to her feet. A million questions and reactions raced across her face.

Then all the women rushed Mora, embraced her a million times, and asked a thousand questions while the women exclaimed over Mora's children.

She tried to explain everything at once, but nothing came out right. The rest of the women and children stood behind her watching and listening in silence.

Katha finally raised her voice. "Be quiet! I can't hear anything!"

The women settled down, but they kept whispering about the band.

"Where's Hangman?" Katha asked. "And Viking, Alien, and Cross?" Her eyes darted to the crowd behind Mora. "Who are all these people?"

"Alien is dead. I'm sorry. We lost him a few months ago in a Renegade attack. Viking, Cross, and Hangman went up to the Ashtaws' valley to see if the Bounty Hunters and the Renegades were following us. Hangman sent us east to see if we could find you. These people....." Mora hesitated. "It's a long story. They're in our band—Hangman's band. He's Kral of this band now. He has been for almost five years."

"Never mind about all that. You can tell us when we get to the camp." Katha raised her voice. "Come on, everyone! We'll take you to the gorges. You can rest there."

The women surrounded Mora again and started bombarding her with questions. Katha had to keep telling them to be quiet so Mora could answer.

She ran through the whole story as quickly as she could from Hangman and the others freeing her from the Renegades, the captive women and children joining them, Red and his party joining the band, and the band's four-year reprieve in Thunder's old mountain territory.

Then she described everything that had been going on with the Bounty Hunters including Kuvik's arrival, his capture and escape from the Bounty Hunters, and then leading the other men back to the Bounty Hunters' village to destroy as many of them as possible.

"That's amazing," Nagana exclaimed. "It's hard to believe it all happened in four years."

Mora squeezed her shoulder. "Viking will be coming home soon. He'll be so happy to see you."

Nagana blinked back tears and looked away. "I never thought I would see him again!"

Katha turned another corner between the cliffs and entered a narrow canyon much tighter than the valley in the mountains. The Godless made their camp here with four-walled permanent shelters for families.

Katha pulled Mora down onto the ground in front of one of the structures. "Now let me see these grandchildren of mine...." She pulled Zaedi toward her. "Do you know who I am, little one?"

Zaedi shook his head.

"This is Katha," Mora told the boy. "She's Hangman's mother—your grandmother. This is Hangman's family band."

Zaedi just stared at Katha. He didn't react to the news.

She laughed at him. "Go play. We'll talk another time."

Zaedi walked away. Thena came right up to Katha and frowned at her. "Did you carry Hangman around—like *that*?" The girl pointed to Maeno asleep in his wrap.

"Just like that." Katha laughed again. "It's hard to remember him being that small—and he wasn't scarred then. He looked just like this little angel." She stroked Maeno's head.

Thena furrowed her brow even more. "He wasn't scarred? He must have been."

"No, dearest, he wasn't born scarred," Katha exclaimed. "He got his scars at his initiation. Didn't he tell you?"

"Of course he did," Mora interrupted. "He's told them a hundred times."

"Your father used to look like Zaedi over there," Katha went on. "He was a beautiful boy."

"Have you all been here the whole time?" Mora asked. "Did you fall back here from the long camp?"

Katha opened her mouth to answer, but no sound came out. A hush fell over the camp when Shadow strode around the corner followed by Hangman and all the men of their combined bands.

Mora struggled to stand up and rushed over to hug Shadow. "You're alive! I never thought I would see you again!"

He beamed at her. "It's so good to see you happy and healthy—and look at this!" He laughed when he petted Maeno on the head.

Mora rushed through the group hugging all of Hangman's cousins. She didn't recognize the young man on the far end until Hangman introduced him and told her the young man was his younger brother Bantam.

"Come sit down," Shadow told her. "I'm sure you've all been on your feet enough these last five years."

He led the way back to the same shelter. Mora sat down next to Katha. Hangman sat down next to Mora. The rest of the party spread out through the camp.

Viking and Nagana rushed into each other's arms and didn't let go. They stood there in the center of the camp with their arms around each other for a long time before she finally broke away and led him back to their own house.

Cross and Bantam both sat near their parents. The rest of Hangman's band found places to sit down and tended their own families.

Hammer and his men scattered through the camp and sat with different people. Hammer went to sit next to Vina near her family. A few of his men joined their sweethearts, too.

Shadow's eyes hardened. "You haven't taken any of these young people to the gatherings. I would have seen you there."

"We couldn't," Hangman replied. "We were too far north or isolated inside Renegade country. There were no other people around from any Clans. We were alone. We only came back far enough south in the last couple of weeks."

"So....these young people.....they aren't married?" Shadow asked.

"Not yet, but they will be as soon as the girls come of age......"

Shadow shot off the ground in a heartbeat. He didn't even wait for Hangman to finish explaining.

A tense hush fell over the camp as Shadow stormed across it to where Hangman's people sat together. Shadow headed straight for Hammer first.

Everyone heard Shadow snap at Hammer in a brutal tone of command. "You get away from these underage girls—all of you. Go sit over there. These girls will go to the gathering this autumn as soon as they come of age. You're all too old to go. Keep away from them."

Hammer stiffened and raised his head to lock his eyes on Shadow. "That isn't the arrangement we made with Hangman. These girls are promised to us....."

"I didn't ask what arrangement you made with Hangman," Shadow snapped. "You're too old to marry—and we don't even know if you're truly Godless. You should all repeat your initiations before you can truly join our Clan. Get away from the girls now or you'll be outlawed from every Clan for the rest of your lives."

Mora cringed when Shadow stormed from one cluster to another pointing at all of Hammer's men and giving them the same order.

Shadow didn't see Hammer get to his feet. He didn't leave Vina's side—not for a second. He stayed where he was until Shadow inevitably saw Hammer still standing in the same spot.

Shadow barged back over there. He didn't see all of Hammer's men stand up, too. The air charged with danger.

No one else made a sound when Shadow stormed over to Hammer again. "I told you to get away from that girl, boy. Don't make me have to take disciplinary action against you."

Hammer took a step forward to confront Shadow. Then Hammer opened his hand and extended it backward toward Vina.

"You can't take disciplinary action against me," Hammer replied in a perfectly calm undertone. "I'm Kral of my own band and we're leaving. We'll never set foot in your territory again. You'll never see our faces. You don't have to worry about that."

Vina took his hand and stood up. She had to shake off her mother when her mother tried to stop her.

Hammer turned to walk away. Shadow dove in and tried to shove his arm between Hammer and Vina. "You walk away with your men," Shadow snapped. "You leave all the underage girls behind. That's the price you pay for going out on your own."

"You aren't Vina's Kral," Hammer replied. "You aren't Kral to any of us if we don't accept you. These girls go where they please. They can stay behind if they want to."

He turned to walk away again. Shadow had no choice but to put his arm down and let Vina walk away, too.

All of Hammer's men stepped out of place and came forward to join him. All the underage girls who had been waiting so long to marry these men also left their families and gathered in the center of the camp.

Lonion and Vuco joined Hammer's band, too—and then the other uninitiated boys stood up, too.

A few more unattached teenage girls joined them. Mora didn't realize so many of these young people followed Hammer's lead—but she should have expected it.

Her throat went dry when Cross stood up. He left his family sitting there stunned when he strode out into the circle and joined Hammer's band.

"Cross—no!" Katha called after him.

Cross ignored her, turned around to stand next to Hammer, and faced his father for the last time.

Cross's sweetheart Sema came out of the crowd and slipped her hand into his. Nothing would ever stop these young people from being together the way they all planned.

Hangman got to his feet last of all. He walked out there and stopped next to his father. They stood face to face with Hammer, Cross, and all the other men of Hammer's band. Hangman actually smiled at his brother and then at Hammer.

"Will you bring these boys in line?" Shadow snarled out the side of his mouth. "You're their Kral. You should make them obey."

"I told you I'm not," Hangman murmured under his breath. "Not even a Kral can tell another Kral what to do. I tried to warn you not to push him. You didn't listen. Now we don't have enough men to defend this camp from our enemies."

Hangman turned back to Hammer. Hangman's eyes softened and he held out his hand. "Travel safely," Hangman told him. "I know you'll be happy where you're going."

"Thank you—for everything." Hammer clasped his hand. "I wish you were coming with us."

"I'm where I need to be. Remember what I said and follow the law. Don't marry before the girls come of age."

"I won't," Hammer replied.

"You'll never get away with this," Shadow snarled. "You'll be shunned by all Godless everywhere—and all Clans everywhere. You'll never be able to bring your children to the gatherings. Your people will die out in the wilderness and everyone will forget you."

"We'll see about that," Hammer replied.

Shadow stormed back to his house and paced up and down, but no one paid any attention to him.

Hammer's eyes swiveled back to meet Hangman's and both men stepped forward to crush each other in a long, deep embrace. Neither of them let go too soon.

Then Hangman hugged Cross the same way. He held onto his brother for a long moment before they parted.

Hammer and his men turned to leave. Mora didn't see Shadow until he broke out of position, stormed up behind Hangman, and tried to make one more dive to stop the party from leaving. Mora couldn't tell if Shadow was trying to pull back Vina or Cross.

Hangman shot out his arm and blocked his father. The two men locked eyes in a moment of unwavering challenge on both sides. Hangman didn't look away until Shadow split off first and stormed back to the other side of the camp.

Hammer waved to those behind him and said, "Let's go."

The men in the rear led the girls out of camp one after the other. Hammer, Cross, and Vina left last.

Hammer waited for everyone else to leave before he paused at the corner where the cliffs led back toward the west. Hangman raised his hand one last time and Hammer's band passed out of sight forever.

<u>End of Book 3.</u>

Keep Reading

R ise of the Giants Series: Book 4: Forged in Blood

The brave warriors of Hammer's band of Godless Clan must forge their own path after separating from their families and the only life they've ever known. The world of dangers doesn't forgive the slightest error and Hammer must overcome countless obstacles just to keep himself and his comrades alive.

Hammer and his people return to the valley and get the idea to domesticate the Ashtaws the way Mora suggested. The project could take years and might even cost the men their lives, but this could be the secret to finally defeating the deadly enemies circling and trying to destroy the band.

Hammer must learn on the fly how to be the leader his people need him to be. He'll face challenges from the dangerous world around him and from internal conflicts and betrayals within his own band. Everything depends on him—including whether he and his people live or die.

You can find it at your favorite book retailer.

Sign Up Once--Get all Theo Mann's free books including brand new releases

S ign Up Once--Get all Theo Mann's free books including brand new releases

In a world where everything is out to kill you, humans must fight for survival every day against huge dangerous creatures and enemy Clans. The Godless Clan has enough to worry about already. They don't need to fight their own.

Sixteen-year-old Shadow knows exactly what to do when he discovers a girl from an enemy band hiding in the jungle. He takes her captive as a prisoner of war, but the Godless have a strict code of honor when dealing with women—even enemy women.

He and Katha will have to fight for their very survival and overcome generations of mistrust before they make it back to their people—who just might be the most dangerous enemies either of them has ever faced.

Sign up at www.theomann.com to read it for free

About Theo Mann

I write 70 books per year—and yes, before you ask, all these books are my original creative work. Nothing written under my name is AI-generated or ghostwritten because I write better than AI and any ghostwriter out there.

People don't read fiction for entertainment or to escape from reality. People read fiction to see their humanity reflected in another person's character and story.

This is my promise to you. When you read my books, you'll see your own humanity reflected in the characters and stories. I take this commitment to my readers very seriously. My books are an intimate form of communication between us. I would never disrespect my readers by turning that over to a machine or another writer. This is my bond between me and you as my reader.

I write 20,000 words per day as my daily work output. If anyone with a public platform would like to challenge me to prove this in a controlled environment, feel free to contact me on this website's contact page.

I worked as a professional ghostwriter for fifteen years. Now I'm on a mission to set a Guinness World Record by writing 700 books over the next ten years and 1400 books over the next twenty years, all originally written by me. See my website for the full book list.

I'm also the author of *Proof for the Existence of God* and the *Crimes Against Fiction* blog. You can find all my nonfiction work at www.crimes-against-fiction.com.

If you have a story idea, or if you would like me to explore a series in more depth, or if you'd like me to explore a character by writing a spinoff series about that character or world, leave me a message on my website's contact page. I answer all reader emails, so ask me anything, tell me what you liked and didn't like, and let me know where you'd like your favorite series to go. I would love to hear your ideas and find out what you'd like to read next.

Find out more at www.theomann.com.

Also by Theo Mann (so far)